To Have
and to Hold

Lauren Layne

To Have and to Hold

POCKET BOOKS

New York   London   Toronto   Sydney   New Delhi

Pocket Books
An Imprint of Simon & Schuster, Inc.
1230 Avenue of the Americas
New York, NY 10020

Copyright © 2016 by LL Book Company

First Pocket Books paperback edition August 2016

POCKET and colophon are registered trademarks of Simon & Schuster, Inc.

For information about special discounts for bulk purchases, please contact Simon & Schuster Special Sales at 1-866-506-1949 or business@simonandschuster.com.

The Simon & Schuster Speakers Bureau can bring authors to your live event. For more information or to book an event, contact the Simon & Schuster Speakers Bureau at 1-866-248-3049 or visit our website at www.simonspeakers.com.

Interior design by Devan Norman

Manufactured in the United States of America

10   9   8   7   6   5   4   3   2   1

ISBN 978-1-5011-3513-2
ISBN 978-1-5011-3514-9 (ebook)

For Anth

Chapter One

"HOLD ON. BACK UP. Back all the way up. What do you mean you're getting *married*?"

It was eleven p.m. on a Wednesday, and Seth Tyler was exactly where he always was these days: behind his expansive mahogany desk at the Tyler Hotel Group, suit jacket slung over the back of his ergonomic chair, tie begging to be undone, impeccably pressed white shirt cuffed at the wrists.

He raked a hand through his thick light brown hair in frustration and fixed his younger sister with his best no-nonsense glare, an approximation—like everything else he seemed to do lately—of his deceased father.

When Seth's father dropped dead of a heart attack eight months ago, Seth had thought the hardest part about his father's passing—other than the mourning, of course—would be taking over the family company.

Sure, Seth had been groomed for the role. He'd wanted the president and CEO title. He'd always wanted it.

Eventually.

But not yet, for God's sake.

Seth had no problem admitting that he was a perfectionist, and he'd been bound and determined to take over the family company *his* way. The right way.

And the right way, as Seth had determined it, was spending at least a year shadowing each of the senior-level Tyler Hotel Group executives. Seth had wanted to learn every possible detail, every in and out of the business, before even thinking about taking over the reins of the Fortune 500 company.

But his father's heart had had other plans. Mainly, up and quitting during a routine round of golf. And so, quietly, per his father's wishes, Seth had become CEO two years ahead of schedule.

Not a day passed that Seth didn't wish his father were still with him, but in truth, taking his place at the head of the boardroom table had been easier than Seth had anticipated. The investors hadn't freaked out. The executive team hadn't left in mass exodus. Even Hank's longtime assistant, Etta, had stuck around, seemingly content to call Seth boss even as she busted his balls about not eating enough vegetables, getting enough sleep, or getting his hair cut.

But if taking over the family company was easier than Seth had expected, there was one ramification of Hank Tyler's death that Seth hadn't been in the least prepared for:

A wedding.

Maya Tyler inhaled a long, patient breath, as though preparing to deal with a difficult child. "Well see, marriage, Seth, is when two people fall in love and decide to spend the rest of their lives—"

"Yes, I'm aware of how marriage works," Seth interrupted. Although, not as aware as he'd like, as it turned out. He wouldn't be getting any firsthand knowledge of how marriage worked anytime soon.

Maya bit her lip. "I'm sorry. I didn't mean to remind you of Nadia."

Seth glanced down at his desk to avoid his sister's too-perceptive gaze. She wasn't wrong. He'd gotten to the point where he could go most days without thinking of his ex, but he hadn't yet figured out how to think about marriage without hearing the incredulous laugh she'd let out when he'd gone on one knee and showed Nadia the ring he'd spent months picking out.

"Can we not?" he said curtly.

"Don't get pissed. It's a wedding. You're supposed to be happy."

"I'm not pissed; I'm just surprised."

That was an understatement. Seth had *not* seen this coming, and for a man who exercised precision in all things, he couldn't say he was enjoying the shock value of Maya's announcement. Especially not on the heels of his father's death. A death that everyone but Seth had seen coming, because Seth had been the lone outsider on the knowledge that was his father's long-time heart condition.

Apparently, Hank had considered his only son a control freak—had known that Seth would have stopped at nothing to try to halt death in its tracks.

His father had been, well, *right*. It was hard to admit, but if Seth had known about his father's condition, he'd have devoted every waking hour to researching experimental treatments and the best doctors.

Hank Tyler hadn't wanted that for his final months. Not for himself *or* for Seth.

Still, Seth resented not having the choice. Resented his father *nearly* as much as he missed him.

But he'd put that behind him. Mostly.

Hank was gone, and Maya was still here. Maya was all he had.

He had known she was dating a new guy—Neil something or other. But Seth hadn't thought a thing about it. Maya had whipped through a constant string of casual boyfriends since high school, and other than a two-year relationship in college, they had never been serious.

And it certainly hadn't gotten close to marriage.

What's worse, Seth hadn't even met this man that was apparently to be his brother-in-law.

But none of this would have mattered, not really, if Seth's instincts hadn't been buzzing that something was amiss with the way this was all going down. Something was off. He knew it down to his gut.

"How long have you been seeing this guy?" he asked.

Maya slumped back in the plush chair facing Seth's desk with a groan. "Don't do this. I *knew* you were going to do this."

He frowned. "Do what?"

"The big brother thing," she said.

"Hard not to, what with me being six years older and all," Seth said.

He didn't add that he was doubly obligated to be protective given Hank's death just months earlier. Maya had definitely been Daddy's Little Princess. She still got tears in her eyes every time their father's name was mentioned.

Maya leaned forward, her pale blue eyes much like his own, although her blond hair was lighter than his, thanks to her frequent trips to the salon.

"I *love* him, Seth. I know you're jaded these days, but Neil is exactly the type of guy we women spend our entire lives dreaming about."

Seth bit his tongue to stop from saying that he bet Maya was exactly the type of girl that guys like Neil dreamed about, too. Young, pretty . . . and filthy rich.

Or so Neil likely thought.

The truth was, most of Maya's money was tied up in a monthly allowance. It had been that way when Hank Tyler had been alive, and Seth's father had stipulated that it remain that way after his death.

Technically, Maya supported herself on the salary from the fancy art gallery where she worked part-time. But judging from the half dozen shopping bags strewn about his office right now, it was safe to say not a penny of that monthly check from their father's estate was going into savings.

Maya wasn't frivolous—she had a good head on her shoulders, gave plenty of time and money to charity—but she also liked pretty things and fancy dinners.

As a result, she tended to attract men who *also* liked pretty things and fancy dinners. Seth was willing to bet the new guy was no different.

It was on the tip of his tongue to beg her to reconsider—to date the guy for at least a year before taking the plunge. But then, time wasn't always the answer, was it? He'd dated Nadia for nearly three years, and look how that had turned out.

Seth sighed at the earnest, pleading look on his sister's face. No wonder she'd had their father wrapped around her manicured finger. The girl was good. No, not a girl, he reminded himself. Much as he thought of Maya as his baby sister, she was twenty-six now.

Old enough for him to start respecting her decisions.

"Tell me about Neil," he said begrudgingly.

Maya grinned and clapped her hands together, launching into something about a meet-cute at the art gallery. Damn it, he *knew* he should have pushed for her to land some desk job here at the hotel group, where he could keep an eye on her.

Seth pushed back from his desk, standing as she chattered away happily, and went to the large floor-to-ceiling windows that had an unobstructed view of the iconic lights of the Empire State Building.

He did some of his best thinking when away from his desk—which meant these days he was barely thinking at all. But when he separated from the office, that was when he was really able to focus: away from email and the phone and the endless to-do lists and memos from his assistant and . . .

"—he's *such* a good guy, Seth. He brings me flowers every day, just *because*, you know? And sweet little gifts. And anytime I mention a new restaurant I want to try, Neil manages to get reservations, like, same day . . ."

And who pays for the dinner?

Seth kept his voice easy as he turned around to face Maya. "What does he do?"

Maya's smile froze for just a moment before it brightened again. "He wants to start his own company—one that makes art more accessible to regular people. You know, like matching up-and-coming artists with new collectors. Eventually he wants to build a mobile app and everything. He's in investment mode right now, but—"

Ah, shit.

Seth had no problem with start-ups. Or art. But a few of Maya's word choices caused the alarm bells in Seth's head to ratchet up another notch:

Neil *wants* to start his own company. He *eventually* wants to build a mobile app.

And the nail in Maya's fiancé's coffin—he was in *investment mode*.

In Seth's experience, a man truly in investment mode of starting his own company didn't have the extra resources to be sending a woman flowers every day. Or buying her little gifts. And certainly not taking her out to dinner on a regular basis at all the hottest new eateries.

Seth ran a finger along the inside of his shirt collar. It did nothing to ease the tension. He tugged at the knot of his tie, loosening it just enough to flick open the top button. Laid-back wasn't something he did often. As a thirty-two-year-old CEO of one of the largest companies in North America, he had an image to uphold.

But it was nearly midnight, and the only person to see him was his sister.

A sister who was getting married.

Fuck.

"Seth, you have to know I hate coming to you with this kind of stuff," Maya was saying now, her voice genuinely contrite. "I know this is all more than you wanted this soon. The responsibility of the company, plus all the logistics of Daddy's estate. The responsibility of *me* . . ."

Seth rubbed at the back of his neck as he sat back down in his chair and faced his sister. "You're an adult, Maya. It's not like I'm having to attend parent-teacher conferences."

"I know, and I'm taking care of myself, I am, it's just—"

"It's just that you want your big white wedding," he said.

Maya grinned in relief. "I *have* been planning it forever."

Seth smiled back. "You forget that I was there for some of those early planning stages. I'm still not sure I forgive you for making Tinkerbell the groom while I was relegated to usher."

"*Head* usher. And it wasn't your fault you didn't look as cute in a bow tie as an overweight pug. Besides, I'm happy to give you a promotion to maid of honor for the real deal," she teased.

"We both know that Tori would kill me if I

took the top spot away from her," Seth said, referring to Maya's longtime best friend. "Plus, teal's not my color." Seth knew his sister loved anything that emphasized her blue eyes and could already see the aqua-themed cornucopia that would be her wedding. He got a headache just thinking about it.

"Oh, please. You can pull off just about any color you want," Maya said. "I hate that you got Mom's olive complexion while I got Dad's pasty shade of pale."

"Buttering me up before you drop the cost of this blessed event?"

Maya pulled her bottom lip between her teeth nervously before scooting toward the edge of her chair. "It's just, well, I have some money of my own, of course, but then Neil pointed out that if Daddy were alive—"

Seth stiffened. *Neil* pointed out, did he? Seth was liking his sister's husband-to-be less and less.

Still, Maya brought up an undeniable point. Though Hank Tyler had left Maya plenty of money, the monthly allotment wouldn't be enough to plan a decent cocktail party in their social set, much less a wedding.

But that wasn't the *real* reason Seth felt himself caving.

He knew that if their father were alive, Hank would have spared no expense for his only daughter's wedding.

And though Seth knew that no fancy flower arrangement or imported champagne could make up for the fact that their parents wouldn't be there to walk Maya down the aisle, Seth was determined to give his sister the wedding she'd always wanted.

"I'll take care of it," he said gruffly. "You know I will."

Maya made a happy squealing noise, but Seth held up a hand. "But just so we're clear. How much are we talking?"

"Oh gosh, I don't know yet," Maya said. "There are so many variables. The venue, the photographer, the caterer, and the dress, of course—"

Of course.

"—but I'm sure I'll have a better idea after this Friday."

"What happens Friday?" Seth asked, somehow fairly certain he wasn't going to like the answer.

Maya did another one of those happy hand claps. "Oh, I didn't tell you! The Wedding Belles have an opening."

Seth stared at his sister blankly.

Maya rolled her eyes. "Come on. The Wedding Belles?"

He shook his head. "Is that, like, a fancy dress shop, or something?"

"Um, try the premiere wedding-planning company in the city. Maybe the country. They have access to all the best venues, the top designers, and they never do the same wedding twice. Everything is custom, original, perfectly tailored to the bride's needs. One of a kind."

That, Seth could translate: expensive.

Still, if their father were alive . . .

"They're super exclusive," Maya said. "You have

to book them, like, years in advance, but I called, and they had something open up!"

"That's great," Seth said, rubbing a hand down his face. He knew full well that the convenient opening had likely been a result of Maya's very recognizable last name.

"So anyway, Friday is just a consultation. They want to hear what I'm looking for and my time-line—"

"What *is* your timeline?" Seth interrupted.

In other words, how long do I have to figure out whether Neil's the gold digger I think he is?

"Well, I've always liked the idea of being a June bride," Maya said, "but that's less than six months away, so we all know that's not going to happen . . ."

Seth blinked. It wasn't? Six months seemed like a hell of a long time to him, but then he wasn't the one who'd been marrying off the family dog when he was six. What did he know?

"So I'm thinking maybe a Christmas wedding," she said. "It's so festive, with the red and green, or I could go metallic, or even blue—you know what that does with my eyes . . ."

Seth tuned his sister out as she ran through pos-sible color schemes.

Christmas. That gave Seth eleven whole months. Plenty of time to get to know his future brother-in-law, and then find a way to get rid of the bastard if he didn't pass muster.

But if Seth was going to make this work—if he was going to have a shot at getting to know the real Neil—it meant he'd have to spend some time with the money-grabbing bastard. He had to be there when the man inevitably slipped up.

"What time?" Seth interrupted.

Maya paused mid-description of the pros and cons of flocked Christmas trees. "What time for what?"

"Your meeting on Friday with the Wedding Chimes. What time is it?"

Maya laughed. "The Wedding Belles. And it's at two, at their headquarters on the Upper West Side. Why?"

"I want to be there."

His sister blinked in surprise. "You do?"

Seth lifted a shoulder. "I want to be involved in all of this. I don't need to come along to dress fittings and whatever the hell else you've got going on, but the big-decision stuff . . . I want to be a part of it."

Maya laughed. "You are so like Dad. He always liked to know how every penny of his money was being spent."

Sure, let's go with that. Easier for her to think he was pinching pennies than checking out her fiancé.

Seth smiled. "Guilty. You want live doves, we'll get live doves, but I want to make sure these wedding planners don't think they have a blank check just because our last name is Tyler."

Maya shrugged and bent down to retrieve her various shopping bags. "Suit yourself."

Seth walked his sister to the office door, dipping his head slightly when she went up on her toes to kiss his cheek.

"Thank you," she whispered.

Seth nodded. "I just want you to be happy."

"I am," she said, beaming up at him. "I'm *so* happy. And I'm really sorry you haven't had a chance to meet Neil, but it all happened so fast."

Tell me about it.

"He'll be there on Friday, right?" Seth asked. "How about the three of us go out for a late lunch after the meeting with the wedding planner?"

Maya nodded. "Perfect. You're going to love him. And he can't wait to meet you."

Me and my wallet, I'd bet.

"Friday, two o'clock," Maya said, kissing his cheek one more time. "Don't be late, 'kay?"

Seth blinked. "Have I ever been late?"

His sister laughed. "Good point. Would you be less grumpy about the whole thing if I told you we'll do an open bar at the wedding, stocked with all your favorites?"

Seth only had one favorite: Four Roses Bourbon. And if the ever-increasing tension in his chest was any indication, he was going to be drinking a lot of it in the coming months. Starting with tonight.

He told his sister good-bye, and then went straight to his bar cart in the corner and poured himself a generous tumbler of his beloved bourbon—hell, he deserved it. Then he went immediately to his computer to search for every possible detail he could find on one Neil Garrett.

Chapter Two

∽

Brooke Baldwin double-checked the weather app on her phone. Then triple-checked it.

Nope. The numbers hadn't changed. Twenty-four degrees freaking Fahrenheit, but "feels like twelve." Really? Once it got below freezing, did it even *matter* what the "feels like" temperature was?

Brooke wouldn't know. She could count the times she'd been in subfreezing temperatures on one hand. A hand that was likely to turn into a Popsicle the second she got outside because she didn't own a pair of gloves.

Reason number 412 why moving to New York City from Los Angeles on a whim had been . . . an adjustment.

So many learning experiences. Wearing stilettos on the subway. Trying to find a taxi in the rain. Finding out that having a washer and dryer in your unit was a Manhattan rarity.

Brooke cast a look downward at the professional-yet-fashion-forward ensemble she had painstakingly

assembled for her first day on the job and sighed re-
signedly. The freeze-your-butt-off weather definitely
required a last-minute wardrobe change. Off went
the sexy but paper-thin wrap dress, on went the blue
turtleneck sweater and leggings. She opted for gray
platform boots instead of the pink Louboutins she'd
splurged on for Christmas last year. Not her trendiest
attire, but it was the warmest thing she owned.

Just like her cute ivory peacoat was the warmest
jacket she owned.

Not warm enough, it turned out.

The bite of the cold January air took her breath
away the moment she stepped outside, and Brooke
wanted desperately to turn right back around.

But there was something else she wanted more.
She forged ahead.

She burrowed her face in her scarf and lifted her
hand for a taxi. In spring and summer, the restaurant
would probably qualify as being within walking
distance.

But in the dead of winter? No. Just no.

Miraculously, a cab took pity on her, and five minutes later she was standing inside MOMA, one of the
most famous museums in the country, as well as the
upscale eatery where she was about to meet her new
colleagues.

Or, as Brooke liked to think about it: Step Two of
Life After Clay.

Step one had been getting the hell out of LA.

Step two commenced today, and involved accepting a job with the uber-elite Wedding Belles.

Brooke wasn't entirely sure what step three would

be, but she was pretty sure it would involve wine and
Celine Dion sing-alongs à la Bridget Jones.

In better news, swanky as the restaurant was, it
was also very LA. The modern decor, efficient wait-
staff, and surplus of designer handbags reminded
her of the upscale haunts she used to frequent back
home, and she felt her shoulders relax as she blew
out a breath she did not even know she had been
holding. Brooke had been one of the top wedding
planners on the West Coast—fancy working lunches
were her jam.

Still, her hands might have been just a tiny bit
clammy as the hostess led her to her table. She might
have been a wedding planner in California, but she
was a long way from the Pacific.

Now she'd be coming face-to-face with the top
wedding planners on the *East Coast*. If Brooke was
at the bottom of her game, courtesy of The Wedding
That Didn't Happen, the Wedding Belles were at the
top of theirs.

*And yet, they wanted you. Buck up, Baldwin.
You've got this.*

A curly-haired blonde spotted her first, smiling in
welcome as Brooke approached the table. Brooke had
practically memorized the Wedding Belles' website,
so she immediately recognized the woman as Heather
Fowler, one of the assistant wedding planners.

Actually, the *only* assistant wedding planner.

The Belles were a tiny company, managing to
climb to the top of the Manhattan wedding scene
with only two wedding planners, an assistant wedding planner, and a receptionist.

In recent months they'd been running even leaner, as one of the wedding planners had left the company to raise a family in Connecticut.

That's where Brooke came in.

Her gaze shifted to the other woman at the table, already knowing what she'd see, and yet somehow surprised that Alexis Morgan looked *exactly* like every picture Brooke had ever seen of her.

In fact, for all the expression on the other woman's face at the moment, Brooke might as well be looking at a photograph now, too, instead of the real thing. A cool customer, this one.

"Brooke," Alexis said, standing and extending a hand. "It's a pleasure to meet you."

Alexis's voice was very much like the woman herself. Smooth, polished, and pretty. Very pretty, Brooke amended. She was shorter than Brooke's own five eight by a few inches, but had that sort of exceptional posture that made her look a good deal taller than she was. Her chestnut-brown hair was pulled into a sleek chignon, her eyes wide and brown with just enough perfectly applied makeup to look put together without being obvious. The outfit was also spot-on. Gray slacks and a white blouse, simple pieces but perfectly tailored to cast a sleek appeal.

"It's so nice to meet you, too!" Brooke said, hoping her voice didn't sound *too* gushing. It wasn't that Brooke was bubbly. Not really. But she was aware of the fact that she was quick to laugh, even quicker to smile, and eager to see the best in people.

Not so long ago, the ready smiles and optimism had been genuine. She hadn't even been aware of them.

Lately, though . . .

Well, fake it till you make it, right?

She shook Heather's hand as well, and the three of them sat down at the low granite tabletop. "We ordered champagne," Heather said with a little wink. "Hope that's okay."

"Definitely. I wouldn't be in this job if I didn't love champagne."

"Have you taken any classes?" Alexis said, leaning forward.

Brooke blinked. "Um. Classes?"

"Champagne classes."

"Maybe we should let her drink a glass before we send her to school, hmm, boss?" Heather asked.

"Yes, of course," Alexis said, sitting back. "I'm sorry."

"Don't apologize, please," Brooke said as Heather motioned for a server to pour their champagne. "I'm on your turf now. If you want me to go to bubbly school, I'm all for it."

"It's actually a blast," Heather said. "They let you drink the stuff, and plenty of it."

"They also have a spit bucket," Alexis said mildly.

Heather waved this away. "Please. Who spits French champagne? Crazy talk."

Brooke smiled, warming to the younger woman. Heather was every bit as pretty as Alexis, although where Alexis looked like she held the world's secrets in some vaulted part of her enormous brain, Heather gave off a friendly what-you-see-is-what-you-get vibe. Her hazel eyes were sharp and intelligent, but there were no pretenses there.

She seemed like the type of friend who'd tell you when your haircut sucked, but only after you'd asked, and the one who'd go on a doughnut binge with you after a breakup and wouldn't breathe a word about the calories.

Not that Heather was a friend. Yet. They'd just met. But Brooke had every intention of making her one. Alexis, too.

"So, Brooke," Heather said. "Tell me honestly. Was your adjustment to New York as rough as mine?"

"If by rough you mean trying to get to Brooklyn and ending up in the Bronx and nearly freezing my face off . . ."

Nodding, Heather picked up a roll from the basket in the center of the table and pointed it in Brooke's direction. "I hear you on the subway bit. Nobody ever really tells you that the entrance to the uptown and downtown trains are rarely on the same side of the street."

"The guidebooks tell you. And the Internet," Alexis said.

Heather rolled her eyes. "Ignore her."

Brooke gave Alexis a nervous glance, curious if the other woman took issue with Heather's informal tone—they were, after all, boss and assistant. But to her surprise, Alexis was smiling. She was not, however, touching the bread basket.

Impressive self-control on Alexis's part, but Brooke had never met a carb she didn't like and followed Heather's lead, grabbing one of the crusty, still-warm rolls and spreading a bit of aioli-infused butter on it.

Before she could dig in, though, Alexis lifted her champagne flute. "Shall we toast?"

"Hells yes," Heather said, lifting her glass. "To the newest Belle."

Belle. I like that, Brooke thought as she picked up her champagne. For the past two years, Brooke had thrown every bit of energy into starting her *own* wedding-planning company, determined to work for herself.

And while being the boss had come with plenty of perks, it had also been . . . lonely. She wondered if this was maybe the way to do it—to belong to something.

"To the newest Belle," Alexis said, echoing Heather. "And to new beginnings."

Brooke met her new boss's gaze, wondering exactly how much Alexis Morgan knew about Brooke's past. Wondered if the other woman knew how true her words were.

She hadn't hid what happened from Alexis during their several phone interviews, she just . . . hadn't volunteered it. Still, it was hardly a national secret. Alexis, and Heather, for that matter, could have found out every sordid detail with a quick visit to everyone's BFF, Google.

Looking at Alexis's face certainly didn't tell her one way or the other whether her boss knew. The woman was like 007 with the unreadable.

"So, Brooke," Heather said, reaching for yet another roll. "You've heard that we East Coasters are known to be a bit more blunt than you West Coasters, right?"

"You're from Michigan," Alexis told Heather. "That's more Midwest than anything."

"I became a New Yorker about five minutes after moving here," Heather said. "We all do. Anyway, what I want to know is—and you can totally tell me to shut my trap, by the way—your, um, spicy past . . . are we talking about it, or not talking about it? I'm fine either way."

"*Heather!*" For once Alexis's voice was anything but calm, and Brooke sensed she'd like nothing more than to kick her assistant under the table.

"I'm sorry," Heather said, going a little bit pale. "Was that rude? I just thought that if we're going to be spending, like, every minute of every day together, we should know what's off-limits and what's fair game."

"Yes, of course it was rude," Alexis said.

Heather gave Brooke a contrite look. "I'm sorry. It's just that it's *totally* not a secret, and if I'm supposed to tiptoe, I have to know now, you know?"

"Good Lord," Alexis murmured, taking a sip of her champagne. "Have you *ever* tiptoed?"

The women's exchange gave Brooke a second to gather her thoughts—to recover from the shock of hearing it mentioned, only to realize that Heather was right.

They would be spending a hell of a lot of time together, and as far as Brooke was concerned, the only thing worse than talking about it was *not* talking about it.

And so, after taking a sip of champagne for courage, Brooke took a deep breath, folded her hands in her lap, leaned forward slightly, and told her new colleagues all about the guy she'd fallen in love with. The one she'd almost married.

Right up until the moment the FBI had arrested him.

At the altar.

Chapter Three

IT'S NOT AS THOUGH Brooke had *meant* to start dating a con man. She certainly didn't intend to get engaged to one.

But that's the thing about con men. The good ones were good at, well . . . the con.

And Clay Battaglia had been a good one. The *best*, actually, if you took the word of the FBI agent who'd debriefed Brooke and her family—while she was still in her wedding dress.

Turns out that while Brooke had been happily building her wedding-planning company, Clay had been quietly and competently getting away with every white-collar crime in the book. While she'd been planning *their* wedding, he'd apparently been knee-deep in yet another Ponzi scheme.

Brooke hadn't even known what a Ponzi scheme *was* when the FBI had told her.

She did now.

Following Clay's arrest, she spent weeks researching white-collar crime. Wanting to know what he'd been up to all those times he'd quietly kissed her forehead late at night and told her he needed to make some phone calls for "work." Wanting to know what her life would have been like if the FBI hadn't taken him down *before* they'd exchanged vows.

Still, while Brooke would be ever grateful that she'd learned the truth before she'd become Mrs. Clay Battaglia, she'd be lying if she didn't admit that the timing of it had stung just a little bit.

If they'd only taken him down a day before. Heck, even an hour before.

But no.

Just moments after Brooke kissed her father's cheek and prepared to marry the man she loved at the wedding she'd poured her heart into, the FBI stormed—yes, stormed—the church.

Clay was in handcuffs before she even registered what was happening.

Numbly she watched as he listened to his Miranda rights at the precise moment he should have been listening to the vows she'd spent months writing.

And as reality slowly sunk in, Brooke waited. Waited for him to look at her. To look at her and say that it was all a lie. All one big misunderstanding, and that they'd be on their way to Bermuda as planned by tomorrow.

He didn't.

He didn't even apologize.

No, the man she'd loved for two years with every fiber of her being merely smiled at her and then shrugged.

There'd been plenty of photos taken that day, but

that was the one that made it onto the front page of every major newspaper on the West Coast.

"The Greatest Con of All." "Arrested by Love." And her personal favorite, courtesy of her very own *LA Times*: "White-Collar Bride."

The stories all read pretty much like you'd expect. About Clay, mostly, and the litany of accusations against him, but also about *Brooke*.

The papers had stopped short of defamation, but the implications were there. She was clueless and ditzy at best, a potentially overlooked accomplice at worst. Completely oblivious to the fact that she'd been sharing a roof with the most nefarious white-collar criminal in a generation—or pretending to be.

None of that had bothered her. What had bothered her was that she'd been a fool. Self-absorbed, naïve, and downright blind.

Brooke had been dodging dumb-blonde jokes for most of her life, but the debacle with Clay was the first time she thought she might really, truly be deserving of the title.

She hadn't been surprised when new clients had stopped calling. Hadn't been surprised when current clients canceled. Nobody wanted to hire *that* wedding planner.

Brooke had even been relieved, at first. In those first weeks after Clay's arrest, she hadn't been able to handle any talk of weddings. Not her own, and not other people's.

But the worst part of all of this, the part that kept her up long into the lonely nights, wasn't the negative effect on her career. No, the worst part was that sometimes, in the very darkest corner of her soul, she feared that she might still love Clay, at least a little. Sure, her *brain* knew that all the things she'd loved about Clay had been a lie. Her *brain* understood that his name wasn't even Clay.

But her heart? Her heart was having a harder time forgetting the way he always let her be the little spoon and tuck her cold feet against his warm calves. Or the way he'd brought her coffee in bed every morning. Or the way she'd come home after a long day with the worst sort of bridezilla and Clay would make them cocktails and sit on the patio with her, and watch the sunset and laugh.

She'd imagined that all their nights would be like that. All the nights for the rest of her life, with maybe a couple of kids thrown into the mix eventually.

Brooke swallowed.

There wouldn't be any more nights on the patio watching the sunset with Clay. Wouldn't be any patio at all, because Brooke's real estate broker had made it quite clear that she should be counting herself lucky to get a dishwasher in New York—a patio was out of the question.

So no patio. No Clay, or whatever his real name was.

No man at *all*, really.

No falling in love.

Not ever again.

Chapter Four

A FTER LUNCH, BROOKE WAS feeling the lightest she had in months, although she wasn't quite sure whether it was because of the champagne or the fact that she'd just spilled her guts to two practical strangers.

She hadn't gotten all personal and weepy or anything, but she'd filled them in on the facts—the *actual* facts, not the tabloid facts—and getting it all out in the open went a long way to making her feel as though she was working with a clean slate.

But the unexpected girl talk, while important for her fresh start, had nothing on the euphoria of the moment she first saw the Wedding Belles headquarters. Other than a delicate silver plaque inscribed with *The Wedding Belles* above the doorbell, it looked exactly like every other house on Seventy-Third Street, which made it all the more charming in its discreetness.

After lunch, Heather and Alexis had headed down to SoHo for a small evening wedding, but Brooke had wanted to get settled at the main office. Her breath whooshed out in a happy sigh as she tentatively opened the front door and poked her head in. If the outside was charming, the inside was perfect—absolutely perfect.

The main reception area had plenty of white, of course. Smart branding, given that the entirety of their clientele was of the bride-to-be variety. But whereas most wedding-related vendors tended toward frilly and formal, Alexis Morgan had taken the opposite direction, opting for clean lines and bright, unabashed pops of color.

The black-and-white-striped wallpaper gave the place an Old Hollywood vibe, and the sleek furniture was made approachable by fun Tiffany-blue throw pillows. Michael Bublé's swoony voice was crooning away from some unseen speaker, the perfect choice for what the Wedding Belles were best known for: a tantalizing blend of the classic and the modern.

It was this sterling reputation that had caused Brooke to consider Alexis Morgan's job offer when she'd brushed off everyone else's. There were hundreds of wedding planners out there and thousands more that *wanted* to be wedding planners.

But for as many women who imagined it to be their dream job, the truth was that getting wedding planning right was hard. Really hard. The key was finding that nearly impossible balance between ensuring the details were taken care of and not being so rigid that you zapped all the romance out of the event. What brides were really after, but never knew how to ask for, was organized magic. The best weddings were the ones that went off without a hitch but also had room for spontaneity.

Not only did Alexis *get* it, she'd figured out how to turn it into a formula. There wasn't a single blight on the Wedding Belles' resume.

Not something Brooke could say about her own now-defunct company.

She swallowed, pushing aside the dark thoughts, which was relatively easy. She'd had plenty of practice over the past four months, after all.

Even when her friends had been pushing comfort wine into her hand, even when her dad was threatening to "show that bastard a thing or two," even when her mom had insisted on crying "on Brooke's behalf," she'd known that she hadn't needed to cry or scream.

She needed to start over. And here she was.

"Hi there!" a perky voice chirped as a petite red-head came into the lobby. "So sorry to keep you waiting. I didn't have anything on the schedule, and I was just eating a late lunch."

"Oh, I'm not a bride," Brooke explained. *Not anymore.* "I'm Brooke Baldwin. I—"

"Oh. My. Gosh!" The redhead came around the side of the desk, and when Brooke extended a hand, the other woman ignored it and went in for a hug. "I am *such* an airhead. I've seen your picture, like, a million times, and Alexis totes just told me you were coming by today. I'm Jessie, the receptionist!"

Brooke blinked in surprise at the hug. Not that she minded hugs, but Jessie was just about as different from her colleagues as could be. Like the others, she was attractive, but where Alexis was elegantly refined and Heather was confidently pretty, Jessie was freaking adorable. She had chin-length orange curls, huge green eyes, and slightly elfish features.

"Tell me that's not all your stuff," Jessie said, gesturing at the large tote bag slung over Brooke's shoulder. "When Mel moved out last month, she had, like, ten boxes."

Mel. That would be Melissa Thompson. Brooke had done her homework. Melissa was nearly as famous in the New York wedding scene as Alexis herself and had become pregnant with twin girls less than a year after giving birth to her first child, a son.

She had, in Heather's words, moved to the burbs.

Brooke couldn't blame her. Being a wedding planner was a full-time job. Nights and weekends weren't just normal, they were necessary.

Brooke continued holding out hope that she'd figure out how to fit a dog into her crazy schedule, but a baby? She couldn't imagine. And three? No—not possible. Even for a glass-half-full kind of girl like Brooke.

"I wasn't sure how much space I'd have, or what the office would be like," Brooke said, patting her bag. "I just brought the essentials."

"Ohmigod, you're going to love. Your. Office," she said, punctuating each word in a way that was, Brooke was quickly realizing, Jessie's default rhythm of speaking. "It's got these big old windows, a *ton* of amazing natural light," Jessie gushed. "Come on up, I'll show you. In the meantime, tell me *everything*. You're from California, right? Can I call you that? California? It suits you!"

"Ah—"

"No, of course not," Jessie chattered on. "It's not like I'd want to be called Louisiana. That's where I'm from."

"You don't have much of an accent."

"I know, right? It just sort of started fading on me this past year. 'Bout all I have left of the South is the occasional 'y'all' and an affinity for fried food. You're not, like, vegan, are you?"

"Nope."

"Gluten-free?"

"Definitely not."

"Thank *gawd*. I mean, we could still be friends if you were, but food's kind of like my thing, and every-thing that tastes good has gluten—that's what Heather and I are always saying. You met her at lunch, right?"

Brooke opened her mouth to confirm, but Jessie kept right on talking. "Anyway, you just let me know if you need anything. Since I moved to New York I've pretty much done nothing but work and tour the city. And eat, of course."

Of course.

"Okay, so up here, this is where the offices are," Jessie said, pausing at the top of the stairs and gesturing around.

The upper level of the Wedding Belles office was mostly just hallways and doors, reminding Brooke of the little house she'd grown up in before her dad had gotten his big break in the Hollywood production world and moved them all to a bigger house in Beverly Hills.

"What's on the third floor?" she asked as Jessie led her to the end of the hall to the left.

"That's Alexis's place."

"She lives here?"

"Yup. And if you're wondering how she manages to separate work and personal life, she doesn't. I just didn't get how a woman who deals with weddings all day long doesn't even seem to want a boyfriend, but then I saw her in action and realized the woman doesn't have time for a hamster, much less a lover."

"What about you?" Brooke asked. "Boyfriend?"

"Eh, yeah. Dean. It's new yet, but I'm feeling good about it. He makes good waffles."

Brooke held a smile. Had to like a woman that could be wooed by waffles.

"What about you?" Jessie glanced over her shoulder as she asked it. "Boyfriend?"

"I'm single," Brooke said, deliberately keeping her voice light. "Super single."

Jessie skidded to a halt and turned around to face Brooke, eyes wide, before putting a hand on her arm. "Oh. My. Gawd. I'm such an idiot. I'd totally forgotten about all that crap and the guy you almost married, and . . . you know what? Let's not even talk about it right now. That's what we do in my house back home. We don't talk about things that pull us down. Not at first. Unless of course you *want* to talk about it."

Brooke's head was spinning. "No. I'm good. I mean, the topic's not off-limits, it's just—"

Jessie held up a hand. "Say no more. Okay, here we go. You ready to swoon?"

Jessie opened the door to Brooke's new office, and Brooke made an involuntary happy noise.

It was bigger than she'd expected—heck, it felt nearly as large as Brooke's entire apartment in Yorkville. A white desk was pushed against the window, and though the view was of bare, leafless trees, Brooke had to imagine that in the spring it would be lovely.

Or even better, what must it be like in autumn? As someone who'd grown up surrounded by palm trees, Brooke had always wondered what it would be like to experience true fall, with all the bright, vibrant colors of the changing leaves and the crisp air . . .

"Right?" Jessie said, correctly reading Brooke's silence. "Mel had a heck of a time leaving. She loved this office. Loved the job, really. But when you push, like, three kids out of your V in just a couple years, I guess maybe you have more important things to worry about. Kegels and breast pumps and stuff."

"And raising children," Brooke said wryly.

Jessie wagged a finger at her. "Right. And that. I like you. I know it's dorky, but the Belles are kind of like a family, so I've been hoping that you'd be awesome. And you totally are. And super pretty."

Brooke rolled her eyes.

"I'm serious! You *look* like you're from LA with that blond hair, blue eyes, and the tan, and I mean that in the best way possible."

"Well, the tan won't last long," Brooke said. "It's freezing out there."

"I want to tell you that you'll get used to it, but you, like, totally won't. Or at least I haven't." The redhead gave her an apologetic smile. "Bet you're missing California right about now, huh?"

"Not really," Brooke said, determined to ward off the wave of homesickness that swelled the second Jessie had mentioned her home state. "I mean, I love it there, but I think I'll love it here, too."

Jessie tilted her head. "A positive thinker. I like that."

Brooke smiled and shrugged. It was how she'd always rolled. Looking on the bright side just seemed smart.

It would take more than one rotten fiancé to change that.

"I should probably get back downstairs," Jessie was saying. "That phone, like, never shuts up, and sometimes we get walk-ins. But let me know if you need anything. And we should for sure grab drinks later. If you're not busy?"

"Not unless you count unpacking my kitchen," Brooke said.

Jessie waved her hand. "Oh, honey. That can wait for weeks. We New Yorkers don't cook much."

"Thank goodness. My fridge is the size of a toaster, and I'm pretty sure the stove doesn't turn on," Brooke said.

"Yeah, well, welcome to New York. Alexis said you found an apartment in Yorkville?"

"That's what they tell me," Brooke said. "I haven't quite wrapped my brain around all the neighborhoods yet."

"Well, like I said, ask me anytime. I dated a broker when I first got here, so I know, like, everything. And mark your calendar for Friday-night martinis. Heather knows all the best places, and I'm her aspiring apprentice in all things slightly dirty."

"I'd like that," Brooke said, meaning it. Jessie was slightly exhausting but fairly impossible not to like.

Jessie left with instructions to make herself at home so she'd never ever want to leave, and Brooke started unpacking the few belongings she'd brought with her.

Her MacBook Pro. Her favorite polka-dot mug. A couple of framed photos, one of her parents, and one of her sorority sisters at the beach house they'd rented for her bachelorette party.

It was one of the few wedding-related items that had made it with her on the move from California to New York. One of the few that didn't make her cringe.

It burned a little. No, it burned *a lot* that the wedding planner had finally gotten the chance to plan her own wedding to the love of her life, and it had ended with the groom in handcuffs, and not the sexy, kinky variety.

Because Brooke had planned the hell out of her wedding.

It had been her best work because it was her most important work. The wedding to top all weddings, even in the land of celebrity nuptials, where one pop star recently gave out purebred puppies as her wedding favor. Brooke was well aware that her own nuptials would be her most telling calling card, and she had been determined to put on the wedding of the century.

Brooke shook her head to clear thoughts of Clay from her mind and continued unpacking the rest of her meager belongings.

It took all of five minutes, and short of trying to guess the Wi-Fi code by trial and error, there wasn't much she could do until Alexis got there and explained how the on-boarding process would work.

Brooke was on the verge of going downstairs to chat up Jessie, or rather have Jessie chat *her* up, when her cell rang.

Thank God. A distraction.

Brooke picked up. "Hey, Alexis!"

"Brooke, hi."

Alexis's voice had the same low, calm tone that Brooke had gotten used to hearing on the other end of the phone, but there was just a slight edge to it this time, and Brooke sat up straighter. "Everything okay?"

There was a rapid *click-click-click* that Brooke guessed was high heels walking across a hardwood floor—quickly.

"Well . . . no, actually," Alexis replied. "Not okay."

"What's up?"

"We've got a wedding tomorrow—Senator Marlow's daughter—and let's just say as far as wedding crises go, it's the big one."

"Oh crap. Missing groom?" Brooke asked knowingly.

"Worse."

Brooke's mouth dropped open. "The bride?"

"Yup. She disappeared sometime between her manicure appointment and final dress fitting. All we have to go on is a text to the maid of honor saying she needed time to think."

Oh crap. Not good.

Although, Brooke wished she'd taken time to think before her own wedding. Maybe had she slowed down, she might have seen warning signs—

Not the time, Baldwin.

"What can I do?" Brooke asked.

"Well, I hate to do this to you on your first day, but I wouldn't have hired you if you weren't amazing, and—"

"Alexis," Brooke said in a soothing voice. "Lay it on me. Tell me what you need."

Her new boss blew out a long breath, and the clicking stopped as though Alexis had come to a halt. "I've got a new client coming in for her initial consultation. Jessie can give you the full file, but CliffsNotes version: the bride is the Tyler heiress, and—"

"As in the Tyler Hotels?" Brooke interrupted, unable to stop herself. To think she'd worried her days of big-name clients were behind her. The Tylers were huge. Hilton huge.

"Yep. Maya Tyler. I don't know much about the groom other than his name's Neil. At this point, I'm not even sure what they're looking for, but she seemed sweet enough on the phone, so hopefully I'm not handing you a total diva as your very first client."

"Wait—my first client?"

"Well, of course," Alexis said. "I mean, I was going to see which of us was a better fit for her style after we met with her, but if you're at the consultation and I'm not, it's all yours."

Brooke inhaled, already feeling the familiar buzz of excitement that took over whenever she was on the verge of a new project.

She wanted to squeal. She refrained. Barely. "Not a problem," Brooke said, impressing herself with her cool voice.

"Excellent," Alexis said, resuming her *click-click-click* walk again. "And Brooke?"

"Yeah?"

"Welcome to the Wedding Belles."

Forty-five minutes later, Brooke had practically memorized the file on Maya Tyler and Neil Garrett that Jessie had Dropboxed her.

Not that there was much to memorize on the latter. Alexis had been right; there wasn't much to know on the guy. The Wedding Belles' details on the man were sparse, and though a thorough Google session had turned up plenty of Neil Garretts, none matched the description Maya Tyler had provided of her fiancé.

Brooke wasn't worried. This early on in the process, it was rarely about the groom anyway. Especially when the bride came from money—big money.

Booking the Wedding Belles was not a cheap endeavor—Brooke's rather impressive salary told her that. But looking through the photos of Maya Tyler that Alexis had pulled, Brooke didn't think budget was going to be an issue. Brooke's designer-trained eye spotted an awful lot of Armani and Jimmy Choo, and the woman had a definite affinity for Louis Vuitton.

By the time two o'clock rolled around, Brooke was all but rubbing her hands together in excitement.

She could work within a budget, of course. Some

of her favorite weddings had been the sweet, smaller affairs. But Brooke couldn't deny that the opportunity to have a blank check and access to all of New York's most glamorous vendors was an excellent way to salvage her career and start her off on the right foot here.

Jessie gave Brooke a quick tour of the consultation room that was off the main reception area.

No wonder the Wedding Belles have exorbitant fees, Brooke thought. There was an espresso machine, eight flavors of macaroons delivered daily. Multiple French champagne options.

The Belles had sophisticated luxury down pat.

"So, you think you can hold down the fort?" Jessie asked as they went back into the main reception area. "I got a text from Alexis. Still no luck on the missing bride, and she wants me to go check the ex-boyfriend's apartment."

"Yikes," Brooke murmured. "Let's hope she's not there."

"Right? Talk about an OMG sitch," Jessie said, pulling her curly red hair into a stubby ponytail. "Wish me luck that I don't find her. Not there, at least. Maybe she decided to get a last-minute Brazilian, you know? For the honeymoon? But you're good here?"

"Absolutely," Brooke said.

And surprisingly, she meant it. This may be her first New York wedding consultation, but she felt 100 percent in her element.

There was nothing Brooke couldn't handle. She'd seen it all. Experienced it all.

She was going to *own* this.

Not two minutes after Jessie left the office, there was a chiming sound at the main door. What better way to demonstrate top-tier service than to open it herself and dazzle the clients from the get-go? Brooke sashayed over to the door and swung it open, then promptly realized that there was one element to wedding planning that she'd never experienced, and it was a bad one.

A *really* bad one:

Wild, instant attraction to the groom.

The man standing on the other side of the door made Brooke's stomach flip in a way she hadn't felt since . . . ever.

Her mouth went dry. Her palms grew sweaty. Her breath drew up short.

It wasn't just that he was gorgeous in the stop-and-stare kind of way, although he was certainly good-looking. His light brown hair was just slightly windblown, with just the subtlest amount of curl.

The long wool coat was perfectly tailored to his lean body, and the navy color made his light blue eyes look all the more piercing. The nose was just a touch long, the brow just a bit intense, and the mouth unsmiling and sexy as hell. His skin was the vaguely gold tone of someone who tanned easily.

But it wasn't his good looks that had her feeling a bit short of breath. It was the look in his eyes—the look of surprise that she knew mirrored her own. Surprise that a perfect stranger could cause such a fierce stab of want.

And he was someone else's fiancé.

No, her client's fiancé.

Crap.

Even Brooke's "look on the bright side" mantra couldn't fix this.

"Hi, you must be Neil," Brooke said, forcing a smile and extending a hand.

"No." His voice was low, his enunciation precise.

"Sorry?"

"I'm not Neil."

Brooke blew out a slow relieved sigh, then quickly tried to cover it up with a little cough.

He wasn't Neil Garrett.

Which meant he wasn't getting married. Which meant . . .

Knock it off. You're so not in a place to be man-hunting right now.

"Oh! I'm sorry. I thought you were my two o'clock appointment," she said.

"I am your two o'clock," he snapped.

The man was literally staring down his nose at her as though she were the ultimate nuisance. Clearly, Brooke had been wrong about their attraction being mutual.

He started to brush past her, but Brooke shifted to block his way. "I don't think so. Not if your name isn't Neil Garrett, and not if you're not marrying a Maya—"

"Maya Tyler," he finished for her.

Brooke's eyes narrowed, but she moved to let him inside, ignoring the way his closeness made her heart-beat quicken.

She shut the door and turned to find him holding out his jacket to her.

Seriously?

Brooke had no problem taking her clients' jackets. Or making them coffee, or pouring them champagne, or frankly, jumping through whatever hoops they wanted her to as long as it related to the wedding.

But something about this man's entitled attitude set her on edge. No, scratch that. Everything about him set her on edge.

She ignored the jacket. "And you are?"

Their eyes locked and held for several moments. God, he was good-looking, in a pretentious, head-of-the-boardroom kind of way.

He tilted his head just slightly, a knowing look on his face as though reading her thoughts. Brooke finally grabbed at his jacket, needing an excuse to turn away from him.

"I'm Seth Tyler," he said quietly as he watched her hang the jacket on a hook near the door. "Maya's brother."

Ah. That explained his sense of entitlement. The man was one of the richest people in the country.

And actually, Brooke was a little surprised she hadn't recognized him. She followed the social scene fairly closely—there was plenty of crossover between the New York and Los Angeles social elite.

But then again, while Maya Tyler made frequent appearances at all the big-name events and dated a handful of celebs, her brother kept a relatively low profile, at least on the social scene. She'd heard his name, certainly, but never seen a picture. Brooke was certain if she had seen a picture, she would have remembered.

"A bride's brother," she said thoughtfully. "That's

a new one. I've had sisters tag along before. Mothers are almost a given. Dads, too, given the whole father-of-the-bride thing. But a brother . . . that's a definite first."

Seth's eyes never left Brooke's. "Maya doesn't have a sister. Or a mother. And as of eight months ago, she doesn't have a father, either."

Brooke forced herself not to look away in embarrassment.

He was trying to make her feel like a jerk, and it was working. She'd forgotten that Maya's file indicated both parents were deceased. She certainly hadn't *meant* to remind him about Hank Tyler's recent death, but her comment had been insensitive all the same. She was usually much better at details than this.

Still, she wasn't about to grovel beneath his icy stare, so instead, she gave a small nod. "Well then, Maya's lucky to have you."

His eyes narrowed as though assessing her statement for mockery, but Brooke merely smiled. Just let him stew on whether or not she was being sarcastic.

"Can I get you something to drink?" she asked. "A cappuccino, water, champagne?"

He glanced at his watch. "Champagne? It's barely past two in the afternoon."

Ugh. So he was like that.

A total stiff.

Good thing he was a ten physically, because his personality was trending toward the negative.

"It's also a special occasion," she said softly. "Your sister is getting married."

Seth grunted and tore his light blue gaze away from hers, and Brooke's curiosity spiked. Whatever Seth Tyler's reasons for being here, they certainly didn't involve being excited about his sister's upcoming nuptials.

Brooke tilted her head slightly and considered him. "You don't want to be here."

His eyes snapped back to her. "I wouldn't be here if I didn't."

"Really," she said, crossing her arms. "So you're telling me that you want to be standing inside a wedding planner's office right now, gearing up to talk about canapés and bustles and tea-length versus cocktail-length bridesmaid dresses, and coupes versus flutes for the champagne toast?"

Seth's gaze raked over her before he took a step closer. He was tall, but she was in five-inch heels, which meant she only had to look up slightly to meet his gaze. She didn't know why, but this man seemed determined to make her feel small. Well, screw him— Brooke wasn't going to roll over and play dead.

She'd experienced plenty of belittling in the past four months from people she actually cared about. She wasn't about to let a perfect stranger—no matter how gorgeous—get under her skin.

"You should know something, Ms. . . ."

"Baldwin," she said evenly.

"Ms. Baldwin," he said slowly, as though tasting the sound of her name on his tongue. Then he dropped his eyes to her mouth as though wanting to taste more than the sound of her name.

Brooke swallowed and forced herself not to take

a step back. "What is it that I should know?" she prompted.

His eyes lifted back to hers, and despite their closeness, despite the heat between their bodies, there was no warmth in his eyes. This was a man who'd long ago mastered the art of perfect, icy control.

"You should know that I never do anything I don't want to," he said in that low, husky voice.

"Is that so?" Crap. Now *her* voice was husky.

"It is," he said slowly. He moved even closer.

"And what is it that you want?" she asked.

His eyes drifted once more down to her mouth, and Brooke ordered herself firmly not to do anything ridiculous, say, like leaning into a man who was proving to be a pretentious ass.

Except . . .

Except, he smelled good. Really good. Like expensive cologne and man and sex, and despite the fact that Brooke was writing off the opposite sex for at least the next year, she wanted . . . she wanted . . .

Another chime at the door sounded, shattering the moment.

If it had even been a moment. A quick glance up at Seth Tyler showed that he didn't look the least bit fazed by the sexually charged encounter.

She turned on her heel, ignoring the heat of his gaze on her back, and opened the door to Maya Tyler and a man who was almost as good-looking as Seth.

Almost.

"Hi, so wonderful to meet you! You must be Maya and Neil," Brooke said, ushering them in with a warm smile as she felt her heart rate return to normal.

"I'm so sorry we're late," Maya said. "I wish I could blame it on traffic, but the truth is, my hair appointment ran long."

"It's hard for us blondes, isn't it?" Brooke said with a wink. "And it was totally worth it, by the way. You look fabulous."

Brooke meant it. Maya Tyler was every bit as gorgeous as her brother. Her eyes were the same piercing light blue as Seth's and a good deal more friendly, while her hair and skin were both lighter. Brooke could tell this was a woman who took full advantage of what must be an unlimited beauty budget—every detail, from the perfect highlights to the subtle eyelash extensions to the creamy complexion, was flawless and expensive-looking.

Brooke turned toward Maya's fiancé. The man was extremely attractive in a vaguely exotic way. His skin was a dark bronze, his eyes dark brown with impossibly thick lashes. The smile was bright white and utterly charming.

It wasn't hard to see why Maya was enamored. Everything about the man seemed likable.

Before Brooke could shake the groom's hand, she was surprised to find that Seth Tyler had stepped forward and was standing beside her, all but edging her out as he stared down Neil Garrett.

"Hi, you must be Seth," Neil said, extending a hand to Maya's brother.

Brooke's eyebrows lifted in surprise. The brother and the fiancé hadn't met?

Interesting. Very interesting.

Her suspicions were confirmed when Maya

stepped forward, a hint of nervousness on her face as she looked between the two men. "Sethy, this is Neil."

"Yeah. Got that," Seth ground out.

Brooke winced at his sharp tone. Neil, however, did not. Maya's fiancé apparently had a good deal more class than her brother, and he merely stood there, hand extended, until Seth relented and shook it.

Maya gave Brooke an apologetic smile, seemingly sensing her confusion. "Neil and my relationship has been sort of a whirlwind. This all happened so fast, and with Seth being so busy with work, he and Neil haven't had a chance to, well, meet."

"It happens like that sometimes," Brooke said smoothly, hoping to temper some of the tension she felt radiating off Seth. "Why don't we all have a seat in our consultation room, make sure everyone's on the same page about expectations, and discuss vision?"

"Excellent idea," Neil said, shooting Brooke a smile as he stepped closer to Maya and put a hand around her waist. "We can't wait to get started on this."

Brooke led the group into the conference room and pulled out a bottle of champagne from the minifridge as everyone sat around the conference room table.

Ignoring Seth's disapproving glare, she caught Maya's eye and held up the bottle. "Shall we celebrate?"

"Yes," Maya said, a little too enthusiastically.

Brooke couldn't blame her. There was way too much tension in the room for what should be a happy, joyous affair.

And she knew exactly who was to blame.

Seth had seated himself across from the happy couple, long fingers tapping against the table as he studied his brother-in-law-to-be.

Brooke made a mental note for her first task of the Tyler-Garrett Wedding: get rid of the brother.

"Just water for you, I assume, Mr. Tyler?" she said sweetly.

His gaze flicked to hers, narrowing slightly.

She gave him a pretty smile. "It is, after all, before five."

His gaze narrowed even further as it drifted over her, as though daring her to continue pushing his buttons. And she shouldn't. She really shouldn't. Not if she wanted to get this account. But he was just so pompous.

"Oh, come on, Seth, have half a glass," Neil said with a laugh.

Brooke realized then that she hadn't even been getting the worst of Seth Tyler's glares. Those he apparently reserved for Neil Garrett.

Brooke pulled four crystal champagne flutes off the shelf—whether he knew it or not, Seth Tyler needed a drink—and listened as Neil tried unsuccessfully to engage Seth in small talk. But despite Neil's rather impressive charm, Seth hadn't done much more than grunt at his sister's fiancé.

By the time poor Neil had resorted to talking about the weather, Brooke was wishing she was skilled enough with a champagne cork to aim it at Seth's head. Something needed to knock some sense into the man. His little sister was getting married, and here he was acting like he was in a board meeting with a bitter rival.

Brooke frowned at the realization that not only was there no satisfying pop of the champagne cork, the damn thing wasn't even budging. Just her luck that she'd get a stubborn cork on her first day.

"Pardon me, I'll be just a moment," Brooke murmured before carrying the bottle into the kitchen Jessie had pointed out earlier.

She needn't have bothered excusing herself. The men were too busy wading through a thick fog of tension and discomfort to notice her departure.

Or so she thought.

Brooke had just wrapped a towel around the cork and started to tug with renewed vigor when the bottle was pulled out of her hands.

She looked up to find herself staring into the unsmiling face of Seth Tyler. Without breaking eye contact, he reached out, tugging the towel out of her hand before tossing it aside.

He stepped even closer, gently pulling the bottle from her grip, and with a quick twist of his large hands, the cork obediently popped off, the sharp sound it made doing nothing to defuse the tension in the room.

He wordlessly held out the bottle, and Brooke took it. "Thank you."

"You're welcome."

The words were polite, but the glare was hostile, and Brooke rolled her eyes.

"What are you doing here, Mr. Tyler?"

"I saw you struggling with the cork. Thought I might be of assistance."

"No, I don't mean what are you doing here in this kitchen," she clarified, lifting her eyes to his. "I mean here, at the Wedding Belles. It's obvious you and your sister aren't close."

His blue eyes flickered, showing vulnerability for the first time since he'd walked in the door. "What makes you say that?"

"Oh, I don't know, maybe the fact that you haven't even met her fiancé until now?"

"They've been dating for all of three months," he said quietly. "Maya and I have lunch twice a week, and she never mentioned they were getting serious."

"Maybe she thought she couldn't talk to you about it," Brooke challenged, lifting her chin. "You're not exactly welcoming the man into the family."

"Ms. Baldwin. You know nothing about it."

"And I'm guessing you don't, either, seeing as you're doing more glowering than actual listening. So I'll ask again, what are you doing here, Mr. Tyler?"

He moved a half step closer. "I'll be the one ensuring that you get paid, Ms. Baldwin. So if you'd like our business, I'm going to suggest you check the attitude."

"So what's the plan? You're going to just shadow my every move?" she snapped.

The question was sarcastic, but to her surprise, his cold expression turned speculative. There were several moments of silence before he responded.

"Let's just say Maya means everything to me, and I'm the only family she has. I plan on being around for the details," he said quietly.

"How much of the details?" Brooke asked warily.

"All of them."

She swallowed, refusing to let herself get flustered.

"I think you should know how this works, Mr. Tyler. Getting involved with the details—all of them—involves more than you getting to spend time with the bride and groom. It also means you're going to be spending an awful lot of time with me."

Seth moved closer, crowding her against the counter in the tiny kitchen until there was nothing but body heat separating them.

Seth lowered his voice to a growl. "How much time with you?"

Brooke licked her lips, hating that it betrayed her nervousness. And her want. "Once a week at least," she said quietly. "More as the wedding gets closer."

"Hmm. Once a week," he repeated. His light blue gaze flicked up to hers. "I think, Ms. Baldwin, that things could get very interesting."

There was that strange charge in the air between them again. But this time, Brooke wasn't going to play—she'd seen enough to know this guy had some serious control issues, and was a jerk to boot.

Not to mention her very first client was in the other room, and Seth seemed to be holding the purse strings.

Brooke wasn't a stickler for rules, but getting involved with a client was a major no-no in every way. *Especially* now, when her reputation was already in tatters. No way was she going to risk her new job with the Belles for some coddled, pretentious asshole—even if he did have killer eyes and the body of a demigod.

Brooke took a deliberate step to the right and edged out from beneath his laser-sharp gaze, effectively severing the moment. "We'll see about that, Mr. Tyler," she said sweetly, then marched out the kitchen door, letting it swing shut behind her.

Chapter Five

IT WASN'T THAT SETH was a loner.

Sure, he'd been an introverted kid—the type to prefer a handful of close friends to dozens of acquaintances, if given the choice. But he'd also played on enough sports teams, been sent to enough summer camps, and been generally well enough liked through his years at prep school and college that he'd had an active social life.

Or rather, he used to.

These days he could barely find the time to go to the gym, much less accept one of the dinner party invitations that trickled in—which was why he had had the company gym fully updated and outfitted with the best equipment. He never had to leave the confines of the building to get in his fitness fix.

But there was one person that Seth could always count on to be around—even when Seth didn't necessarily want him to be.

"Dude. *Your* turn to spot."

Seth didn't even pause as he added more weight to the bar. "I have some energy I need to work out."

"Right, because I'm just a delicate canary with no life stress whatsoever," Grant muttered. Still, he didn't protest when Seth lowered himself to the bench and rested his hands on the familiar silver bar, taking a deep breath before Grant helped him lever the weight over his chest.

Seth wouldn't go so far as to say he liked working out. It was a sweaty, time-intensive affair. But somewhere along the line he'd gotten hooked on the habit. Five days a week, at least, and twice a week he and Grant went together.

His friend always joked it was the manliest possible way for two adult men to maintain a friendship.

"You're doing more than last week," Grant observed as Seth moved through his reps. "You want to talk about it?"

Seth didn't reply. This sort of interaction was pretty typical: Grant talking at him. Seth ignoring, Grant pestering anyway.

From anyone else, it would have driven Seth up the wall, but since friendships didn't come more loyal than Grant Miller, the least Seth could do was let the guy talk at him.

Still, more than two decades' worth of unshakable friendship didn't stop Seth from rolling his eyes as his friend started humming what seemed to be an awkward attempt to rap to some Top 40 nonsense in which every other word seemed to be *ass*.

And Grant was right about the weight. He had

added extra, and it *was* because he had something to work through.

Namely a certain blond wedding planner who seemed determined to haunt his every waking thought despite the fact that he didn't even know the woman.

He finished his reps, panting as he sat up and holding out his hand for a towel. Grant was now adding dance moves to his song, so Seth leaned down and fetched his own towel.

"Hey, did you see that email from the Sydney branch?" Seth asked. "About the check-in touch screens being shit."

Grant stopped "dancing" and motioned to Seth to move before he folded his lean, six five frame onto the bench, making it look uncomfortably small.

"The screens aren't shit. The people are."

Seth stared down at him. "That's what I get? This is what I pay you for?"

Grant wiped down the bar before tapping his temple. "This. You pay me for my big-ass brain."

Seth rolled his eyes. But Grant's claims about his big brain were, in fact, annoyingly true—Grant had started at the company as a college intern, just like Seth, and had been promoted to CIO a couple of years earlier by Hank, who in a very controversial and widely criticized decision had passed over older and more-seasoned candidates to give Grant the position. Lucky for Grant, Hank had never given a damn what people thought or said about him. "You sound like a douche."

"Impossible," Grant said solemnly. "You've always

cornered the market on douche bag. I can't bear to take it away from you."

"Such loyalty," Seth said.

"Right? Okay, but seriously, dude, you are extra pissy lately. All your bad vibes are harshing my mellow. What's up?"

"Harshing your mellow? Really?"

His best friend pointed a long finger at him. "Don't change the subject. Speak."

Seth crossed his arms, half wanting to tell his friend to shut the hell up, half wanting to unload some of the tension that had been hovering around him ever since Maya had dropped her getting-married bomb.

A tension that had only increased once Seth had realized that he had a serious boner for the Barbie-esque wedding planner who was not at all his type, and yet who he hadn't been able to stop fantasizing about in the week since he'd seen her.

Brooke Baldwin.

Even the name was bubbly.

Grant gave a knowing laugh. "Oh damn. I should have figured it was a woman that's got you tied up in knots."

For once, Seth wished his best friend didn't know him quite so well. It was bad enough that he and Grant had been able to read each other from the moment they'd been assigned as science partners back in the fifth grade.

Most of the time he was grateful for having his best friend working just a couple of floors below him in a corner office nearly as impressive as Seth's. But right now, when Seth wanted nothing more than to brood in silence over his sister's marriage to a gold-digging playboy, and maybe, just maybe, fantasize about a hot blonde with a fantastic rack . . .

"Oh, come on," Grant persisted as he took a slug from his water bottle. "You can't get that look on your face and then not spill."

"I can," Seth replied mildly. "Seeing as we're no longer thirteen, eagerly counting the days until we get to touch an actual breast."

"Speak for yourself. I touched my first tit at twelve."

"You did not."

"I did. Crystal Perkins, remember?"

Seth snorted. "You keep trying to sell that one, but I refuse to believe it. She was a year older and hot."

Grant lifted a finger to gesture over his tall, fit physique. "Chicks dig this."

"Yeah, *now*. But back then you had braces, acne, and walked like a newborn foal."

Still, Grant had a point. Women did seem to go crazy for him. Somewhere around twenty he'd grown into his tall frame, going from awkwardly lanky to athletic and ripped thanks to a rigid workout schedule. Add in a crooked smile, messy reddish-brown hair, and light brown eyes that his more besotted female fans deemed gold, and Seth's best friend was pretty much a bona fide ladies' man.

It was annoying as hell.

"Whatever, man," Grant said good-naturedly. "You going to tell me what your deal is, or what?"

Seth rubbed the towel over his face and relented. "Maya's getting married."

Out of the corner of his eye, he watched as Grant's mouth dropped open. "You're shitting me."

"I wish," Seth muttered.

Grant leaned forward slightly, arms resting on his knees as he stared at the floor, looking shocked.

You and me both, bro.

Seth understood Grant's reaction. Maya was almost as much of a sister to Grant as she was to Seth. Grant had more or less grown up at the Tyler residence. His own parents had lived in a lavish penthouse in Midtown, but it was a lonely, miserable existence. Grant's mom had been a semi-successful fashion model who'd traveled more often than not, his dad an equally self-involved Wall Street magnate who hadn't wanted kids in the first place.

And while the Tyler house had hardly been all bear hugs and homemade cookies, Hank Tyler had at least paid attention to Grant. Whenever Grant had stayed for dinner, which was often, he'd been included in the dinner table inquisition of "How was your day?" and "Did you get your test results?" and "Is your homework done?"

For a kid that would have been otherwise raised by a string of indifferent nannies, it had made a big impact on Grant. Which is why it made so much sense that Grant's career had taken off under Hank's protective wing—the Tyler Hotel Group was widely known as being a family-run business, and Grant Miller was, in fact, family.

Seth had never been more aware of that fact than right now, staring at his friend's horrified face.

"Who the hell is she marrying?" Grant asked.

"His name's Neil Garrett. They've been dating for three months."

"Three months? And you're letting her fucking marry this guy?"

"Hold on, champ," Seth said, holding up a hand irritably. "First of all, seeing as this isn't the eighteenth century, I don't 'let' Maya do anything. I'm every bit as pissed off about all of this as you are, if not more so, so quit trying to convince me to hate it. Right there with you."

Grant dragged his hands over his face, and then sat up straight. "Okay, so what's our plan? How we going to get rid of the guy?"

"Easy, Capone."

"Come on. I know you've thought about it."

Seth lifted a shoulder. "I may have entertained some ideas. But since getting arrested for murder's not really on my bucket list, I'm starting simpler. Figure out who the hell the guy is, if he's good enough—"

"He's not."

Seth ignored the interruption. "Look, I'm doing the best I can. You know how Maya is. If I flat out tell her not to, she'll probably go elope."

Grant grunted in agreement to this assessment.

"I don't suppose you know of any private investigators," Seth asked, deliberately not meeting his friend's eye.

Grant's gaze sharpened. "You wouldn't."

I would.

Seth spread his hands to the side and tried to explain. "I'm not getting anywhere on my own. I'm good enough with Google when it comes to looking up the time of the Giants game, and I know how to update my own LinkedIn profile, but I'm not getting anywhere on finding dirt on this guy."

"Dude, anything more than looking up the dude on Facebook is a no go. She's your sister. She'll kill you."

"It's because she's my sister that I have to," Seth snapped back. "I can't let her marry a guy she's known for all of three months. I hadn't even met the guy until after he put the ring on her finger."

Grant sat up straight. "Switch this around. Pretend that you're the one getting married, and Maya hires a private investigator to research your girl. How do you feel?"

"Wouldn't happen," Seth said automatically. "For starters, you of all people know why I'm not getting married anytime soon. Probably not ever. And if I did, it wouldn't be to a woman I just met. And if it was to a woman I just met—"

"Never mind." Grant laughed, holding up his hands in a gesture of submission. "You're impossible to talk to."

"I can't let her marry someone I don't know anything about," Seth continued quietly, silently begging his friend to understand. "If this guy turns out to be an ass, and I let her walk down the aisle, if he hurts her—"

Grant blew out a breath and rubbed a hand over his face. "I know, man. I get it. I care about Maya, too. But you know—you *know* that there are some things in life you don't get to control, right?"

Seth looked away, knowing exactly what his friend was referring to.

When Seth's father had dropped dead of a heart attack eight months earlier, the shock of it had knocked the wind out of Seth.

Only, Seth had been the only one who was shocked.

Hank's preexisting heart condition had been common knowledge to everyone except Seth. Because that's the way his father had wanted it. He'd wanted Seth in the dark. He'd said as much in a brief letter delivered posthumously that had very nearly ripped Seth's heart out.

You care too much, son. It would have consumed you, trying to fix me, and some things aren't for you to fix.

His father was wrong.

Seth could have helped. He could have taken over the reins earlier. Could have flown his father to any fancy research facility in the world. He could have saved him, if only he'd known.

But this thing with Maya had been brought to his attention before permanent damage could be done. He could have enough time to stop it, to save her. He just needed the proof.

Grant cracked his knuckles, and Seth raised his eyebrows in surprise. He'd seen his friend crack his knuckles plenty back in high school—anytime Grant was agitated.

"There's got to be another way," Grant mused. "A way to talk some sense into Maya without completely invading her privacy."

"Go for it," Seth muttered. "But she never listens to you any more than she does to me. Less, possibly." Grant and Maya had all of the closeness of blood siblings, but all of the squabbling, too. Hell, half the time Seth felt like the one breaking up their arguments, rather than the other way around.

Crack, crack. Again with the damn knuckles. "This is the time when we need a woman around."

"Why, because Maya would listen to someone with ovaries?" Seth asked skeptically.

"More than she'd listen to us. Maybe we go through Tori. If anyone can talk sense into Maya, it's her best friend."

"You've met Tori, right?" Seth asked dryly. "You really think there's a chance in hell she'd sabotage her chance of being maid of honor?"

"You're right." *Crack. Crack.* "Hell, this was probably her idea," Grant said darkly.

Seth looked at Grant askance. His friend was getting even more pissed off about this than he'd anticipated. "You okay, dude?"

"Yeah. Just . . . I can't believe she's getting married, you know?"

Seth rolled his shoulders in a futile attempt to get rid of the tension that seemed to follow him everywhere these days. "Don't remind me. I'm trying to get myself in there as much as possible. I'm helping with the fucking wedding planning."

At that, Grant tilted his head back and let out a loud laugh. "God, I'd kill to see you picking out flowers. Can I tag along?"

"No," Seth grumbled. "The damned wedding

planner already thinks it's weird enough that I'm tagging along; it'd only be worse if you were there, too."

Grant was still smirking. "My assistant got married last summer. She carried around this pink binder thing everywhere. Want me to ask where she got it? See if they have one in blue glitter?"

Seth shot him the finger. "I think that's what we're paying the damned wedding planner for. So none of us have to carry the binder."

Grant's gaze turned speculative, before his smirk grew even more shit-eating.

"What?" Seth ground out.

"Twice now it's been the *damned* wedding planner. That's a lot of heat for someone you've only met—once? Twice?"

"Once."

"And yet she's the *damned* wedding planner. Either you're taking out your frustration with Maya's engagement on this poor woman, or . . ."

Seth held up a hand. "No. No *or*."

Grant laughed. "There is so an *or*."

"Shut up, man."

"Is she hot?"

"Is who hot?"

Grant snickered and stood up, apparently abandoning the bench press. "So let me get this straight. Maya's marrying a douche bag out for her money, and you're trying to run interference by getting involved in the wedding planning, except this wedding planner's got your dick in a tangle." He flicked his towel at Seth's head. "I'm hitting the showers, man." He started to walk away.

Seth glared at his friend's back. "You're such a dick."

Grant turned back and smirked. "Tell me I'm wrong. About any of it."

Seth ground his teeth and tried not to think about Brooke Baldwin. About how full her mouth had been or the way he'd longed to wrap her long hair in his fist, to pull her head to him.

Or how her blue eyes held secrets.

His friend shook his head as he turned away. "Good luck with the damned wedding planner, man. From the look on your face right now, you're gonna need it."

But Seth wasn't listening. His friend, without realizing, had put an idea in his head that was rapidly taking shape.

Maybe Brooke Baldwin could be more than a late-night fantasy.

Maybe she was *exactly* what he needed to get the inside track on Neil. And to stop his sister from potentially making the biggest mistake of her life.

Chapter Six

◦～◦

IF THERE WAS ONE thing a wedding planner learned to master early on in her career, it was the gape-mouthed reaction to a really fabulous venue. Nothing was a larger vote of confidence to the client than a planner who swooned openly with the bride and groom over the lavishness of a beachfront villa, a perfectly manicured garden, or an honest-to-God castle.

But whereas Brooke had become mostly immune to all of the most elite reception sites in the Los Angeles area over the years, and so at least some of her boundless enthusiasm for every site was a bit feigned, New York was still very new to her.

And so it took every bit of self-control she had not to whip out her cell phone and take a picture of the Starlight Observatory that she was currently showing to Maya, because it was exactly the type of view that belonged on Instagram.

"So what do you think?" Brooke said as she forced herself to turn away from the floor-to-ceiling windows and smile at her bride and groom. "Keep in mind that this is the first one, so there's no obligation. This will just give us a starting point so you can start to get a sense of what sort of vibe you're looking for."

She watched as Maya turned in a slow circle, chewing her bottom lip as she took it all in. Maya was dressed in a pale pink sweaterdress and cream-colored knee-high suede boots that she somehow managed to make look Manhattan-chic instead of go-go-girl revival.

Brooke for her part was also feeling pretty damn fabulous. She'd dragged Heather out shopping the weekend before, demanding to be schooled in the art of looking good *and* staying warm. Turns out that was a bit of a unicorn in New York fashion. You could be warm or cute, not both, not *truly*.

Brooke had opted for cute. Naturally. But with Heather's help, she'd at least taken a step in the right direction toward surviving the East Coast winters. The socks were key, she'd learned. She'd tripled her boot collection courtesy of Stuart Weitzman, and her socks were now all thick, ugly affairs that nobody would ever see but that did a reasonable job of warding off frostbite.

The most important upgrade was the coat. Turns out puffy down coats could be fashionable, and Brooke had happily given her credit card a workout to splurge on a white puffer coat with a gorgeous fur trim and a leopard-print belt.

Slowly but surely she was starting to feel like a real New Yorker.

"I like it," Maya said, pursing her lips. "But I'm

worried that it's not different enough. I've already had two friends get married here, and it feels a little done, you know?"

Brooke nodded in understanding, fully prepared for this. She'd discovered that for most brides, there was no worse fate for a wedding than to have been done before. This was especially true the higher you went in the society food chain, and Maya was at the tippy-top.

"Absolutely," Brooke said, making a note in her planner. "Of course, if that's your main concern, I'm confident that we can make any site completely your own—with the right theme, the right vibe, we can make people forget that they've been here before."

Maya glanced at her curiously. "What are you thinking?"

Brooke opened her mouth to launch into her pitch when Neil crossed from where he'd been inspecting the far side of the room. "It's too small."

Maya wrinkled her nose at him. "What do you mean too small?"

"Well this fits what, two hundred people?" Neil asked, glancing at Brooke.

She nodded in confirmation. "Two hundred for a seated dinner."

He was already shaking his head as he placed a hand on Maya's back. "We need something bigger."

Maya let out a little laugh, but Brooke thought she saw just the slightest strain around the other woman's smile. "Really? How many people were you thinking?"

He glanced down at her, his handsome face the

picture of confusion. "I was just assuming you'd want a big wedding."

"Two hundred *is* a big wedding."

"Sure, it's good-sized, but you're a Tyler, sweetling. Half the city is going to want to see you get hitched. Plus, the press, and the—"

"Whoa," Maya said, holding up a hand. "No press."

Uh-oh. Brooke smiled politely and took a step back. "I'll give you two a moment to discuss."

"No, it's okay," Maya said. "I'd actually prefer we wait for Seth anyway. I'm sure he'll have some thoughts on this."

Brooke barely bit back a groan, but she kept her voice casual. "Oh, is he planning on joining us today?"

"Yeah, he should be," Maya said, glancing at her watch. "Said he was running a bit late, but I'm sure he'll be here any minute."

Brooke would be hard-pressed to say who was more displeased with this news, her or Neil, who despite being a grown man seemed oddly on the edge of a tantrum.

She knew why *she* didn't want Seth around, but why didn't Neil? Although she couldn't quite blame him, given the awful way Seth had treated him at the Belles headquarters.

Then she watched his handsome features relax, the tension seeming to disappear, and Neil gave Maya a gentle smile before kissing her temple. "Of course, let's wait for Seth. And if you want a small wedding, then I want a small wedding. You just can't blame a guy for wanting the whole world to see his girl in that white dress, you know?"

It was the right thing to say, Brooke thought admiringly as Maya melted against her fiancé, and then averted her eyes as the two of them locked lips in a dreamy, drawn-out kiss, partly to give them privacy and partly because, frankly, the sight of a couple in love made her stomach turn a little bit these days. Not the best thing for a professional wedding planner, but that's just the way things were for her right now.

Unfortunately, Brooke averted her eyes in the wrong direction, and her gaze landed in the doorway of the Starlight Observatory, where an angry-looking Seth Tyler stood glowering at the scene before him.

At first Brooke thought he was irritated by his sister's public display of affection, but the goose bumps along her spine told her that, nope, Seth's anger seemed focused on *her*.

Maya and Neil were still wrapped up in their kiss and hadn't yet noticed Seth, but Brooke was noticing him.

All week she'd been clinging to the fantasy that the strange and instant awareness between them had been a fluke—that the next time they saw each other, they'd respond to the other like normal human beings.

But from the way her stomach flipped when their eyes met, she knew the hope was a futile one. Whatever this thing was—insta-lust, insta-hate, whatever— it was very much present.

Still, just because it was there didn't mean she had to acknowledge it.

Brooke tucked her planner under her arm and walked toward him, a polite smile firmly in place. "Mr. Tyler. Glad you could join us."

"Ms. Baldwin. Nice to see you again." He said this without a smile, his eyes raking over her. Somehow he managed to look both annoyed and aroused. Which was perfect, since that's very much how she was feeling at the moment. Maybe they would cancel each other out.

Their forced pleasantries caught the attention of Maya and Neil, and Maya skipped over to give her brother a warm hug. Brooke noticed the way his harsh features softened when he hugged his sister, only to re-harden into their usual scowl when Neil extended a hand.

Seth didn't snub the other man, but from the slight hesitation before he took his future brother-in-law's hand, Brooke got the sense that he wanted to.

"Seth, what do you think?" Maya asked, tugging him further into the bright open space.

"About?"

"About this." Maya spread her arms to the side and spun. "For the wedding."

Seth's cool blue eyes flicked over the room, taking only about five seconds to assess before turning his attention back to his sister. "If you want to get married at the top of a skyscraper, we can do it on top of one of the Tyler Hotels for free."

Maya's smile vanished completely, and Brooke's palm itched with the urge to slap him upside the head. Neil didn't respond at all other than to move closer to Maya and rub a hand soothingly over her back.

Seth seemed to realize his mistake. "It's not that I don't want to spend money on your wedding; I just think—"

Maya glanced away, and Seth's shoulders slumped slightly, clearly at a loss for how to get himself out of the mini-hole he'd dug.

Brooke stepped forward, a soothing smile in place. "Well, I for one think we can do better. This place is fine, it's lovely, but none of you are over the moon about it, which tells me it's not exactly right."

She looked at Maya for confirmation as she said this, knowing that if Maya were to put her foot down and say the venue had to be this one, both men would concede.

But as Brooke expected, Maya's delicate features flashed in relief at having someone else make the decision for her.

"Agreed." She nodded her head enthusiastically. "I want some place that I fall in love with the first minute. Not one where I have to squint my eyes and tilt my head to the side in order to see the magic, you know what I mean?"

"Not really," Seth muttered under his breath.

Maya and Neil clearly missed his sarcasm as they pulled in for another of those dreamy, mildly nauseating kisses, but Brooke leveled Seth with a gaze that, she hoped, could not be clearer: *Knock it off. Be nice.* Seth quirked an eyebrow and offered up an innocent smile, which made her all the more infuriated. God, this guy was a pain.

"So what's next?" Maya asked, pulling herself away from Neil.

Brooke opened her notebook. "I've got four more options today. If you didn't love this one, I think I'll cross one off the list. Another skyscraper on a high floor, but a bit more intimate, and if you thought this one was too small, the next one definitely is not going to work—"

"Who said it was too small?" Seth interrupted.

There was a moment of awkward silence. Maya nervously glanced between her brother and fiancé, and once again, Brooke was the one to speak up. "Neil mentioned that perhaps the guest list might be more than what this venue can handle."

Brooke was braced for a snide comment, but Seth didn't say anything at all, and that was somehow much worse. There was no question about it—in order for any of them to enjoy this planning process, she'd have to get rid of the brother. Still, they were stuck with him for today, so maybe if she could just keep Seth and Neil separated as much as possible, nobody would lose an eye or a limb.

"I think we'll head uptown," she said. "The Miller Museum can be rented out, and it's beautiful. It could be just the thing."

"How do you know? Didn't you just move here?" Seth asked snidely.

"Seth!" Maya gave her brother an exasperated glance, but Brooke just ignored him altogether and turned to Maya, her wide smile feeling painted on. She would not let this grade-A jerk get to her, no matter what. "What do you think, Maya?" she asked brightly. "Shall we check that one out next?"

"Absolutely," Maya said. "I've never been, but I've heard great things."

"Fine," Seth said, already moving toward the door. "Maya, you have your car?"

"Yes, of course. We all—"

"Excellent. You and Neil take that. I'll take Ms. Baldwin in mine. There are some budget details I'd like to discuss with her."

Brooke refused to let her footsteps falter as they stepped into the elevator. "You have a car?"

He glanced at her. "Yes. Why?"

Oh, nothing. Just that it's very Mr. Big and I might swoon.

One of her favorite parts of the *Sex and the City* fantasy was when Carrie's mysterious Mr. Big would arrive in that sexy town car with his personal driver. One of the ultimate status symbols in New York.

Or any city, for that matter.

Too bad the car's owner was a super-douche who she had no desire to spend time with.

"I really should ride with Maya and Neil," she protested as they exited the fancy lobby out into the brisk New York afternoon. "There are a few things to discuss and—"

"There definitely are," he said smoothly before wrapping strong fingers around her bicep and pulling her gently to him. "And we can all discuss them together, once we get to the museum."

Brooke shot a desperate look toward Maya, but the younger woman gave her a happy, oblivious wave as she preceded Neil into her waiting town car. "Text me the address!"

"This way, Ms. Baldwin," Seth said.

Brooke jerked her arm free and glared, making it clear that she didn't appreciate being manhandled any more than she liked being manipulated.

He lifted his eyebrows in challenge, and in answer, she lifted her chin and walked toward the sleek black car he indicated, smiling in thanks as the waiting chauffeur opened the door for them.

Then Seth slid in, his warm hip subtly brushing against hers as he got situated beside her.

The door closed.

They were alone.

Chapter Seven

SETH REALIZED HIS ERROR in judgment the second his hand had locked around Brooke's arm to usher her toward his town car. An error that became even more prominent when he'd climbed into the car beside her, and his leg had pressed against hers.

Now his hand and his leg burned just from simple contact with the woman, through their clothes. God knew what would happen if he ever got his hands on her for real.

He'd probably combust.

As for the effect those grazing touches had had on her . . .

Seth glanced out of the corner of his eye at Brooke's profile. Noted the way her cheeks were a touch pinker than before, her breath a bit shallow.

Brooke cleared her throat and glanced down at the minimal space between them. "You're on my coat."

Seth glanced down, and sure enough he was sitting on her coat, which in turn was holding her captive against his side. "Right," he said gruffly. "Sorry."

Even as he said it, they both stayed perfectly still. Seth had to order his body to cooperate, shifting slightly so she could pull away, and the second she did, he felt the urge to yank her back again. To pull her to him, to kiss that full bottom lip, maybe pull her up and over him so she was straddling him, and just—

The privacy screen separating them from Dex, his longtime driver, came down slightly. "Pardon the interruption, Mr. Tyler. I didn't get the address of where we were heading."

"Oh!" Brooke said, fumbling with her book. "Let me get that for you."

"The Miller Museum," Seth interrupted.

Dex nodded. "Very good, sir. Traffic's especially bad today. A concert at Times Square, some rally in the park, plus construction on Third. Might take us a while."

"Wonderful," Brooke muttered as she typed something on her phone.

Dex slid the privacy screen back into place, and Seth almost wished he'd asked the chauffeur to leave it as is so he wouldn't be tempted by the blonde beside him.

His grand plan of getting close to her with the hope of talking her into doing some digging on Neil and Maya may not have been one of his best. He could barely think around the woman, much less speak coherently.

Hardly like him.

Seth tapped his fingers slowly on the leather seat beside him, forcing himself to look out the window instead of at her.

Out of the corner of his eye, he saw her slide her phone into her bag, and was surprised when she shifted her body around to face him. She didn't even try to hide the fact that she was studying him. He half expected her to start jotting notes about him in her little book.

Uptight.

Control freak.

Unlikable.

He clenched his jaw, staring out at the slowly passing city before he gave in and looked over at her. "You're staring."

She shrugged, unapologetic. "You've been to the Miller Museum before?"

He lifted a shoulder. "Once or twice."

"Your sister said she'd never been."

He gave her a look. "Do you do everything with your siblings?"

"I don't have any siblings."

"Ah."

She rolled her eyes at that. "Ah, what?"

"Ah, the only-child thing. Explains the pampered-princess bit you have going on."

"Just like you being a big brother explains the overbearing thing you've got going on?"

He shrugged, unperturbed by the accusation. "I'm not going to apologize for wanting what's best for Maya."

"Uh-huh. So the only reason you're tagging along with wedding-planning tasks that you clearly despise is because she asked you to?"

Seth narrowed his eyes at the sweetness in her

tone. "It's like I told you before: Maya doesn't have a mom or sister or father to do this with her."

"But she has Neil."

Seth couldn't stop his grimace, and now it was Brooke's turn to narrow her eyes. "That's why you're really getting all up in this business, isn't it? You don't trust Neil."

Seth drummed his fingers more rapidly against the seat in irritation, suddenly far more annoyed with the traffic than he had been a few moments earlier.

This was his chance to convince Brooke to help him, to explain that he just had a feeling Neil was bad news and wanted her help in confirming that before his sister committed herself to a totally untrustworthy jerk—or worse.

He chose his words carefully. "What do you think of him?"

Brooke scrunched her nose. "Of Neil?"

He nodded.

"He seems to make Maya very happy."

The words rolled right off her tongue, sweet and cheerful, and Seth recognized it immediately for what it was.

A line.

"Tell me something," he said, turning more fully toward her. "Do you care even a little bit about whether the people you're marrying off are right for each other? Or is it all about the check at the end of the day?"

It was an insulting question, and as expected, her placid smile disappeared altogether, before reappearing, this time with an edge. "Oh, come now, Mr. Tyler.

It's never only about the check. It's also about the write-up in all the biggest bridal magazines."

She batted her eyelashes as she said it, and though her tone was thick with disdain and sarcasm, Seth couldn't help but wonder if there wasn't a bit of truth there. He'd seen the Wedding Belles' office. Knew enough of their reputation to know that Brooke and the women she worked with weren't in this as a hobby. It was their career.

They might like what they did, but there was ambition there, too. A pride in what they did, and did well, from the looks of it.

Normally he'd have admired it.

But since Brooke's ambition would very likely see his sister marrying the wrong man, he wasn't about to applaud her for having lofty career goals.

"There's something you should know before we go any further," he said, his eyes locked on hers.

"I can hardly wait to hear it. You sure you don't want to wait until we're out of the car? Maybe you can crowd me against a kitchen counter again and invade my personal space?"

Seth's fist clenched at the memory her jab evoked—remembered just how good it had felt to lean into her, how satisfying it had been to watch her bright blue eyes go dark and stormy with want. And she did want him. She may be fighting it just as readily as he was, but there was heat between them.

A heat that was once again threatening to burn him. To burn both of them.

"I can crowd you in here, too, if you want," he said, flicking his eyes meaningfully at the privacy screen that prevented Dex from having the slightest clue as to what was happening back here.

Brooke made a slight sniffing noise. "Do these moves usually work for you? Does threatening to manhandle women turn them on?"

His eyes locked on her lips. "Sometimes. Only when they like to be handled."

Brooke's expression remained unchanged, but he could have sworn he saw a slight twitch of her hand, as though she was itching to pull him toward her just as much as he wanted to haul her across his lap and lose himself in that perfect pink pout, to slip his hands under that fussy sweater to where he just knew she'd be warm and soft.

A tense moment stretched between them before she cleared her throat and lifted an eyebrow. "You were saying there's something I should know?"

Right. Right.

"I don't think Neil Garrett is the right man for my sister," he said quietly.

"Well that comes as a huge surprise. It wasn't at all obvious from the way you glower at him every chance you get."

"I just don't want to see her get taken advantage of and make a mistake."

Brooke's eyes softened slightly. "Of course you don't. But Maya's, what, twenty-six? Twenty-seven? Plenty old enough to be making her own decisions."

"I realize that. I just want her to make her decisions with all of the facts."

She shook her head in confusion. "What do you mean?"

"I mean that I think the Neil that Maya thinks she's in love with isn't the real man. Or at least not all of the man. He's hiding something, and I need to figure out what it is before he traps her into a marriage."

For a moment something awful and real flashed across her face—as though his comment struck a raw nerve. But then she merely shook her head and let her eyes go perfectly blank as the car finally came to a stop outside the Miller Museum.

He held her eyes as he waited for Dex to come around to open the door. "Do we have an understanding, Ms. Baldwin?"

She blinked. "Seriously? No, we don't have an understanding. On the one hand, you're hiring me to plan a wedding—not only that, you're actively participating in the planning. On the other hand, you're telling me you don't intend to let the wedding actually happen. What exactly is it I'm supposed to do with that information?"

"Stay out of my way," he said, without hesitation. "Let me do what I do best."

"Which is what?" she said as the door opened, the rush of winter air providing a merciful reprieve from the building heat between them. "Controlling everything around you?"

He lifted a shoulder. "Pretty much." *When I can.*

She rolled her eyes and started to scoot toward the door, but he used his body to block hers, since he was closest to the curb.

"Brooke."

She paused and looked at him, exasperated. "What?"

"Stay out of my way," he repeated.

"Under one condition," she said with a wide, fake smile.

He narrowed his eyes and waited.

"I'll stay out of your way, big brother"—Brooke reached a hand up to his cheek, patted it with a condescending familiarity—"if you stay out of mine."

Chapter Eight

❧

AFTER SPENDING A COUPLE more hours with the happy couple and the not-so-happy brother, Brooke was more certain than ever that Seth was completely off base about his sister's fiancé.

Sure, Neil had been just a bit pushy at their first stop about wanting a large wedding, but the second he'd realized that Maya hadn't wanted that, he'd backed off completely. In fact, from what Brooke had seen so far, Neil Garrett might be perhaps the ideal groom. And she would know, having been in the business for a while and encountering virtually every type of groom out there. Generally speaking, they could be grouped into three main categories:

1. The passive-aggressive nightmares who swore up and down that they had zero opinions, that the bride could pick whatever made her happy, only to wait until after the DJ had been selected to announce they wanted a live band, or until after

the red velvet cake had been selected to announce
they wanted chocolate, and so on.

2. The guys who *actually* had zero opinions and had
to be physically dragged to their suit fittings and
rehearsal walk-throughs.

3. The more forward-thinking dudes who cared as
much as—or more than—the brides about the
flowers, who had strong feelings on crab cakes
versus mini tartlets, and who had their personal
tailor working on their wedding tux even before
they'd bought the ring. These ones often cried.

From what Brooke could tell, Neil didn't fit into
any of these. He demonstrated that he cared, in that
he provided input when explicitly asked, but he
also seemed to be more concerned with what Maya
wanted. He was polite and friendly, easygoing, and
most important, completely smitten with Maya.

He seemed . . . decent.

If Maya did have a guy problem, it wasn't on the
romantic front.

On the sibling front, however, Maya had a serious
issue to contend with. Seth alternated between silent
and glaring and pissy and opinionated. If one place
was too small, the other was too large. If one was
too fussy, the next was deemed pedestrian. The only
good news about the man being a complete ass was
that he was making it very easy for Brooke to move
past whatever this weird thing was between them.
But she couldn't ignore the effect he was having on
her bride, whose smile was growing more strained by
the minute, or her groom, whose skin had taken on a

distinctly pale pallor. By the time they were on their third and final venue of the day, it had become clear that they couldn't keep going like this.

Seth, for his part, seemed completely unfazed by the fact that he was the storm cloud on an otherwise sunny occasion, and he walked a few paces behind them, typing distractedly on his phone while Maya quietly conceded that maybe they needed to call it a day.

Brooke walked Maya and Neil through the lobby of the lavish Biltmore Hotel that had been one of the front-runners for a possible reception site, assuring the distraught bride that it was only the first day and that they would of course find the perfect venue.

She didn't add that they'd need to leave the overbearing big brother behind in order to do so, but that wasn't Maya's problem to deal with. People like the Tylers paid companies like the Wedding Belles a premium not only to identify problems such as this one but to solve them.

Although, Brooke had to admit, this particular problem was trickier than most—that the person who was paying her to solve problems *was*, in fact, the problem.

But she wasn't worried. She wasn't one of the best wedding planners in the country for nothing.

It was time to prove herself worthy of that title.

The dejected group filed outside and prepared to separate, Seth staying behind in the lobby to finish up whatever apparently super-important call had his phone attached to him like a third ear. Acting on instinct, Brooke pulled Maya into a quick hug before the other woman could slip into her waiting town car. "I'll talk to him," she whispered.

Maya didn't pretend to misunderstand. "He means well," she said to Brooke in a hushed tone. "Seth's just so used to controlling everything, and now that Daddy's not here, he thinks he has to be my protector and my brain, and . . . I love him to death, but he's driving me crazy."

Brooke squeezed her tighter before pulling back and giving Maya a reassuring smile. "He loves you to death, too. But maybe I can convince him to show his love in other ways than all this hovering."

"Yes, please," Maya said gratefully, grabbing Brooke's hands. "Let's find a way to make him feel involved without having him be so . . ."

"Involved?" Brooke rejoined with a knowing smile.

Maya nodded. "Exactly."

Neil came up beside them, sliding an arm around Maya's waist and kissing the side of her head tenderly. "Let me take you to an early dinner?"

Maya smiled up at him gratefully and nodded, and Brooke's heart twisted just a little in jealousy. Yes, she was a very self-assured woman. Yes, she could take care of herself, support herself, the whole enchilada, but sometimes after a long day when you were aching, it was nice to know that someone else was there. To share a cocktail with and let the day's tensions fade away.

She missed that.

"Maya!"

Brooke glanced over to see an unfamiliar man

headed their way, but from the way Maya's face lit up, it was obvious she knew him.

"Grant!" She rushed toward the man and wrapped both arms around his waist in a friendly hug. Brooke appraised the man with interest—he was handsome, in an easy, likable sort of way. He was unusually tall, but carried his height well, his movements smooth and easy as though he was accustomed to maneuvering all six-plus feet in whichever way he pleased. He had medium-brown hair that Brooke imagined would glint a bit red in the sunlight, warm whisky-colored eyes with thick lashes, and a good smile.

A *great* smile, Brooke amended as he grinned down at Maya.

Maya returned the happy smile. "What are you doing here? I haven't seen you in weeks, and I see you outside a hotel of all places."

"I was just on my way home from the office," he said. "What's your excuse?"

"Oh my gosh," she said, laying a hand on his chest as though it was second nature. "I haven't seen you in so long, you might not have heard." Maya reached for Neil's hand, tugging him forward. "I'm getting married!"

It was hard to say which man disliked the other more. Neil, for his part, clearly hadn't missed the easy familiarity with which Grant and Maya greeted one another, and it didn't seem to be sitting well. And there was no mistaking the flash of agony on Grant's face at Maya's pronouncement.

"Seth told me the good news. Congratulations,"

Grant said, his flat tone indicating he was feeling anything but celebratory about Maya's announcement.

The men silently shook hands, and the unspoken challenge there was like déjà vu from when Seth and Neil had first met.

Maya looked at Neil lovingly. "Neil, babe, this is Grant Miller. He's my brother's best friend. Well, and one of mine, too. We grew up together, so he's practically like a second brother."

Neil nodded in acknowledgment of this. Grant said nothing.

Maya finally seemed to realize that something was amiss but was clearly clueless as to how to fix it as she looked helplessly between the two men. Brooke stepped forward and extended a hand to Grant. "Hi there. I'm Brooke Baldwin. The wedding planner."

Grant's smile returned, not quite as bright as it was when he'd seen Maya but friendly nonetheless. "Ah yes. The *damned* wedding planner. I've heard all about you," he said with a little wink. "Speaking of, where is the magnanimous Seth?"

Now it was Brooke's turn to be confused. Seth had talked to his friend about her?

"He's on the phone," Maya said with a dismissive wave of her hand. "As always. Neil and I were just about to grab an early dinner. You should come!"

"Thanks, but I have plans later," Grant said, in what Brooke would have bet money was a smooth lie.

"Ah," Maya said. "Who's your latest lady?"

He clucked her playfully under the chin. "Nobody you know, Miss Nosy."

Maya giggled, Neil frowned, and Brooke was

suddenly feeling a little bit parched for a drink herself, preferably of the alcoholic variety. There was
always drama in the wedding-planning world, but so
far the world of Manhattan's rich and famous had a
whole other layer of subtext. She'd always thought
the East Coast was made up of a bunch of straight
shooters, but so far she'd only seen a whole lot of
what people *weren't* saying.

"Shall we get going, sweetie?" Neil said, rudely
interrupting Maya's animated description to Grant of
the various venues they'd looked at today.

She glanced at him, her smile dimming. "Right.
You must be starving. You sure you don't want to tag
along, Grant? Or Brooke?" she added politely.

"Definitely not," Grant said.

Brooke shook her head with a polite smile.

"Okay, well then. I'll see you both later?" Maya
said as Neil ushered her into the car. "Bye!"

Then the car door closed, and Brooke lifted a
hand in send-off. Grant, for his part, didn't move as
the town car pulled away from the curb.

Brooke sighed and dropped her wedding planner
into her oversized bag, and then, even though she'd
known the guy for less than five minutes, found herself
turning toward Grant. "You want to talk about it?"

His eyes snapped to hers, and she watched as
surprised wariness was quickly replaced by a mischievous grin. He glanced over her, although not in the
lecherous, checking-her-out way, more in an "I have a
plan" kind of way.

He jerked his chin toward the hotel before them.
"Seth still inside?"

Brooke shrugged. "I suppose so. He said he had a phone call, and I haven't seen him come out."

"Huh." His expression turned even more speculative as he scratched his chin. "Brooke Baldwin, would you like to have a drink with me?"

"Ah—"

Grant held his palms out. "No funny business. Just two people in need of a drink. I'll buy."

It was tempting. Very tempting. She did want that drink. But . . .

"I'd like to," she said, giving a regretful glance over her shoulder. "But there's something I need to take care of first."

Grant gave a soft laugh. "If it's giving Seth the dressing-down I'm sure the bastard deserves, can I be there to watch?"

"I thought you two were friends."

"Oh, we are. Best friends," he said, looping an arm casually around her shoulder and pulling her in the direction of the lobby bar. "Which is why I can't wait to see his face when he sees us having a drink together."

Chapter Nine

❧

SETH LIKED TO THINK he was a man who was prepared for all things.

Hurricanes. Market crashes. Breakups.

But twice in the past month he'd found himself
blindsided.

First, by his sister's engagement announcement.

Second, by his instant and slightly insane attraction to the Malibu Barbie wedding planner.

And now, just as he was hanging up the phone
with the Tyler Hotel's Tokyo office, there was a third
shock: the sight of his best friend and said wedding
planner having a cozy cocktail in a hotel lobby bar as
though it was no big deal.

"Oh, hell no," he muttered, dropping his phone
back into his suit pocket and charging toward them.

The hotel lobby at the Biltmore was one of Seth's
favorite places to drink in the city. The high price tag
of their drinks scared off the vast majority of tourists,
ensuring that the bar was generally quiet enough to
have a conversation.

Something Grant and Brooke seemed to be managing quite well as they sat hip to hip on the small love seat by the fire.

"Well, this looks cozy," Seth blurted out the second they were in hearing distance.

Brooke glanced up in surprise at the interruption. Her hands had been waving wildly as she'd been talking to Grant, but the second her eyes met Seth's, her hands dropped to her lap, and her smile froze in place.

He wasn't surprised at the obvious change in her demeanor, but he was a little . . . stung. Seth knew he'd never been quite as charming as Grant, not quite as smooth with the ladies, but he usually didn't cause someone with so much light to dim the second he got near.

"Hey, man!" Grant said in a more enthusiastic greeting, taking a sip of his cocktail and seeming completely unaware of the strange tension between Brooke and Seth.

Then he glanced up and met Seth's eyes, and Seth saw from the slight smirk that his friend wasn't unaware at all. The asshat had planned this.

Seth sighed and sat in the leather chair across from his best friend and his sister's wedding planner, and tried to ignore the fact that they looked like the perfect couple. He also tried to ignore how much that bothered him.

"Explain," he said, lifting a hand to gesture between the two of them as his other hand reached for the small black leather drink menu on the table in front of him.

"Ran into your girl here while she was ushering off Maya and that complete tool she thinks she's marrying."

Brooke groaned just as she was about to take a sip of her cocktail. "Oh God. Not you, too."

"What?" Grant asked, looking at her in confusion.

Brooke jabbed a finger in Seth's direction. "It's bad enough that I have to deal with *his* unfounded anti-Neil campaign. Now you're hating on the poor guy, too?"

"Well, he—"

"Is perfectly wonderful to Maya," Brooke said, interrupting Grant. "And I can maybe, *maybe*, get how big brother here would be all spoiling for a duel, but what's your deal?"

"I . . ." Grant glanced at Seth for help, but Seth could only shrug. If he knew how to wrangle the wedding planner, he would have done so by now. "I'm like her brother," Grant said finally.

"Riiiight," Brooke said skeptically as she took a sip of her martini.

Grant shrugged. "It's true."

Seth's eyes narrowed at the too-casual note in his friend's tone. He knew when Grant was faking it, and something was off there. But before he could figure it out, Brooke had directed her attention back to him. "Mr. Tyler. I'm glad you found us, because we need to talk."

Grant grinned and rearranged himself in his seat as though settling in for a show. His arm was around the back of Brooke's seat, and Seth gave him a warning glare, but Grant merely grinned wider.

"Can I at least get a drink first?" Seth muttered as he looked around for a server.

She nodded as though granting her subject a brief reprieve.

Seth ordered a Manhattan to match Grant's before he shrugged out of his suit coat and set it on the chair next to him.

"All right. Let's have it," he said, leaning forward slightly and rolling up his sleeves to hear whatever lecture Brooke Baldwin was going to throw his way.

His eyebrows lifted when she didn't respond right away, and he saw that her eyes were tracking the motion of his fingers, watching as he navigated around his cuff links and rolled the white dress shirt to his elbows.

"Ms. Baldwin?"

She swallowed. "Right. Okay. Here's the thing."

"The thing," Grant repeated, unhelpfully.

Brooke slapped Grant's leg in mock scolding, and Seth gritted his teeth.

"I know that you want to be involved in Maya's wedding planning," Brooke said. "But we both know your overinvolvement has nothing to do with you caring about how every penny is being spent and everything to do with you lurking over her and Neil because you don't like the guy."

Seth shrugged. "So? No secret there. I told you as much in the car today."

"Wonderful. So here's what *I'm* telling *you*. Back. Off. Even if Neil is the scum of the earth you two seem to think he is, Maya needs to discover that for herself. And"—she held up a finger when she saw he was about to interject—"if you're wrong, if he *is* a nice guy who loves your sister and will make her blissfully happy until they're both old and gray, then you need to know this: you are ruining what should be some of the happiest memories of her life."

"Now hold on," Seth said, his temper spiking. "You don't get to—"

"No, you hold on," Brooke shot back. "She's planning her wedding. A once-in-a-lifetime opportunity in which she gets to be the princess and everything she's ever wanted, and instead of walking on sunshine, she looks ready to crack every time you open your mouth to bark out some complaint."

Seth winced at the picture she was painting, and he let his mind flit back to the day that had just passed, realizing rather uncomfortably that Brooke was right. He'd gone out of his way to be an ass, mostly as a means of punishing Neil, but in the meantime he'd been punishing the one person he was trying to protect.

His head dropped forward in defeat, and he could barely muster a gruff thank-you when the server returned with his cocktail.

He took a deep pull of his drink and decided to try to explain himself. "I can't—I can't just turn it over to her and that bast— and Neil. I know you think I'm a penny-pinching asshole, but if I'm right, the wedding would be the perfect excuse for him to spend God only knows how much on caviar and the most expensive champagne, and I don't know, fucking doves and shit."

"Doves really aren't that expensive," she murmured, and Seth gave her a look.

"Sorry," she said, holding up her palms. "Irrelevant."

Seth took a sip of his drink, then ran his hands through his hair, feeling suddenly tired. "I don't know how to give up complete control and still be . . ."

"In control?" she said with a small smile that felt friendly instead of antagonistic for once.

"Yeah," he said quietly. He returned her smile, and it was, well, not a moment, exactly, but it was something. It was something to be spending time with her and not feeling like he had to shove her away out of fear that he'd pull her close and have his way with her.

"Just pretend I'm not here," Grant said in a stage whisper. "Oh wait, you already are."

Brooke gave a nervous little laugh and broke eye contact. The moment was over, but that was okay, because she still looked happy, and happy Brooke was, well . . . interesting. Attractive.

And rare, he realized as he studied her.

She was smiling, which she did often. But whether it was the drink, or the fact that she was off-duty, or the company, she was relaxed now in a way he hadn't seen her since they'd first met. Her laugh a little looser, her eyes less guarded, her gaze more open.

Seth realized then that maybe he'd misjudged the Barbie. He'd thought that the other Brooke was all there was, with her perfect smiles and inane platitudes that disguised sharp edges. But seeing her now, he realized there was another Brooke.

Perhaps the real Brooke.

The perfectly composed Brooke had made him want to do dirty, nasty things with her, and well, this one did, too.

But this relaxed, friendly Brooke who was currently looking at him with unshuttered eyes . . . he wanted to know her in ways other than just naked ways. Wanted to know what made her laugh, what made her cry . . .

Grant cleared his throat, and Seth jerked slightly.

Right. They weren't alone. But someday soon, maybe.

"So what do you suggest, Ms. Baldwin?" Seth said, sitting back in his chair and trying to pretend that this was just another business transaction. "How do you propose I control how my money gets spent, ensure my sister's not marrying a money-grubbing asshole, and make sure that Maya enjoys the process, if in fact, Neil is a decent sort?"

Brooke pulled her full bottom lip beneath her front teeth, biting down softly as she pondered this.

"Okay, don't say no right away," she said slowly.

Seth shook his head and took a sip of his drink. "Never start a negotiation that way."

"Shush," she said. "We wedding planners do things differently. Hear me out. You need to take a step back from the minutiae. Tag along to the big-money decisions, sure. The wine, even the dinner style. But when it comes to everything else, give Maya some distance. Let her shop for her dress and her cake and her bouquet without you hovering. Let her and Neil go cake tasting and ooh and aah over buttercream frosting versus fondant without her sulky big brother sucking all of the romance out of every single moment."

"But what if—"

"I'm not done," she said calmly, holding up a finger. "And, so that you're not feeling like you're spending money blindly, you and I can discuss what Maya and Neil decide after."

Seth froze at this, at the exact same moment Grant sat forward with the mother of all shit-eating smirks. "*After*? Explain."

Brooke's smile faltered a little, and Seth wanted to slap his friend upside the head for potentially ruining something that could be good. Something that could be just along the lines of what he'd been thinking of asking her to do earlier today, in fact.

"I just meant that maybe after I met with Maya and Neil on wedding-related things, I could discuss them with Se— Mr. Tyler."

Grant spread his hands to the side. "Well, I think that's a great idea. You guys could do, what, daily dinner? Drinks? Nightcap?"

"Grant," Seth said, keeping his voice mild.

"What?"

Seth ignored his troublemaking friend, keeping his attention on Brooke. "Would you tell me what happens between the two of them during the day?"

"What do you mean?" she asked.

"I mean that my problem isn't the money so much as the man. I would spend millions if it meant Maya marrying the love of her life, who'd be good to her. But if he's not that man, I want to know about it so I can do something about it."

"I'll watch him like a hawk, if you agree to take a step back," Brooke said. "That's the deal."

He gave a grim smile. "With all due respect, Neil's a good-looking guy, and he's proven himself more than adept at convincing women that he's legit. What makes you think that you can spot a phony?"

Brooke's smile turned brittle as she picked up her drink and avoided eye contact.

Aha.

So he was right about those eyes holding more than just an arresting shade of blue.

Brooke Baldwin had a secret.

Chapter Ten

WHEN BROOKE FINALLY LIFTED her eyes to meet Seth's, she knew she'd made a mistake. Even without saying a word about Clay, or her ruined wedding, he was onto the fact that she was hiding something, and was determined to figure it out.

Well, too damn bad, Mr. Tyler. I'm not going to dwell on my past failures, and I'm certainly not going to let you dwell on them.

Her past with Clay was far from a secret. She'd gone out of her way to ensure that it was out in the open, letting the wound get oxygen.

As a result, Brooke rarely felt vulnerable these days—she'd been carefully building a shield around her ever since Clay had been arrested, and most of the time it worked.

But this man . . . Seth made her feel vulnerable. She didn't like it.

Seth's gaze narrowed, and even as she was braced for him to eviscerate her, target her right where it hurt and prey on her most vulnerable inner secrets, Seth surprised her by nodding slowly, and then sitting back in his chair. "Okay."

"Okay, what?"

"I'll go along with your plan. I'll back out of the wedding planning if you promise to keep me apprised about everything—the planning, and the guy. Those are my terms."

Brooke let out a little laugh. "Done. That was easier than I thought."

He held her gaze. "I'm trying to trust you, Ms. Baldwin. Don't make me regret it."

"And don't let your guard down, either," Grant advised her. "You know Seth's just going to Google you the second he goes to the bathroom. In fact, I'm surprised he hasn't already."

"I thought about it," Seth said, his eyes never leaving Brooke's. "But some mysteries are far more interesting to unravel by yourself."

"I'm not a mystery," she said quickly. Damn it, she sounded defensive. "And don't pretend you're at all interested in peeling back my layers, or whatever. You had me all summed up as a ditzy airhead within moments of meeting me."

"Right. And I'm sure you withheld all judgment on me," he said. "No snap assumption about who I might have been, hmm?"

She pursed her lips. He knew she'd thought he was the groom.

Fair enough.

Maybe getting it out in the open would make this whole thing feel less . . . tense.

She turned to Grant. "I thought Seth was the

groom when I first met him. He's all riled up about it since clearly he's a classic marriage-phobe."

Grant's usually at-ease expression flickered, and he gave Seth a wary glance as though Brooke had her foot hovering over a land mine.

"Sorry," she said quietly. She didn't even know what she was apologizing for, but instinct told her she'd jabbed a sore spot. And even though her brain was racing with curiosity, her heart knew all too well what it could be like to have someone pick at your wounds when you weren't prepared.

Still, the thought of Seth Tyler having wounds seemed implausible, to say the least. He was so rigid, so deliberate in everything he did. It seemed impossible that anyone would get the drop on him to hurt him.

But someone had hurt him, she realized as she studied him under her lashes. It was written all over the tense lines of his mouth.

"Don't apologize," Seth said curtly. "My idiot friend here is apparently under the impression that I was once closer to the altar than I actually was."

Grant opened his mouth as though he wanted to argue but snapped it shut and picked up his drink.

"I proposed to my ex," Seth said in the same bored monotone voice someone might use if they were announcing that it was raining. "She said no. End of story."

Brooke tried to keep her expression blank, but poker face had never really been her thing. Her heart hurt for him, but more than that, she hurt for the way he thought he had to hold it inside.

She knew all too well what it was like to put on a brave face when your insides were in splinters.

"Stop that," he muttered quietly.

"Stop what?"

"Feeling sorry for me."

"Seth hates pity," Grant explained.

"Who doesn't?" Brooke said quietly.

For a moment, her eyes met Seth's, and a brief spark of understanding flashed between them. Two people who'd been hurt but who would go to their grave before admitting it, even to themselves.

Then the moment was over, and he lifted his glass in a silent, mocking toast.

Grant leaned forward to grab his cocktail off the table, finishing the last sip in one swallow before slapping his palms on his knees and standing. "Well. This has sure been fun."

"Where the hell are you going?" Seth asked.

"Got a date," Grant said, pulling out his wallet and extracting enough bills to cover all of their drinks plus tip.

"With whom?" Seth challenged.

Grant ignored this, instead reaching down for Brooke's hand and raising it up to his lips as he bent, kissing the back of it in a gentlemanly gesture that Brooke found oddly charming. "Ms. Baldwin, you are beyond lovely. It was a pleasure."

Seth rolled his eyes, and Grant gave Brooke a sly wink before stepping back, clamping his friend on the shoulder in farewell, and strolling out of the hotel bar without a backward glance.

"Do you think he really has a date?" Brooke asked.

Seth shrugged. "I doubt it."

"Why, because he's in love with your sister?" Brooke asked sympathetically.

Seth's face went blank in stunned confusion. "What?"

Brooke froze. Was this not common knowledge? It had taken her exactly five minutes of being in Grant Miller's company to figure out that he had it bad for Maya, but judging from the stricken look on Seth's face, he had no clue.

"He's like her brother," Seth said.

"*Like* her brother, but not," Brooke said, keeping her voice gentle. "But you would know better than me. Maybe I read the whole situation wrong."

"I'd like to think that you did." Seth dragged a hand over his face. "But . . . Grant didn't handle it well when I told him about Maya's engagement. I didn't think a thing of it, because I didn't handle it well, either. I assumed his motives were protective. Brotherly." His eyes widened as he registered the full implication of what Brooke was insinuating. "Holy shit."

"Maybe they were," Brooke rushed to interject. "Look, I shouldn't have said anything, really. It's the dang martini, loosening my tongue. It's why I don't usually drink with clients."

Seth's smile was slow and dangerous as he leaned forward. "Don't drink with clients, huh? And yet here you are."

"I'm here because Grant asked me to drinks, and Grant is not my client."

"Huh," he said. "But you could have told Grant

you wanted to grab a drink elsewhere. And yet you came right back into the hotel where you knew I'd be."

"Because I wanted to talk to you. About the wedding, and us working something out so your sister can actually enjoy her wedding planning," she added quickly.

"And we've come to a mutually satisfactory agreement," he pointed out.

She hesitated, feeling like it was a trick statement somehow. "Yes."

His smile was slow and confident. "Yet, you're still here."

She opened her mouth to retort, but . . . he was right. She was still sitting here, and even stranger, she didn't want to leave. A part of her didn't want this moment to end, even though she wasn't sure if it was actually pleasant.

He gave her a knowing smile. "Rethinking your strategy?"

She finished the rest of her drink. Sure. They could go with that. "Let's just say that willingly putting myself in your company on a regular basis brings a whole new level of meaning to 'taking one for the team.'"

His smile dropped, and for a second, Brooke could have sworn he looked almost hurt. Which made no sense, because the man didn't even pretend to like her. He might want her, yes—Brooke wasn't stupid—but he'd made it clear he didn't *want* to want her.

And yet the expression on his face right now looked suddenly, horribly, lonely, and for the life of her, Brooke couldn't figure out how she felt about that.

Seth gave a curt nod and finished the rest of his own drink. "So we're done here, then."

"Mr. Tyler."

His eyes flicked up, cold and ice-blue as always, and yet . . . maybe they weren't cold so much as wary. And perhaps she could understand that. Just a little.

"Do you want—" Brooke licked her lips and tried again. "Do you want to have another drink with me?"

His eyebrows lifted. "Here? Now?"

She nodded.

Seth studied her in that cool, assessing way he had so perfected. Then he stood, and Brooke's heart sank—both from the disappointment of having taken a risk that hadn't paid off and from the strange pang she had at the thought of watching him walk away.

But he didn't walk away.

Without so much as a hesitation, he rounded the small cocktail table to sit beside her, settling into the seat Grant had vacated just a few minutes earlier.

His distance was perfectly respectable. He didn't crowd her, didn't touch her, and yet somehow he seemed so much closer than Grant had been.

"This okay?" he asked quietly, suddenly looking adorably unsure of himself.

Brooke smiled. "Yeah. Yeah, this is just fine."

Seth held her gaze until the arrival of the waitress ended the moment.

"Martini?" he asked, jerking his chin at her empty glass.

"Yes, same thing, please," Brooke said, smiling up at the waitress. "Belvedere, slightly dirty."

"I'll take another Manhattan," Seth said.

When Brooke turned back to him, he looked amused.

"What?" she asked.

"A dirty vodka martini . . . somehow that seems to be exactly the perfect drink for you."

Brooke tilted her head. "Do you always mean for things to sound the way they do when they come out of your mouth?"

"How's that?"

"Provocative."

"What's provocative about repeating your drink order?"

"The dirty part," she muttered, looking away.

His laugh was low and sexy. "Ms. Baldwin, I assure you that I didn't mean it inappropriately, but I'm intrigued that you took it as such."

She ignored this, deciding that if she was going to survive this—whatever "this" was—she'd need to get the upper hand.

"So tell me about this woman," she said, keeping her voice light. "For someone who's so anti-wedding, it sounds like you came rather close. Grant seemed to agree."

"Grant's delusional. Although, I never said I was anti-wedding."

She snorted. "You don't have to. You wear your skepticism like a scarf."

His expression turned considering. "I think marriages can work, absolutely. I just don't think they work for the lovey-dovey reason you see in the movies."

"Lovey-dovey? Really?" Brooke asked. "Also, could you be any more cliché right now?"

He gave a little laugh. "You get that a lot, huh?"

"Let's just say the whole 'true love is a fantasy' routine is a bit tired."

"And what would you have us all subscribing to?" he asked as the server approached with their two cocktails balanced perfectly on a tray. "That we're all just waiting to be tamed by the right woman?"

Brooke waited until the server had placed their drinks down and moved away, buying herself some time.

"Not tamed," she responded finally. "We women just want—we hope . . ."

Brooke trailed off, and Seth shifted his body to face her more fully, his expression turning earnest. "What? What do you hope?"

"That someone good will love us," she said quietly.

He blinked in surprise, and she gave a little sigh as she picked up her drink. "I know. It's sad, really, how simple it is. But the truth is, I don't think any of us women really want or need the roses and the fancy dinners or even the poetry so much as we just want the love."

Seth said nothing as he watched her take a sip of her martini. She should watch herself. Martinis packed a punch, and the glasses at this bar were large. And yet, while she certainly felt the buzz from her last one, she also wasn't entirely sure that it was just the alcohol at work.

She was pretty sure the man next to her was every bit as intoxicating as the vodka. Maybe more so.

"Okay, so what's your take on it?" she said, embarrassed by how vulnerable she felt after her overshare. "You said that marriages could work, but not for the 'lovey-dovey' reasons. Why do you think some of them last, then?"

"For the same reason any merger works. When both parties stand to benefit equally, there's no reason it shouldn't work."

Brooke stared at him. "That's . . . that's . . . hideous."

"How so? Everybody wants something, Ms. Baldwin. It's just a matter of ensuring each side can offer the other what they want."

"All right," Brooke said, turning toward him and matching his posture. "I'll play along. What is it that your ex wanted that you couldn't offer?"

His head snapped back a little, and Brooke gave him a victory smile. He hadn't seen that one coming, and that was exactly her point. It drove her crazy when people talked about relationships in that cool, emotionless tone right up until the point you talked about *their* relationship.

"Nadia . . ." His gaze drifted to somewhere over her shoulder as he considered. "I don't know what Nadia wanted. I'm not sure that Nadia knew what Nadia wanted. Maybe that was the problem."

"What about you? What did you want that she wasn't offering?"

His eyes came back to her, and Brooke suddenly felt just a tiny bit breathless. No, it definitely wasn't the vodka that was her main problem. It was him.

"I want stability," he said quietly. "I want someone who won't offer up any surprises. Not that Nadia was volatile; I just didn't know what she was thinking. I like to know. Everything."

"So, your ideal mate is a robot," Brooke said.

He gave her a rueful smile. "Believe it or not, I do understand just how unreasonable I must sound. It's why I'm not exactly holding my breath to get married anytime soon. Or ever."

"At least until they come out with an attractive cyborg model," she said with a little wink.

They were sitting closer now. Just inches separating them. When had that happened? *How* had that happened?

And yet Brooke didn't move away. Neither did he.

Belatedly, she realized they were steering into personal territory. She had to think of this as a business meeting between two associates, that was all. So she had to get back to the business at hand.

She cleared her throat. "So where does Maya fit into all of this? What if Neil can give her what she wants?" she asked. "What if she and Neil both benefit from the marriage? Excuse me, *merger*."

He gave her a ha-ha look, but he answered her question seriously. "Maya wants what any woman with no parents and a crusty brother wants. A companion. My sister is . . . she's lonely."

"Not a word I'd use to describe her," Brooke said slowly. "But I suppose you'd know better."

He shrugged, looking uncomfortable. "She has plenty of friends. And me, of course. But even when she was young, Maya was always one of those people who flocks to others. Not because she needs them; she just likes them. She gets her energy from those around her—specifically, from people who love her."

"And you don't think Neil Garrett is that guy?"

"Honestly?" he said, rubbing a hand over the back of his neck. "I'm not even sure Neil Garrett is Neil Garrett."

Brooke stiffened. Seth meant his comment off-the-cuff. As far as she knew, he didn't have a clue about her history with Clay beyond what she'd told him.

But his words brought up bitter memories, memories of a man who wasn't who she thought he was. Not in person, not in intentions . . . not even in name.

"Since I'm going to be practically spying on the poor guy, I need to know—what makes you think that about Neil? Why don't you trust him?" she asked Seth, keeping her voice calm.

He picked up his drink, studied the dark cherries before taking a thoughtful sip. "I don't know. Hunch, mostly. Everything about him is so vague. His family. His job. His past. All of his social media profiles were created at the exact same time, about a year ago."

"Plenty of people were late to the social media game," she said. "Including yourself."

He gave her a curious look, and she blushed as she realized what she'd just given away.

Seth leaned toward her slightly, his smile devilish. "Why, Ms. Baldwin. Have you been researching me?"

"I research all my clients," she answered in a clipped voice.

His smile only widened. "What is it that you wanted to know?"

She didn't look away. "What made you tick. What your angle was."

"My *angle*?"

"That first day," she said, not breaking his gaze, "you were so reserved and yet so forward. The contradiction was puzzling, and I wanted to know what you wanted."

"I think you know exactly what I wanted, Ms. Baldwin." Very slowly, Seth's hand extended toward her, his large finger gently touching her jaw. "What I still want. And perhaps more to the point . . . I think you want it, too."

Chapter Eleven

❦

SETH HAD PUSHED HER too hard.
Too fast.

The entire ride back to Brooke's apartment, he
kicked himself for misgauging the situation.

It was rare for Seth to make a misstep, but he'd
definitely made one tonight, and Brooke was making
him pay for it with the silent treatment.

The second he'd touched her and pushed her to
admit she wanted him, she'd turned skittish on him
and clammed up, offering only a tight little smile
that didn't come close to reaching her eyes before she
abruptly changed the subject. They'd stayed at the
bar long enough to finish their drinks, but the mood
had been deliberately impersonal on her part as she'd
rambled on about flowers and bows and canapés, in
what he knew was a deliberate attempt to keep him
at bay.

Which was fine.

He didn't have time for a dalliance with anyone,
much less his sister's ditzy wedding planner.

But then she wasn't ditzy, now was she? Behind those practiced smiles and guarded eyes, Brooke Baldwin was . . .

Well, she was a surprise.

She was a romantic, sure, but she was also deliberate in her romanticism. As though her unshakable belief in happily ever after was a conscious decision rather than a default fantasy born out of naïveté.

And even more puzzling was her admission that what she wanted—*all* she wanted—was someone good to love her.

The simplicity and earnestness behind her words had nearly taken his breath away, and now as she sat stiffly beside him, keeping her face pointed resolutely away from him, he wanted very much to pull her toward him and beg her to explain what she'd meant.

To figure out how to be the kind of *good* that she wanted.

He supposed he could find out. He could research her in the same way he was researching Neil. Find out what made her tick. What secrets she held. But he was realizing he didn't want to find out that way. He wanted her to tell him. Wanted her to confide in him.

Why he wanted that, he didn't know. He didn't want a relationship. Hell, he wasn't even sure he wanted a friendship.

And yet, neither was he ready for her to get out of the car. To walk away from him with all this strange tension lingering between them.

"When will I see you again?" he blurted out.

She looked at him in surprise.

"For our deal, I mean. To discuss the wedding."

"Oh. Right." She dug around in her bag and pulled out her planner. "Um, Maya and I are doing an initial consultation at a couple of dress shops on Friday, but you won't want to know about any of that, so . . ."

"Friday is perfect."

She glanced up. "What?"

"What time is your appointment?" he asked, ignoring her surprise. The car had just pulled up outside her building, which meant he had to act fast.

"Two," she said begrudgingly.

"And it'll last how long?"

Her eyes narrowed. "There are a couple of shops I want to take her by, see what sort of vibe she likes. Factoring in traffic, we should be wrapped up by five or so."

"Five. Done."

"No, not *done*. I'm not seeing you on Friday."

"You said that if I butted out of the wedding planning, you'd keep me apprised."

"Sure, of the stuff that's relevant to you and that has to do with Neil. Neil won't even be there. Maya's dress is completely irrelevant."

"And going to be terribly expensive."

Her mouth snapped shut, her teeth making an irritated little clicking noise. "Yes, I suppose it's likely to be expensive, depending what she's looking for."

"And I'll be paying for it," he said with finality. "So let's make it five thirty on Friday."

He pulled out his phone to schedule it in, refusing to look Brooke in the eye for the irritation he knew he'd see there. Yes, he was controlling the situation, pushing her too hard. But Seth didn't back down. He didn't know why, but making time for Brooke Baldwin in his life felt necessary somehow, and he didn't much care whether she liked it or not.

"Fine," she snapped. "Five thirty. I can come by your office, we can review whether or not your sister wants a sweetheart or halter neckline—"

"And then I'll take you to dinner."

Her hand was on the door handle, and she shoved the door open, likely catching Dex by surprise.

Seth leaned over and caught her arm before she could go storming out of the car. "Ms. Baldwin."

She shot him an angry glare. "Do you realize how many times you just interrupted me? How pushy you are at trying to achieve your agenda?"

He opened his mouth, and then shut it as he realized he had been horribly high-handed with her. "I'm sorry."

Her mouth opened to retort, but then she shut it and gave him a suspicious look as she jerked her arm free from his grasp.

His fingers itched to touch her again, but he clenched his fist instead and took a steadying breath and forced himself to make the request of her. "Ms. Baldwin. Will you have dinner with me on Friday? Please?"

"To discuss Maya's wedding dress?" she asked warily.

Fuck no. He didn't give a shit about his sister's wedding dress.

But he'd set himself up for this bullshit, so he forced himself to nod. "Yeah."

"All right," she said slowly. "We can do dinner. But, Mr. Tyler, I really need you to understand . . . I'm not looking for anything . . . romantic. Or sexual. This thing between us—I'm not going to pretend it's not there, but I'm also not going to act on it. My career with the Belles is too important to me to risk screwing it up over something like this."

His fist clenched harder, and he pulled his hand back at the rejection. He wasn't surprised. Hell, he didn't want anything, either; it was just . . . the straight-up dismissal burned. Not only because he was turned on as hell every time he looked at her, but because he got so much damned energy just from being around her.

And the feeling, apparently, was not mutual.

"It'll just be a business dinner," he said, his voice low and quiet. "I have them all the time."

Which was true. Just not with people who looked like her. Not with people who made him feel the way she made him feel.

"Perfect," she said primly. "I'll see you Friday at five thirty, then. Shall we meet at the restaurant?"

"At my office, just in case I'm running late," he said. "If that's okay."

She nodded. "Okay, then. Have a nice night, Mr. Tyler."

"You too," he said gruffly as she shut the door behind her.

But he wouldn't have a nice night.

He'd be too busy trying to get her out of his damn head.

Chapter Twelve

⮑

I CAN'T BELIEVE YOU got us an appointment at Blanche," Maya said admiringly as they stepped out of her town car onto the sidewalk outside one of the city's most elite bridal shops.

"This is what you get when you hire the Belles," Brooke said with a smile. "The best."

"I know, but I have friends—famous friends—who couldn't even get in," Maya said, sounding slightly awed.

Brooke wasn't surprised. Small, tony shops like Blanche very carefully cultivated their air of exclusivity. She knew they'd rather needlessly turn someone away than give them the impression that they were overly available.

But that's why people hired the Belles. Half of a wedding planner's job was wooing not just the brides but the vendors.

And lucky for Brooke, Alexis Morgan had gotten her stiletto-clad foot in the door of all the most elite vendors.

Brooke smiled indulgently, proud of herself for clearly impressing her client. They'd had a great day so far, a complete one-eighty from the disastrous venue-scouting day. It turned out that spending time with Maya Tyler without the presence of her hovering fiancé or domineering big brother was actually quite fun.

Brooke had liked the woman before. It was hard not to like someone who seemed so determined to be pleasant at every turn. But after the two of them had started their wedding dress consultation day with a Starbucks run, just the two of them, she was delighted to find signs of a sharp wit hiding beneath that angelic face. There was a tartness to Maya that had Brooke realizing that in addition to being an easy-to-work-with client, Maya was also the type of woman that could become a friend.

"Look at these potted plants," Maya crowed as the climbed the steps to the discreet brownstone that housed the dress shop. "Everything's so white. The flowers, the pots. I'm surprised they didn't spray paint the freaking stems. I mean, how *dare* they be green."

Brooke snickered. If she was being perfectly honest, she wasn't overly excited about this particular appointment. The woman on the phone had been perfectly civil—ingratiating, even—but there was a fine line between exclusive and snobby, and her instincts told her that Blanche would be coming out on the latter side of the scale.

Still, Maya was a hotel heiress who'd probably literally used silver spoons growing up—Brooke couldn't not at least show her the place.

Brooke rang the bell.

"Hello?" The voice that answered managed to sound upscale and refined even through the intercom crackle.

"Hi, Brooke Baldwin here with Maya Tyler for our two o'clock appointment?"

"Let me check the books."

Brooke saw Maya roll her eyes and smiled. "By all means. Please check them," she said sweetly.

"Ah yes, here you are. Someone will be right down to greet you."

The door opened not two seconds later, and Brooke and Maya exchanged a glance at the ridiculous pretense of the whole thing. An attractive brunette dressed in a white pantsuit held a silver tray with two glasses of champagne and a plastic smile.

"Welcome to Blanche," she said, all but bowing as she extended the tray toward them. "I'm Marietta, assistant to Ms. Boulud, who graciously awaits your presence upstairs."

Brooke didn't hesitate in grabbing for one of the glasses. She'd need a drink to get through this.

Maya must have had the same thought, because she too gratefully snatched up one of the elegant flutes and didn't hesitate to take a rather large sip. The two women's eyes met and they smiled.

Unsurprisingly, the entire foyer was white marble. As were the stairs. Brooke and Maya exchanged yet another skeptical glance as they followed Marietta's curvy backside up the winding staircase.

The upstairs was slightly less sterile-looking in that the hardwood floors had been left in their natural, dark wood state rather than being white-washed like everything else.

The woman that waited at the top of the stairs, however, was anything but natural. Her blond hair was platinum to the point of being nearly white. A perfect match for her blindingly white smile and her equally white wrap dress.

Shoes? White. Manicure? White. Jewelry? White.

The only part of her not white was her skin, which was a very unnatural orange shade.

Brooke took a quick sip of her champagne to keep from giggling outright and saw Maya do the same.

The white-and-orange woman approached. "Ms. Baldwin. Ms. Tyler. A pleasure. I'm Stacy Boulud, one of the lead sales specialists here at Blanche."

They did the requisite handshakes before Stacy glared at Marietta and shooed her away with a one-fingered wave.

"This way, please. To the salon," Stacy said, turning on her heel.

"I feel like I need to confess that I'm terrified right now," Maya whispered.

"Me too," Brooke whispered back.

The salon was in fact a large circular living room that kept with the white theme right down to the coasters.

"So, Ms. Tyler," Stacy said the moment Brooke's and Maya's butts hit the white couch. "Have you given any thought to which designer you'll be using?"

"Hmm." Maya furrowed her brow. "No, not quite."

"Because we have access to all of them," Stacy

interrupted. She held up her hands to gesture around at the Spartan room. "Do you see any dresses here?"

"Well, no."

"No, you do not," Stacy said proudly. "Because we would never display anything off the rack. We offer only custom confections."

Confections?

Brooke had seen her share of uppity dress shops, but this was a whole new level. Still, if there was ever a bride that was at the top layer of society, it was certainly Maya Tyler, so Brooke kept her smile firmly in place lest this be exactly the kind of ass-kissing Maya was accustomed to.

"At this point I'm not ready to commit to a dress shop, much less a designer," Maya said sweetly.

Brooke felt a little stab of appreciation. Nicely done, letting Stacy Boulud know that she was a long way off from having secured their business.

The other woman gave a stiff smile. "Who else are you looking at? Because I can assure you we're the best in the business."

"Brooke is taking care of managing all my options," Maya said smoothly. "Why don't you tell me a little bit about your process?"

"Of course. Well, for starters, we have several brainstorming sessions on style and materials and vision before we even think about coming at you with a tape measure. We know that a wedding dress isn't just a dress. It's part of the decor."

Oh dear Lord.

"Um. Wow," Maya said. "That's an interesting take on it."

Stacy's phone rang, and she winced as she glanced down. "I'm so sorry, Ms. Tyler. This number has been calling constantly, and I really need to address it promptly, if you don't mind?"

"Sure, of course," Maya said a little too readily.

The second Stacy stepped away, Maya turned toward Brooke and mouthed, *Yikes*.

Brooke bit the inside of her cheek to keep from laughing and gestured with her chin toward the champagne chilling in the bucket in front of them. "More?"

"God, yes," Maya muttered.

Brooke topped off both of their glasses, their gazes catching as snippets of Stacy's conversation drifted toward them. The other woman was making no effort to keep her voice down, and she was clearly not pleased with whomever was on the other end of the call.

"I'm sorry, who referred you to us?" Stacy said in an impatient tone and then paused. "Mmm. I see. Well, we only accept appointments from people who've been personally referred by past clients."

Stacy examined her manicure as she listened to the person on the other end. "Well, if you were able to give us a reference. Perhaps someone who could recommend your . . . connections?"

This time she barely gave the person on the other end a chance to respond before cutting them off once more. "I'm sorry, but it seems we're all booked up for the next couple of years. Best of luck finding a shop that fits your needs."

Brooke swallowed her anger. She'd seen this

plenty of times—but while she was fine with vendors who were picky about finding the right clients, there was a cruelty to Stacy Boulud that was hard for her to stomach.

"Sorry about that," Stacy said, returning to her seat across from them. "Sometimes desperate brides can be so persistent."

"Mmm. Yes, shocking that they'd want access to the best dresses, just like the rest of us," Maya said sarcastically.

Stacy gave a nervous laugh. "Yes, well . . . as I was saying, about our process—"

"Actually." Maya sat forward and set her champagne flute on the coffee table. "I don't think your process is going to work for me."

"I'm sorry?"

Stacy looked so stunned, Brooke wished she had a camera.

"Well, it's just that you said you're booked up for the next couple of years. My wedding is in just a few months," Maya said in a sweet, anxious voice.

Stacy's made-up eyes widened as she realized she'd essentially just put her stiletto-clad foot in it. "No, I was just—"

"And, you said you only take clients with referrals, and I don't have any referrals, do I, Brooke?" Maya asked, turning toward Brooke with comically wide, innocent eyes.

"No," Brooke said, all too happy to play along. "I'm sorry, but I'm new in town. No referrals."

"Shoot," Maya said, slapping her palms gently against her thighs in dismay before popping up.

"Well, looks like we'll have to find a shop that fits our needs."

Stacy shot upright. "Ms. Tyler, please, I'm sure that we can find you the perfect dress. Something beautiful and custom and befitting of your status."

"The only status I care about right now is my status as a bride. And that makes me no different from that woman on the phone who deserves to have her dream dress every bit as much as I do."

Maya had dropped the soft-and-sweet routine, looking outright fierce, and Stacy's cheeks turned pink even beneath the orange of her fake tan. "But, Ms. Tyler—"

"I think we're done here," Maya said to Brooke, ignoring Stacy altogether.

Brooke had never really seen any similarities between Maya and her brother before, but she saw it now, as Maya's straight spine and cool eyes mimicked her brother's almost exactly. Brooke was positive this was what Seth Tyler must look like when doing business with someone who'd pissed him off.

Which she was guessing was most people, knowing how difficult the man was to please.

Brooke gave Stacy a little shrug as though to say, "What can you do?" and then followed Maya down the stairs, past a fascinated-looking Marietta and into the cold winter afternoon.

Only when they'd descended the steps did Maya slow down and turn around. She put a hand over her mouth and let out a startled little laugh, and just like that, she was back to being sweet, pleasant Maya. But the fact that she had some steel beneath all those soft curves made Brooke like her all the more. Especially since Maya had used the ice-princess routine for all the right reasons: to put an outright snob in her place.

"Can you believe her?" Maya said.

"I'm so sorry," Brooke said. "I promise the others won't be like that."

"Oh, stop." Maya waved her hand as the driver opened the door for them. "You had to show it to me, of course. Blanche is the best, and I did say I want the best, just . . . not like that, you know?"

Brooke slid in beside Maya. "You lied about not having referrals, didn't you? I'm guessing you must have friends who got their dress there."

"Oh, dozens," Maya said. "And their dresses were gorgeous, but the whole thing in there just didn't feel good. It didn't feel like me."

"What does *good* feel like for you?" Brooke asked, hoping to finally be able to get a read on what Maya was looking for.

Maya sighed. "I . . . is it weird that I don't know?"

Brooke smiled. "Not at all. Plenty of brides are surprised to realize that daydreaming about a hypothetical wedding is a lot different from planning an actual wedding."

"But it's not just the wedding," Maya said, sounding a bit tired. "It's . . . everything."

"Explain?"

Maya touched a hand to her forehead. "Do you think . . . do you think it'd be okay to skip the rest of the dress appointments? Or are we on a short timeline?"

"No, of course that's okay," Brooke said. "We have

plenty of time, and you haven't even set a date yet, so everything can be as flexible as you need it to be."

"Not everything," Maya muttered, staring down at her hands.

Uh-oh. Brooke knew that voice, and it was not the voice of a bride with wedding stress. It was the voice of a woman who was feeling a bit lost.

"Maya. Do you want to talk?" Brooke asked gently.

Maya glanced up. "Yes, actually. I would love that. What do you say we exchange the wedding dress shopping for a glass of wine?"

"A fabulous trade," Brooke said.

Maya rolled down the window of the partition between them and the driver and directed her chauffeur to a wine bar over on the Upper West Side.

Twenty minutes later, Brooke and Maya were seated at a cozy high top near the window, armed with a glass of sauvignon blanc for Maya and a class of cabernet franc for Brooke.

"So what's going on with you and my brother?" Maya asked with a mischievous smile.

The question was so unexpected that Brooke didn't quite have a chance to come up with an evasion. "Hmm? Oh, um. Huh. Nothing, really. Why do you ask?"

Maya laughed. "I knew it. You two totally have a thing."

"No, no thing," Brooke said quickly.

"Right. So you're telling me you're not seeing him later to report back on this meeting?"

"He told you that?"

Maya snorted. "Of course not. Grant did."

I'm sure he didn't tell you I'm supposed to spy on your fiancé. Brooke tried to divert the conversation back to Maya. "Tell me about Grant."

Maya's blue eyes narrowed just slightly. "What do you mean?"

Brooke took a sip of her wine, keeping her face neutral. "I'm just curious about him. He's ridiculously likable."

"Oh?"

Brooke didn't think it was her imagination that Maya's gaze went just slightly guarded at Brooke's comment, and somehow she was very sure that this— Grant—was exactly what was causing Maya's cold feet.

"Did you two ever date?" Brooke asked casually.

"No!" Maya looked horrified. "Why, did he tell you we had?"

"Why would he tell me you had if you hadn't?" Brooke asked, tilting her head in confusion.

Maya pointed a finger in Brooke's direction. "Oh, you're good. You're really good."

Brooke winked. "I know."

Maya heaved out a breath and took a sip of wine. "Okay, you want to know what went down with me and Grant?"

Brooke didn't respond. She just waited.

"Nothing," Maya said, slapping the table a little with her fingers. "Nothing went down. Not in the dirty way, not in the romantic way. It's just he . . . we . . . I always thought that . . ."

"That you'd be more than friends?"

"Yes!" Maya said gratefully. "I mean, I had a crush on him for most of my life. He was my older brother's best friend, you know?"

Brooke nodded. "Classic."

"Exactly. It's a classic, and I always waited for that moment where he'd do what he was supposed to do and wake up and see me differently. As a woman, instead of as Seth's little sister."

Oh, he sees you, Brooke thought silently. *He definitely sees you.*

It also hadn't escaped Brooke's notice that Maya had yet to utter her fiancé's name once throughout this chat. In fact, the entire day, the word *Neil* had not passed Maya's lips.

And now, seeing how animated Maya got talking about a man she wasn't going to marry, Brooke had to wonder if maybe, just maybe, Seth might be onto something about this impending wedding being bad news. But not for the reason he thought.

"Did you ever tell Grant how you felt?" Brooke asked carefully.

Maya studied her wine. "There were a couple of times where we had . . . moments, I guess you could call them. These tiny little heartbeats where I swear maybe he felt something, too, but then the moment was over, and I just . . . I don't know. It's cliché, but I don't want to ruin a good thing, you know? He's almost like family, in a way. And he means everything to Seth." She shook her head. "If something were to go wrong between us, it could ruin their friendship, and I couldn't live with myself if I did that to them."

"And then you met Neil," Brooke prompted.

"Right." Maya smiled. "I met Neil."

Brooke bit her lip, knowing she should use the opening to talk about wedding things, but she couldn't get Seth's skepticism over Neil out of her mind.

"How'd you and Neil meet?" she asked, even as she silently screamed at Seth for planting the seed of doubt in her mind.

True love did exist. It *did*.

She needed it to. Needed to know that what had happened with Clay was a fluke, and that there was hope for her to fall in love and get married and have happily ever after.

"Oh my gosh," Maya started gushing. "It was totally one of those random moments where you know it's just meant to be. I was at Starbucks, waiting for my usual triple grande two-pump vanilla, one-pump almond latte, and when the barista set it on the counter, I went to reach for it just as he went to reach for it, thinking it was his."

Brooke blinked. "You ordered the exact same drink?"

It wasn't that odd, she supposed, given Starbucks's popularity, but Maya's drink order was a unique one. Quite the coincidence.

"Yes! Weird, right? I've never met anyone who likes the same drink as me, and then he ends up behind me in line at Starbucks, and he's hot."

Apparently, Seth Tyler was officially all up in Brooke's head, because it took all of her self-control not to point out that if Neil had been in line behind her, he very well could have heard her order and repeated it as an excuse to talk to her.

But Brooke was a wedding planner, and wedding planners sold romance just as much as they did their organizational skills, so she merely smiled and asked what happened next.

Maya lifted her shoulders. "We got to talking. He asked me out, and I said yes. And then he kept asking me out, and I kept saying yes. And then he asked me to marry him, and . . . well, I said yes to that, too."

Brooke blinked. "That's . . ."

"Boring?" Maya said with a smile.

"No, I was going to say that that's very, um, efficient."

Maya laughed. "Efficient. You remind me of my brother, only he's not so pleased with my efficiency."

"It's pretty typical older-brother stuff," Brooke said. "You can't blame him for being a little overprotective. Especially with how quickly everything happened."

"I just don't know how to explain to him that he and I don't . . . we don't want the same things."

"How so? What do you want?" Brooke asked, genuinely wanting to know what made this contradictory woman tick. One moment she was all bubbles and romance, and the next she was almost startlingly pragmatic.

"I want to get married," Maya said unabashedly. "I'm tired of the socialite scene. I mean, I'm sure I'll always do that a bit, and don't get me wrong, I do love the nice stuff, but I'm tired of dating. I'm even more tired of the lonely nights. And I want babies, and I want to bake cookies, and I want . . ." Her voice trailed off as she circled the stem of her wineglass with her manicured fingers.

"You want something real," Brooke said.

"Yes," Maya said enthusiastically. "That's exactly it. I want something real. Something that will be there even if the money and the penthouse were to disappear."

"And that thing—that's Neil?"

Maya's smile was a little forced. "The way you keep mentioning Neil's name. It's like there's something you want me to say that you haven't heard yet."

Whoops. Brooke should have known better than to go down this path. Her friends were always joking about what a bad actress she was, and Maya had clearly seen right through her plan. Well, Seth's plan.

It was time to get honest. Really honest.

Just not about what Maya expected her to be honest about.

"I'm sorry," Brooke said, reaching across the table and touching her fingers to Maya's arm. "I'm letting my own issues taint your happiness, and I shouldn't."

"Issues?"

Brooke blew out a breath and decided to give Maya the truncated version. "So you know that I'm new to New York, but you don't know why."

"Because you moved here to join the Belles."

"Yes," Brooke said, tracing a nail around her cocktail napkin. "But the truth is, I didn't have much of a choice after my own career went belly-up back in LA."

"What happened?"

Brooke sipped her wine. "Let's just say the biggest wedding job of my life—my own—ended up as front-page news after my fiancé was taken away in handcuffs."

Maya's eyes went huge. "Holy crap. I heard that story. Oh my gosh, I thought you looked familiar, but I totally did not put two and two together." This time it was Maya who reached across the table. "I'm so sorry that happened."

Brooke forced a smile. "Me too. But it's not fair for me to let my own experiences with Clay taint your experiences with Neil."

"Oh, Neil's nothing like that," Maya said automatically.

Well, of course you don't think so, Brooke thought to herself with a surprising hint of bitterness. Nobody supposes their fiancé is anything other than what they want them to be.

"Does my brother know?" Maya asked curiously.

"No," Brooke said quickly. "And I'd really appreciate it if you kept this between us girls."

"Happy to," Maya agreed. "Plus, it'll be much more fun this way. You'll be like a sexy puzzle he'll want to solve himself."

Brooke grunted in skepticism.

Maya laughed. "When are you seeing him next?"

Brooke glanced at her watch. "Tonight, actually. I'm supposed to meet him at his office at five thirty, and then we're doing dinner."

Maya wiggled her eyebrows. "And what about after dinner?"

"There is no after dinner. It's a business meeting."

"Poor Brooke," Maya said, patting Brooke's hand. "I don't think you realize just how much trouble you're in."

"How so?"

"Let's just say when my brother wants something, he gets it. Always."

Chapter Thirteen

⁓

IT WASN'T UNTIL BROOKE was a full eleven minutes late to their meeting that Seth had the uncomfortable realization that he didn't have her phone number.

Here he'd been, obsessed for days with the prospect of seeing her again—of having her to himself—and he didn't even know how to text her.

He glanced at the clock. Five forty-two.

She didn't seem like the type to be late. Was she going to stand him up?

There was a brief knock at the door, and he sat up straight from where he'd been semi-slouched in his office chair, only to slump again when he saw that it wasn't Brooke coming through the door.

"You wanna tell me what's got you acting like you're seventeen again?" his assistant asked as she strode into his office as though she owned the place. And sometimes it felt like she did. Etta Manza had salt-and-pepper hair, almond-shaped hazel eyes, and the build and personality of a linebacker. Seth didn't know how old she was. He'd known her since he was a kid doing homework at her desk, and she'd always just seemed "sixty, give or take twenty years." Neither did Seth know how his father had found her; God knew she wasn't the clichéd prim and proper secretary of her day.

He'd never been more grateful than the Monday morning after the funeral when he'd wandered into the office feeling a little bit sad and a whole lot lost and seen Etta just sitting behind her desk, her red-rimmed eyes the only signal that something was different.

Then she'd made him a cup of strong black coffee, set it in front of him, and told him he had a conference call with the German office in ten.

They'd never talked about her staying on as his assistant; it had been a foregone conclusion. But she was more than that to him. It wouldn't be quite right to describe Etta as a mother figure. She'd never be the type to make a warm cup of tea or homemade muffins. But she'd pour him a shot of whisky when he needed it. Listened when he didn't even realize he needed to talk.

But right now, at this moment, Etta was absolutely not who he wanted to see.

"Have there been any calls this afternoon?" he asked, ignoring her question.

"No, none," she said. "We're one of the largest hotel chains on the planet, but no phone calls. No emails, either. I've just been playing spider solitaire all day."

His glare was meant to show her exactly what he thought of her sarcasm, but Etta had always been one of the few people to remain unfazed by his moods, and she didn't flinch.

"You going to answer my question?" she asked.

"What question?"

She crossed her arms and studied him. "You couldn't get off your four o'clock fast enough. I rescheduled after-hours calls and canceled your business dinner with Pete Corella and his wife."

"So?"

"So. You and Nadia back on?"

Nadia?

It took Seth a second to reorient his thoughts to his ex-girlfriend.

"No," he said curtly. "Nadia and I are over. Who's manning the phones?"

"Jared."

"Who the hell is Jared?"

Etta jerked her head back toward the main reception area. "My new intern. You met him last week."

"Oh. Right. Tall, skinny, a little hyper? Tries to give me vitamins every morning?"

"That's the one. You expecting a call, Sethy?"

He spun slightly in his chair and refused to answer.

She turned her head slightly and called over her shoulder. "Jared, you get any calls from a woman looking for Seth?"

There was the sound of a chair toppling over, and a tall blond kid appeared in the doorway, slightly out of breath. "What was that, Ms. Manza?"

Seth rolled his eyes. He was surprised the intern didn't salute.

"At ease, Intern," Etta said, echoing Seth's thoughts. "Did a young lady call for the boss recently?"

"Ahhhhhhhh." Jared's eyes rolled toward the ceiling as though he was mentally going through the last phone calls. "No, ma'am. There have been four phone calls since you left your desk, none from women. But earlier today, there were plenty from women. Shall I go back through the call log and print out a list? I can even—"

"Jared. You got a girlfriend? Boyfriend?" Etta interrupted.

"Yes, ma'am. Me and my girlfriend, Sammi, have been dating since high school."

"Which was what, yesterday?" Seth muttered.

"Well, think back to how it was before Sammi responded to the note you left in her locker," Etta prompted.

"Oh, I messaged her," Jared interrupted. "On Snapchat. Or was it Twitter?" he mused.

Etta held up a hand. "Do I look like I'm up on the latest social media trends? Be quiet and listen. Think back to how it was before you and your girl got together. Did your face look an awful lot like this?" She pointed at Seth.

Jared glanced nervously at Seth for the first time since coming into the office. "Ah, yes, ma'am. I'd say I did have that look."

Seth threw up his hands. "What look?"

"That special mix of blue balls and puppy eyes," Etta said smugly.

Seth grunted. "That's not what's going on here."

"With all due respect, sir . . ." Jared said.

Seth cut the younger man off with a searing glare, and he backed out of the office, all but bowing before returning to his desk.

"Don't take it out on him that some girl stood you up," Etta said.

Seth glanced at the clock on his computer. She was now nearly half an hour late. It was just as well. Maybe she'd chickened out, or forgot, or simply decided to back out of their deal. Maybe now he could finally stop thinking about her lush curves and big blue eyes . . .

"Excuse me, Mr. Tyler?" Jared said, coming back into the doorway.

Christ. "What?"

"Downstairs reception just called. Said there's a Ms. Baldwin here to see you, but I don't have anything on the calendar."

"Send her up," Seth said, sitting up straight.

Before he could catch himself, he ran a hand through his hair, trying to smooth some of the unpredictable waves, only to realize his mistake.

Etta made a crowing noise. "I knew it. My little Seth does have a crush. Who is this Ms. Baldwin, pray tell?"

"It's a business meeting, Etta. She's Maya's wedding planner, and we're simply getting together to discuss the financials of the upcoming nuptials."

"Oh, honey. I know you're in trouble when you start using words like *nuptials.*"

Seth looked pointedly at the door, but although he knew full well that Etta understood the hint, she made no effort to move. Instead, she tilted her head and studied him before giving a brief nod. "It's good to see you like this."

"Like what? Irritated?"

"You're always irritated," Etta said matter-of-factly. "No, what I mean is, it's nice to see you *alive*."

Seth had been in the process of straightening his tie, but his eyes flew to the older woman. "What the hell is that supposed to mean?"

Her expression was just a little bit sad as she gave him a pointed look. "I think you know exactly what that means."

She turned on the heels of the brown loafers she wore every day and marched out of the room, leaving Seth to stare after her.

What did she mean, I'm alive? Seth thought angrily as he turned to face the window and gather his thoughts.

Of course he was alive. He was thriving. He exercised daily, had the sort of high-powered, successful career that most men could only dream about. He had every necessity, every luxury. There was nothing else he possibly needed.

Well, except for stopping his sister's asinine plan to marry this Neil character. But that's what he had Brooke Baldwin for. He knew that Brooke thought she was in the right about Neil, and he had every intention of proving her wrong.

"Mr. Tyler?"

Seth turned toward the sound of the soft, familiar voice, and for a second he forgot all about why he'd called her here. Forgot about Neil and his sister and the fucking wedding.

There was only her, as she was, standing there in a slim-fitting blue dress that perfectly matched her eyes, her slim calves tapering down into dangerously sexy fuck-me heels.

And suddenly, he knew exactly what Etta meant about him not being alive.

Not until now. Not until this minute.

Or at least the bottom half of him was.

Shit, he hadn't had a boner this unprovoked since puberty. The woman was just standing there, and all he could think about was sliding his hand under that dress and finding out if her ass was as perfect as it looked.

He was betting yes.

Fuuuuuuuck, this was inconvenient.

"I'm really sorry I'm late," she said, coming into his office and looking sweetly frazzled. "I was with Maya, and then we were going to be done with the shopping, but then there was wine, and she decided she wanted to go to the appointments after all, only we'd missed the appointments, so they had to squeeze us in, but it took a while, and—"

He shook his head. "It's fine."

She gave a crooked smile. "You looked mad when I walked in."

Horny. Fucking horny.

He shrugged. "That's just my face."

She burst out laughing. "Well, that's good to know. Here I've been thinking I just always bring out the worst in you."

"I'm not entirely sure that's not true," he said, walking past her to shut the door to his office.

She looked at him in surprise. "I thought we were going to dinner?"

Yeah, well, that was before I realized I couldn't be around you without getting a fucking hard-on.

Of course, he wasn't at all sure that them being alone in his office was the right solution, either, but he felt like he couldn't even think, and he needed a moment to clear his head.

A moment he wouldn't get when they left the quiet of his office.

"I thought we might have a drink first," he said. "But if you're hungry, we can get going."

"No! No, I'm . . . a drink would be nice. And a chance to sit down. I had a half glass with Maya, but it wasn't nearly enough to prepare me for the world of New York bridal shops."

"Different from Los Angeles?" he asked.

"Yes. LA is certainly intense in its own way, but vendors over there at least pretend to be chill about things."

"No such thing as chill in Manhattan," Seth said, walking to the left side of his office, where he kept a few bottles of wine and liquor alongside his precious espresso machine.

"Yes, I'm learning that," Brooke said.

He glanced back in time to see her sinking into the leather couch against one wall of his office with a little sigh and rubbing her temple, and he realized that all of her talk about the stress of the afternoon wasn't just small talk, and he had the uncomfortable urge to comfort her, even though he'd never been good at any of that.

"What can I get you?" he asked. "Martini? Wine?"

"I'll have whatever you're having," she said, still rubbing her temple.

Seth poured vodka into two crystal tumblers, topping them both with tonic and a lime wedge.

She smiled in thanks as he walked over to the couch and handed her the drink. Their fingers brushed, and for a second their eyes met and held before she glanced down. Tempting as it was to sit next to her, Seth forced himself to sit in the side chair.

Not nearly close enough, but with the added benefit of being able to better see her.

Get a grip Tyler, you're acting like a stalker.

She took a sip of the drink and then closed her eyes in gratitude. "It's almost wrong how right this vodka tastes right now."

"How's the head?"

Her eyes opened and her nose scrunched. "Huh?"

"You were rubbing your temple. Headache?"

"Oh, just the beginnings of one," she said, rolling her neck a bit. "But I think it's on its way out rather than its way in. It feels good to sit." Then she laughed. "You must think I'm ridiculous. A wedding planner who can't handle an afternoon of dress shopping."

Seth smiled. "You forget that I've been shopping with Maya. I'm pretty well-versed in the headache and cocktails that follow."

She smiled back even as she shook her head. "It's not your sister. Truly. She's great. It's more getting used to this city. Manhattan looks so small and orderly on a map, but it's not, is it?"

He smiled into his drink. "Definitely not."

"You like it here?" she asked.

"Love it," he said without hesitation. "But, that's not to say I don't feel the need to get away sometimes."

"Do you? Get away, I mean?"

"Not as often as I'd like, although I do have a vacation home on the coast of North Carolina."

"No Hamptons beach house for you?"

"Nah. When I want to get away, I want to get all the way away. The Hamptons scene is a little too happening for me."

"Shocking, what with you being so social and all," she said with a wink.

Seth felt a little surge of satisfaction at the playfulness in her tone. While her words were as tart as ever, he didn't think it was his imagination that some of the antagonism between them seemed to have faded.

Brooke reached down and surreptitiously ran a finger over the arch of that damn sexy stiletto-clad foot. Seth gave her a knowing look. "You can take them off, you know."

"Oh gosh no," she said, sounding horrified at the prospect.

"Ms. Baldwin, you can't tell me those five-inch spikes are comfortable."

"Of course they're not," she muttered. "But I certainly can't take them off around someone who calls me Ms. Baldwin."

"All right, then," he said, his voice coming out low and gruff as he held her eyes in challenge. "You can take them off. *Brooke.*"

Chapter Fourteen

❧

SINCE WHEN HAD A man suggesting she remove her very stylish, very expensive, very uncomfortable shoes become just about the biggest turn-on in her adult life?

Since now, apparently.

Because when Seth Tyler was looking at her with those ice-blue eyes, and her name—her first name—on those lips, Brooke wanted to take off a hell of a lot more than her shoes.

She bit her lip and took another sip of her drink. "I really—no, I'm fine."

He nodded once, setting his drink on a small end table. She assumed he was going to drop the topic, but to her utter surprise, he slowly bent forward, and, slipping a hand around her calf, he pulled her leg gently forward, just enough so that he could ease the shoe off.

The cramped bones in her toes immediately sighed in relief, but even as her foot relaxed, the rest of her went on high alert.

Seth reached for her other leg, not meeting her eyes as he repeated the same motion with the other foot. Only when both shoes were carefully set aside did his gaze lock with hers, and Brooke's breath caught, not just at the warmth in his eyes, although there was plenty of that.

No, what made her heart beat just a touch faster was the shyness there. It told her that the boldness was uncharacteristic of him, and she felt . . . damn it. She felt a wave of tenderness.

Her smile felt tremulous. "A bit of a reverse-Cinderella thing we have going on here," she said, trying to lighten the mood.

"Reverse indeed," he said, seeming relieved at her response. "Since I'm no prince."

"You sure about that?" Brooke said as she made a sweeping gesture at his office. "Because if where you work looks this much like a palace, I can't even imagine where you must live."

Seth sat back in his chair and reached once again for his drink as though they hadn't had a moment more akin to a couple that had been together for years rather than business acquaintances who'd known each other for a few days.

He grinned a little evilly. "Ms. Baldwin, are you trying to wrangle an invitation to my home?"

They were back to Ms. Baldwin, then. That was okay though. He could call her whatever he wanted as long as he kept smiling at her all friendly and familiar like that.

"Where do you live?" she asked, taking advantage of the rare easy mood between them.

He glanced down at his drink. "My dad was big into real estate. Maya and I inherited a few properties around the city."

"That's not an answer."

"That's because I hate this question." Seth blew out a little breath. "Okay, fine. I live in one of my hotels."

"What's wrong with that?"

Seth blinked. "You don't think it's . . . cold, or impersonal?"

Brooke laughed and took a sip of her drink, pulling her feet up beneath her on the couch before she could think better of it. She felt a little stab of embarrassment, but reversing the gesture would be even more awkward, so she decided to just roll with it in the name of comfort.

"No, not really. I mean, do you like living there?" she asked.

He chewed a piece of ice thoughtfully. "Nobody's ever asked me that before."

"Dude, you need to get some new friends," she said. "You seem to know a lot of people who either don't like where you live or don't care."

He winced, and Brooke immediately regretted her words. She'd meant them jokingly, but obviously it had struck a nerve. "I didn't mean—"

Seth held up a hand. "Don't apologize. Please. And you're right. I do need some new friends, probably. As far as whether or not I like where I live . . . I do. I don't know that I want to live there forever. Or even next year. But where I'm at in my life right now, I like the convenience of it. I'm close to the office, I can get room service whenever I want . . ."

"And you own the building," she said.

"Yes, there are perks to the job," he said.

They were both silent for a moment, and Brooke let herself relax into the quiet.

Finally, however, she realized they probably couldn't put off the inevitable, and she reached into her bag for her planner. "So, let's talk wedding, shall we?"

He groaned. "Do we have to?"

Brooke glanced up, startled. "This was your idea, Mr. Tyler."

"I know," he said, draining the rest of his drink. "And at the time, it seemed like a good one. Hell, it's still a good one. I want—need—to know what's going on with Maya, but with you all curled up on my sofa with your shoes off, I find that it's not what I want to be talking about at the moment."

Brooke's belly flipped at his words—at the picture he painted.

And even more so because he looked embarrassed by the admission.

"What do you want to be talking about?" she said, her voice a little bit lower than she was used to hearing it.

He nodded at her drink. "Another?"

She glanced down. "I better not. I haven't eaten much today, so I should probably wait to get some food in me."

"Is that a hint that you're ready to get going?"

Brooke didn't think she was misreading the regret in his voice, and she definitely wasn't misreading what her own instincts were telling her: that she was in no hurry to leave whatever was happening here, despite the fact that every inch of her knew it was a bad, bad idea.

"Not at all," she said softly.

He leaned forward again, his face taking on that slightly urgent look that she suspected he must get before closing a big deal.

"Would it be out of line to suggest that we eat here?" Seth asked.

"Here? In your office?"

He nodded. "We could order in. Sushi, Italian, whatever you want. Unless of course you'd prefer something less . . ."

Intimate, she silently finished.

"If you want to go out, I've made reservations at a few places so we had options. I wasn't sure what your tastes in restaurants are."

"You, or your assistant?" she said with a smile.

"Me. Etta doesn't manage my personal life."

She tilted her head. "But this is a business dinner, isn't it, Mr. Tyler?"

He smiled. "Well, it certainly feels like it when you continue calling me Mr. Tyler."

She glanced away. She couldn't call him Seth. Not yet. It was bad enough that she was barefoot, curled up on his couch, debating eating dinner just the two of them, in his cozy office, with nobody around, no audience to ensure they kept their distance.

"I can call the car around," he said gruffly, misunderstanding her silence.

"No!" she said, holding out a hand. "Please don't. The thought of putting those shoes back on . . . I'm not ready. Staying in sounds great."

They both knew the shoes were an excuse, but he didn't call her out for it. "One of my favorite Italian places in the city knows me. They'll be here in thirty if I ask them to."

"I'm betting everyone in the city knows you," she said dryly. "But Italian sounds great. I pretty much like it all, so whatever you think are their best dishes, go crazy."

He nodded before pulling his phone out of his pocket and dialing a number as he picked up his glass and returned to the bar to fix himself another drink.

Brooke sipped the remainder of her own drink as she studied him from the back. He was broader than she'd realized. His facial features were narrow to the point of being sharp, so she'd always sort of assumed that the rest of him was, too, but seeing him now from this angle, she saw that he had the broad shoulders of someone who knew the inside of the gym, tapering down to a narrow waist and long legs.

His brown hair curled down over the edge of his shirt collar, and she smiled as she realized that Seth Tyler needed a haircut. A strange little quirk for a man who was so exacting in every other way. Brooke somehow found it endearing that he hadn't made time for it.

It made him more . . . human, somehow.

Oh, honey, she chided herself. *You have it bad if you're getting all panty-dropping hot about his over-long hair.*

She checked her email as she half listened to him order a bunch of things she didn't recognize. His Italian accent seemed on point, at least to her un-trained ear, and she wondered how many languages he spoke. For some reason she was guessing it was at least three. If the man was this controlling over his sister's wedding, there was no way he wouldn't want to know what was going on with his international team.

Her phone buzzed with a text from Heather. How'd the dress shopping go?

Brooke responded, As you warned me. Completely scary.

Don't worry, it'll get a bit easier once they know you. Wish I could have been there for your first experience at Blanche.

OMG. Is it always like that?

Always. But some of my brides eat it up. #bridezilla

Brooke snorted. Did you just hashtag via text?

Sorry. Updating our social media accounts. Can't turn it off. So who'd Maya end up going with?

TBD. Not Blanche though. She shut those bitches
DOWN.

Love it, **Heather responded.** So you get a free pass
on dinner with Big Brother then since Maya didn't
commit?

Brooke bit her lip, wondering how to respond.
She'd told Heather about her unusual arrangement
with the Tyler wedding, and her friend had seemed
unfazed. And it wasn't all that uncommon in wedding planning for the planner to run interference with
meddling family members in order to keep the bride
and groom happy.

And yet, somehow what she was doing with Seth
felt completely different from the times she'd soothed
a high-maintenance mother of the groom or sweet-
talked a penny-pinching father of the bride into The
Dress for his little angel.

Your silence has spoken, **Heather** texted before Brooke could come up with a response. And I
approve. Looked him up. He's HOT.

Brooke rolled her eyes and put her phone aside
as Seth hung up his call and walked back toward her.

"All right, I lied. They said forty-five minutes," he
said.

"No problem." She patted her planner. "I really do
need to get an actual budget from you. It's all very hypothetical at this stage, but this stuff tends to happen
fast."

"Don't remind me," he grumbled, setting his glass
on the table and shrugging out of his suit jacket and
loosening his tie.

Brooke tried to keep her eyes trained on his face and failed. His upper body, nicely accentuated by his crisp dress shirt, was, well, spectacular. "We don't have to do this tonight. Talk about the wedding, I mean. We can reschedule for next week."

His eyes met hers. "I'll get there. Give me a minute."

"Sure," she said warily. "What do you want to talk about in the meantime?"

Seth's gaze drifted hotly over her at the word *talk*, and she felt an answering surge of lust at the things they could do *other* than talk.

Brooke hadn't had a casual hookup since college. She was more of a third-date kind of girl, preferring to make sure she actually liked a man before getting naked with him.

She wasn't at all sure she liked Seth Tyler.

She also wasn't at all sure she wanted to get naked with him.

Liar.

Okay, so she definitely wanted to get naked with him. But there were some people you just didn't sleep with, and a client was absolutely on the list.

Seth seemed to read her mind, and the heat dimmed from his gaze as he lowered to the chair beside her. "You asked what I wanted to talk about."

She nodded, grateful to be back on conversational rather than horizontal terms with the man.

He was studying her gaze. "What I'm about to ask might be construed as prying, so you can absolutely tell me to go to the devil."

"Who I'm pretty sure is a friend of yours," she joked gently.

Seth didn't rise to the taunt.

"I'd like to talk about you," he said quietly. "I'd like you to tell me about Clay."

Chapter Fifteen

BROOKE STARED AT HIM for several seconds. She was surprised, although she didn't know why. A two-second Google search of her name brought up no fewer than a dozen articles about Clay's spectacular arrest.

For a brief moment, Brooke gave into the surge of resentment. She let herself acknowledge that it was unfair that she'd worked damn hard to build her wedding-planning career only to have it all erased by one man's misdeeds.

As far as the general public was concerned, she was no longer Brooke Baldwin, Wedding Planner Extraordinaire. She was that poor clueless girl whose criminal mastermind fiancé got arrested at the altar.

Most of the time, Brooke accepted this. What was the point in dwelling, after all?

But sometimes . . . sometimes the unfairness of it all clawed at her throat.

Right now was one of those moments. She didn't want Seth Tyler to look at her as Clay's ex. She wanted to be . . .

What did she want to be in the eyes of Seth?

A competent wedding planner, certainly. The man was gearing up to fork over no small amount of money for his sister's wedding. But she wanted to be seen as a woman, too. And not the kind that had dated a man for two years without knowing who he really was.

But . . .

She *was* that woman. Much as she'd like to re-write history, she couldn't. She couldn't change what happened any easier than she could change the fact that the news was out there. Hell, she even had her own meme, for God's sake.

The best she could do was convince the world that she was over it. That Clay might have surprised her, but he hadn't hurt her.

Brooke met his eyes and smiled slightly. "You looked me up."

"I didn't, actually. I'll admit I sensed there was something amiss. But it didn't seem my place to snoop."

"Interesting. I had you pegged for a control freak who hated surprises."

He gave a short laugh. "Spot-on. And true. But it was different with you."

She blinked. "Why?"

"Hell if I know," he said, holding her gaze.

Except he *did* know. They both did.

"So if you didn't go snooping, how'd you know about Clay?"

"Grant. He thought I should know before I said something idiotic."

She snorted. "Is that even possible?"

"Play nice, Ms. Baldwin. I'm feeding you."

"And playing nice means spilling my guts?"

"Only if you want to."

Brooke studied him, realizing that he meant it. He wasn't going to badger her, wasn't going to pry. There was simply an invitation to talk. To share.

"How much do you know?" she asked, taking a sip of her drink.

"The CNN version, I guess. I've never met the guy, but we moved in some of the same circles back when he was in New York. His name is familiar enough that I recognized it when I read the story."

"You and everyone else," Brooke muttered.

He sighed and rubbed a hand over the back of his neck. "I hated him before, but knowing now that it was you he screwed over royally . . . let's just say that I wish we still lived in a time where it was acceptable to take a man like that out back and put him and the people around him out of their misery."

Brooke's lips parted in surprise. "That's very . . ."

"Uncivilized."

"I was going to say sort of *gratifying*," she admitted. "I mean I don't *actually* want Clay dead, obviously, but I'll confess that the fact that he's been turned into some sort of celebrity can be a bit grating."

"Because he hurt you."

"No," she said quickly. "He didn't, really. I mean I suppose he did, but I'm over it. No use dwelling on what can't be changed, right?"

His eyes narrowed slightly as though he didn't believe her, but she stared back at him, silently daring him to challenge her so that she could flip it around and ask him if *he* was still dwelling on the woman, Nadia, who had turned down his marriage proposal.

She was willing to bet money that they were the same in their determination to move forward.

"I don't know that there's much to say other than what you already know." She twisted her glass slowly as she stared at the melting ice. "I thought I was marrying the love of my life, obviously. And he . . . well, he wasn't the man I thought he was. Literally and figuratively."

"Have you spoken with him since his arrest?"

"No."

"Perhaps you should."

"He's in *prison*," she snapped. "His first phone call was to his lawyer, and I'm sure you can understand why I wasn't falling all over myself to visit him."

Seth held up his hands in surrender. "I struck a nerve. Apologies. I just think it could be healthy to get some closure."

Brooke rolled her eyes. "Gosh, thanks, I haven't heard that one before from people who actually know me. And on that note, are you all chatty with your ex? On good terms? Got closure, have you?"

His eyes narrowed as he studied her. "You're not at all as sweet as you look, are you?"

"Usually I am. You bring out the worst in me."

He smiled at that. "Perhaps we should steer clear of personal topics, then. It makes you surly."

"I'm not surly," she ground out. "I'll talk about the Clay thing. What do you want to know?"

"Promise not to lose your shit?"

"Nope, I do *not* promise that," she said sweetly. "So tread carefully."

Seth leaned forward and held her gaze. "A man you were in love with—a man you were planning to marry—was lying to you. For years. Using you in the worst possible way, pretending to be something he wasn't. And deny it all you want, but he hurt you."

Brooke swallowed and said nothing.

"That's your business, and I won't pry," he said quietly. "As you pointed out, we're practically strangers. But what I want to know is why you refuse to consider the possibility that Neil Garrett might be just like Clay. Not a con man, per se, but if Clay wasn't exactly everything that he said he was, what makes you think Garrett is? What makes you believe that Clay's the only shithead out there and that you're the only woman who's been betrayed in the worst kind of way by a man?"

To her utter horror, Brooke felt tears pricking at the back of her eyelids, and she blinked quickly to force them back before lifting her chin and looking at him defiantly.

"Because I want to believe it. My job is putting people on the path toward happily ever after, Mr. Tyler. In order to do my job well, I have to believe it. I *have* to."

He stared at her a moment longer before giving a short shake of his head.

"Come on," she cajoled lightly. "Surely you don't think that, just because your ex wasn't the one, happy endings don't exist."

Seth tossed back the rest of his drink and stood. "Actually . . . that's exactly what I think. I also think I'm the only one in this room that has my head on straight."

Chapter Sixteen

❧

SETH'S HARSH DECLARATION HUNG between them for several seconds.

Brooke itched to argue—to tell him that he was wrong. That happy endings do exist. That just because they hadn't happened for them yet didn't mean that they wouldn't someday.

The angry stubbornness on his face stopped her. If she didn't want him prying into her life, she couldn't very well go prying into his.

But she wanted to, and that puzzled her. The man wasn't even likable. He was uptight and irritable and went from being deadly sexy to outright cold in the blink of an eye. He was also the type of man who took one nasty setback in romance and decided to forgo all hope. Exactly the type of pessimist she'd always abhorred.

However, there was something in his expression beyond the stubbornness that beckoned to her. A pain that he refused to acknowledge. A pain that she felt strongly compelled to fix, even as common sense told her to steer the conversation back to his sister's wedding and put professional boundaries between them.

Seth's phone vibrated with an incoming call, breaking the tense silence, but just barely. He picked up. "Yeah . . . Yeah, please send the food up. Thanks, Christian."

Seth blew out a long breath as he hung up, dropping the phone back on the table, not looking at her. "Food's here."

He looked about as happy about it as a man on death row.

Whatever easy mood had settled between them just a few minutes before was long gone.

Brook set her glass aside. "I should go. I think this was a mistake."

He didn't argue.

Brooke reached down to put her shoes on. "For what it's worth, I think you're wrong about your sister. Neil. All of it."

Seth snorted. "Because you're such a good judge of character. *And* quick to face your demons."

Brooke gave him a plastic smile as she snatched up her planner and purse and stood. "I think we're done here. From now on I'll give my full report of the wedding progress to my boss, and she'll keep you apprised of the details."

"That wasn't our deal," he snarled.

"Well, I made a mistake when I made that deal," she said, heading toward the door. Brooke shot him a glance over her shoulder. "And as you so kindly pointed out, I'm clearly not a good judge of character. God knows I misjudged *you*."

Brooke reached for the door handle, jerking it open just as a male hand lifted and slammed the door shut again.

"I never lied to you about who I was," he said, his voice low and angry. "About what I was."

"And who and what is that, exactly?" she shot back. "A cold, rigid control freak who not only refuses to let himself be happy but doesn't seem to want it for his sister, either?"

"Cold, am I?" he said, his breath warm against her cheek. "You sure about that?"

Brooke's heart was thumping now, and she jerked at the door handle again. His big hand stayed where it was, keeping the door closed. Locking her in.

Her hand dropped to her side, and she inhaled. "Let me go."

She saw his fingers flex slightly, as though wanting to remove his hand but incapable of it.

"I'm trying," he growled.

"Try harder," she said, her voice urgent.

"Why?" he shifted slightly closer until the center of his wide chest crowded against her shoulder. "Scared of what might happen if you stayed?"

Brooke opened her mouth to deliver a tart response only to realize that her face was too flush, her mind far too addled to come up with a worthy lie. The truth was she was terrified what was going to happen if she didn't get out of this room. Terrified that she was going to cross some terrible professional line that she'd never recover from.

Seth's lips touched her cheek. Not a kiss, exactly. Just an erotic touch that sent fire rippling from the spot his lips touched to lower on her body. Spots she wanted his mouth to touch. And linger.

Brooke ordered her body to move, and when it didn't obey, Seth pressed even closer, his mouth brushing her cheek once more, but closer to her mouth. Another non-kiss that was sexier than any *actual* kiss she'd ever received.

She kept her gaze locked on the back of his hand as it continued to hold the door closed, even as she felt his other hand move toward her.

Seth palmed the back of her head, gently turning her face toward him. Their eyes locked, and for a second, neither moved.

He dropped his head and kissed her.

Brooke moaned as his tongue slipped into her mouth, hot and confident, his hand continuing to hold her head as his other hand dropped from the door to her hip, turning her toward him so they were chest to chest, man to woman.

She heard a thud, realized it was her purse dropping to the floor. Heard another moan, realized it was her own.

Her hands were on his face, her fingers digging at his hair as she kissed him back. Brooke fought for control of the kiss and failed miserably. He was too big, too controlling, too damn hot in the way he took the kiss from slow and sensual to hot and raunchy and then back to slow again.

She heard a knocking noise, embarrassed to realize it might be her heart. The knock grew louder, and reality crept in, albeit slowly.

He lifted his head, breathing hard.

Another knock. At the door. Someone was knocking at the door, her addled brain finally put together.

She immediately stepped back out of the way of the door—out of sight from whomever was on the other side.

Seth swore under his breath before jerking the door open.

"Good evening, Mr. Tyler. I have your food order here, sir."

Seth made a noise that might have been a thank-you, might have simply been a grunt as he pulled out his wallet and shoved a fifty-dollar bill at the delivery boy.

"Thanks, let me just get you your change—"

Seth grabbed the plastic bag and shut the door in the kid's face, then turned back to Brooke.

Neither of them moved. Neither of them even spoke.

The magnitude of what she'd just done was starting to penetrate the haze of want and she slowly bent to retrieve her bag before standing again and forcing herself to meet his eyes.

She tried to figure out what he might be thinking, but as usual there was nothing on the straight, icy planes of his face.

Brooke reached for the door handle, and he stopped her again, but only with words this time.

"You should stay. Eat."

"I shouldn't. And we both know it," she said as she pulled open the door, peeking her head out into the darkened hallway to make sure the delivery guy was already on the elevator.

"I promised you dinner," he tried again.

"I'm not hungry. Really."

Well, she was, but not for food.

Brooke stepped out into the hallway.

"Ms. Baldwin. Brooke."

She paused in her stride but didn't look back.

"For what it's worth, I'm not sorry," he said. "Not in the least."

"Well, that makes one of us," she whispered. "That shouldn't have happened. It was unprofessional, and for what it's worth, I'm embarrassed and hope you'll understand that this was a misstep on my part and not a reflection on the Belles."

"Oh for God's sake, you really think I care that you're—"

"Planning your sister's wedding?" she interrupted, finally forcing herself to look at him. "Because I am. And if sticking your tongue in my mouth was some messed-up attempt to bring me around to your way of thinking about stopping the wedding . . ."

Seth's expression went from icy to furious in a second. "That's bullshit, and you know it. That kiss was about a man and a woman who wanted each other, but by all means, keep lying to yourself. You're good at it."

His words struck a chord. Big-time.

Brooke turned on her five-inch heel and marched toward the elevator.

She half expected him to call her back. Maybe even follow her.

Instead, she heard the door slam shut a second before a messy-sounding thud hit it, and she knew the expensive takeout had just been hurled against the door.

Had she not been in so much turmoil, she might have smirked at the fact that the ice king had a temper.

Instead she stepped into the elevator, turning to face the closing doors before she slowly lifted a hand to cover her face, as she wondered what the hell she had just done.

Chapter Seventeen

B ROOKE HAD BECOME ACCUSTOMED to the Wedding Belles offices being a women-only zone.

Sure, there were the reluctant grooms who stopped by from time to time, and the occasional father of the bride.

Or even more unusual, the brother of the bride.

A brother who had piercing blue eyes and a sharp tongue and was the best damn kisser she'd ever encountered.

Brooke shook her head to banish the thoughts. Nope. No way.

She'd done a hell of a lot of thinking over the weekend and had decided to forgive herself for kissing the guy. Mistakes happened, and beating herself up over it would help no one.

But . . . neither was she going to put herself in the situation where they could have a repeat scenario. Since she was clearly incapable of maintaining professional distance with Seth, she'd have to put *actual* distance between them.

She wasn't exactly looking forward to having this conversation with Alexis, but she hoped being up front about the conflict of interests might earn her brownie points with her new boss.

So Brooke had deliberately gotten to the office early, knowing that Alexis started her workday at the ungodly hour of seven and hoping to catch her before the usual bustle of the day started.

Only, it wasn't her boss who stood in the quiet reception area of the Belles' office.

It was a man.

She skidded to a halt, blinking in surprise at the dark-haired guy rummaging around in Jessie's desk. He glanced up, straightening glasses with one hand as the other held a yellow sticky notepad he'd just pulled out of a drawer.

"Oh, hello there," he said with a slight smile. "You must be Ms. Baldwin."

Oh *yummy*. The man was handsome *and* British.

"That's me. Although, I'm afraid you're a step ahead of me," she said with a cautious smile, still a little unsure who he was or what he was doing here.

"Right. Of course." He came around the side of the desk, and Brooke was impressed to see that in addition to the sexy glasses, chiseled jaw, and moody brown eyes, he also wore his navy pinstripe suit quite well.

The man had it going on, in a bookish, quiet kind of way.

"I'm Logan Harris. The Belles' accountant."

"Oh!" Brooke said, shaking his extended hand. "Somehow I just assumed Alexis handled all of the books herself."

He smiled rakishly. "That's what she wants everyone to think."

Brooke laughed, because it was clear this man knew her boss well. "Where does she keep you, chained up in the basement with one of those old-school visors?"

"Please don't tell her I've escaped. I just wanted a bit of sunlight."

"And a sticky pad, apparently," Brooke said, gesturing at his left hand.

"So I can write my SOS message," he replied.

Brooke giggled. Yes, *giggled*. She'd always been a sucker for accents. What woman wasn't?

"Seriously though," she said, "how come I haven't seen you around?"

He shrugged. "Alexis and I meet twice a week, but always before eight. It works best for both our schedules."

"An accountant that does house calls. I'm impressed," Brooke said, taking a sip of the latte she'd picked up on the way in.

"Most clients come to my office downtown. But Alexis and I go way back."

"Huh," Brooke said, studying the man more closely. His tone was completely professional, but there was something there . . . an intensity when he spoke of Alexis.

And speak of the devil . . .

There was the familiar *click-click-click* of Alexis's stiletto heels coming down the staircase. "Logan, did you find— Oh! Hi, Brooke."

"Morning," Brooke said, drawing out the word

and searching her boss for any sign that there'd been hanky-panky with the handsome Brit but finding none. Alexis was every bit as put together as always. Not a strand out of place, no lipstick smudge, no mis-aligned buttons.

Disappointing. Highly disappointing.

"You're early this morning," Alexis observed.

"And a good thing, too. Otherwise I wouldn't have known that we have a handsome British accountant working with us."

She said it casually, flirtatiously but harmlessly so, and was doubly intrigued when Logan blushed. God, he was cute.

"A handsome British . . . ? Ohhhhhh," Alexis said. "You mean Logan."

Logan gave her an exasperated look. "Really? You have more than one accountant?"

Alexis shrugged. "I guess I'm just used to your accent."

"And his handsomeness––you're used to that, too?" Brooke teased.

Alexis only blinked at her in semi-confusion. Brooke snorted. For a woman who was so on top of things, sometimes her boss could be strangely obtuse.

Either that or she had a damn good poker face.

Maybe a bit of both.

"Well, much as I'd love to sit and crunch numbers with you two, I should probably get to work," Brooke said as she lifted her drink in farewell and headed toward the stairs. "But Alexis, whenever you're done, I was hoping we could chat before the day gets too crazy."

"Of course," Alexis said, studying Brooke with that too-sharp gaze. Brooke had the most unsettling feeling that Alexis somehow knew what she wanted to talk about, which made no sense.

But then, that was Alexis for you. One step ahead of everyone.

"Lovely to meet you, Ms. Baldwin," Logan said.

"Lovely to meet you, too, Mr. Harris. Hope you're allowed above board long enough to see the sun come up."

"Above board?" Alexis asked.

"Inside joke," Brooke said with a wink at Logan.

Alexis's eyes narrowed, and Brooke hid a smile. Maybe her friend wasn't quite so unaware of Logan as she was pretending, because she clearly wasn't loving the fact that there was an inside joke she wasn't in on.

There was a story there, with Logan and Alexis, but Brooke would bet serious money that Alexis didn't even know it yet.

Up in her office, Brooke booted up her computer as she sipped her latte and stared out at the chilly New York morning that was just beginning to show the first traces of life as people trudged to work and started on their daily post-weekend grind. She was still struggling like hell to get used to the frigid weather, but Brooke was surprised to realize that she liked having an actual winter.

The year-round sunshine in California had its benefits, certainly, but there was something lovely and quiet about a true winter. The short days and cozy nights curled up under a blanket were relaxing

and reflective, allowing her a chance to sit and con-
template in a way that the long LA days and nights
hadn't really permitted. Not that Brooke allowed
herself to do much of that lately. It had been hard
enough to keep her feelings about the Clay situation
at bay, and now there was Seth Tyler muddying things
up even further.

For starters, the man was too damn serious. Yeah,
he had a sense of humor lurking under that sharp
gaze, but he also wasn't easy. He'd demand more
than she was willing to give just by being *him*, but he
wouldn't give anything back.

Pleasure, certainly. She was positive that they'd do
just fine in bed.

But what about after that?

Seth didn't want to get married. Hell, the man
barely looked like he wanted to *date*.

And Brooke . . . Brooke *did* want that. She so
desperately wanted a nice man who'd take her to dinner, buy her pretty things, and most of all, who'd hold
her. Who'd pull her close, wrap his big arms around her,
and just let her lean. Without plan or agenda.

A kind man, a gentle man, who wanted to build a
life with her.

That's all she wanted. Not so much to ask, really.

Seth Tyler was *not* that man.

But he could kiss. Holy hell, could he kiss.

Brooke's phone rang, and she winced when she
saw the caller ID. Nothing like seeing one's mother's
name pop up on the screen to ruin what could have
turned into a good X-rated daydream.

She flicked her finger lightly against her forehead,

willing the filthy images of Seth Tyler to fade from her mind before she picked up the phone.

"Hey, Mom! You're up early. Like, really early."

"I started this new predawn yoga class," her mother said in a voice that was far too energetic considering it was barely five a.m. in California. "And they have a juice bar connected to it featuring a really lovely collection of sea vegetables."

Um, gag.

"Yummy," Brooke managed in response.

Brooke considered herself to be a fairly health-conscious modern woman. She exercised regularly, tried to eat assorted salads for lunch most days. But Heidi Baldwin was a whole other level of health nut. Calorie counting, juice cleanses, clean eating, the whole deal.

"How's New York, darling? Are you making sure to get plenty of fresh air?"

"You live in LA, Mom," Brooke said, picking up her latte. "Not exactly known for being smog-free."

"Well, tell me you're at least carrying your pepper spray with you. That many people crammed into a tiny space, and you're practically begging to get mugged."

"I wonder which one will kill me first," Brooke mused. "The pollution or the mugging?"

"Or a runaway cab," her mother said. "I've heard some of them don't even have their driver's licenses."

"Where?" Brooke challenged. "Where have you heard that?"

"At least tell me you're happy," her mom said, ignoring the question.

"Of course!" Brooke said, the response rolling off the tip of her tongue before she had a chance to even consider the question.

But it was true—she really was happy. She loved her apartment. Loved her job. Loved her clients, and her work colleagues, who were slowly but surely becoming her friends. She was even growing to love the city, which, while admittedly completely different from what she was used to, was a bit addictive.

So what if she was a little lonely sometimes? If she ached for the unmistakable caress or touch of a lover at the end of a long day, someone to listen to her stories and pour her a drink as she walked in the door and kicked off her shoes? Brooke firmly believed that happiness was a choice, and she was choosing to be happy, therefore . . . she was.

"I'm glad," her mother said cautiously.

"I really like it here," Brooke said, consciously quieting her voice so it didn't come off quite so manic.

"Good," her mother said with an audible sigh of relief. "I mean, don't get me wrong, the selfish in me wants you to come back home so I can make you my homemade kale cakes while we watch *Real Housewives of Orange County*, but the part of me that's a rather exceptionally well-adjusted parent is glad to see you thriving."

Brooke laughed. "I miss you guys, Mom."

"We miss you, too, sweetie. Did I tell you I found a package of Oreos in your father's sock drawer?"

"No! Not Oreos," Brooke said in an exaggeratedly scandalized tone. "What's next? Cocaine?"

Brooke's father went along with his wife's health-nut crazes, but only to a point. He'd embraced meatless Mondays, developed a taste for quinoa, and could choke down a smoothie in the morning, but he refused to give up his Saturday-morning bacon, his Friday-night martini, or, apparently, his Oreos.

"He said he was stress eating," Heidi said. "Because he missed you."

"Aw, that's sweet," Brooke said. "Good to know I can be replaced with chocolate wafers and fake sugary cream."

"That's what I said!"

Brooke smiled at the legitimate outrage in her mother's voice. "So other than your new yoga place and Oreo-gate, how are you guys? Anything new?"

There was a moment of silence, and Brooke's smile slipped. Her mother's moments of silent were rare, and they almost always were a precursor to not-great news.

"Well, sweetie."

Brooke closed her eyes. "Lay it on me, Mom. Whatever it is, I can take it."

"It's about Clay," her mother said in a rush.

Brooke sucked in a breath, even though she'd known that that's what any bad news must be about. It was just that she wasn't used to hearing his name. Her friends and family went out of their way to avoid mentioning him, so if her mom was bringing it up now, it must be important.

"You know his trial's coming up," Heidi continued quietly.

Brooke said nothing. She'd known, of course, in

the back of her mind, and had even started to prepare herself for hearing his name in the news again, maybe even hearing her own name. But she resented his intrusion on her life just as she was starting to get her feet back under her.

"Well, I guess we knew it was coming," Brooke said, keeping her voice calm. She started to take a sip of her latte, but the sugary, foamy taste suddenly turned her stomach, and she set it aside.

"That's not all, honey," her mom said. "The thing is . . . well, we had a meeting with the prosecutor last week."

Brooke tensed. "Why did the lawyer want to talk to you guys?"

Her mother fell silent again, and Brooke groaned. "Mom. Please. Rip off the Band-Aid."

"Your father lost most of our retirement fund in one of Clay's scams," her mother blurted.

No.

Must breathe. Must get air.

There was no air in this office.

Brooke put a hand to her chest and forced herself to draw in a ragged breath.

"Sweetie, say something," her mother begged.

"Tell me you're joking," she said when she was convinced she was no longer going to pass out.

"I wish. We didn't want you to know. You'd already been through so much, and we both felt so foolish, but they want us—your father—to testify."

Brooke let out a little manic laugh. Her dad was going to be testifying against her fiancé. Ex-fiancé.

Brooke's father was the senior vice president of

marketing for a major Hollywood studio. His income wasn't insignificant, which meant that his retirement account likely hadn't been, either. And Brooke's mother had sold her organic bakery for some hefty sum a couple of years earlier, most of which they'd set aside . . .

For retirement. Which they'd now lost, thanks to Brooke's stupidity.

"Oh my God," Brooke breathed.

"In Clay's defense, he did seem reluctant about taking your father's money," her mother said.

"Wait, I'm confused," Brooke said sourly. "Are we defending Clay or testifying against him?"

There was a moment of silence, and Brooke knew why. It was the first time she'd expressed any kind of bitter emotion about what had gone down with her and Clay. She took a deep breath, pushing the anger back. Knowing that if she let it in, even a little, it would consume her.

"I just mean that I think he really did care about you," Heidi said gently. "And by extension, I don't think he wanted to hurt us."

"And yet he took all your money."

Okay, so maybe the anger was a little bit there. Lurking.

"I know. It's just, we practically threw it at him," Heidi grumbled. "We were so determined to support our new son-in-law, and . . ."

Heidi broke off, seeming to realize she was only making Brooke feel worse.

"Is Dad—is he going to testify?"

"Well, that's what we wanted to talk to you about," her mom said.

"You mean to gauge my level of bitterness?" Brooke said. "Like on a scale of one to ten, how badly do I want him to rot in jail?"

Her mom laughed, but it was one of those sad, "this sucks" kind of laughs. "Pretty much."

Brooke blew out a breath. "I don't know. I mean, I want him to pay for what he did, obviously. But I'm trying to put it behind me."

"I know you are, honey. I just sometimes wonder . . . have you thought about talking to someone?"

Brooke frowned. "I talk to people all the time."

"About Clay?"

"Well . . . no. Not if I can help it. There's no point in dwelling on the negative, Mom. You taught me that."

"Sure, sweetie, but I never meant that you weren't allowed to mourn. I worry that you—"

"I'm fine," Brooke interrupted. "Really."

There was a long moment of silence.

"So Ms. Farley hasn't contacted you, then?" her mom asked.

"Who?"

"Irene Farley. The lead prosecutor."

"No. Why would she?"

"We've just been worried that they might try to bring you on the stand."

Brooke froze. "They wouldn't. Would they? I mean, I didn't know . . . I didn't have anything to tell them. Why, did she say anything about me?"

"Just that they might be in touch," Heidi said miserably. "Apparently Clay himself will be getting on the stand, and they're worried about him being able to charm the jury. They think their best shot is to discredit him on a personal level. Make him seem not only a thief, but, well . . . a callous jerk."

But he's not.

Damn it.

Brooke hated that that was her first thought—to defend the man who'd broken her heart. It was just so damn hard to erase the memories she had of Clay. Of the man she'd known. Loved. That Clay might not have been real, but their time together was. Her memories were. Her happiness with Clay . . . that had been real to her, even if it had ultimately also been an illusion.

"I haven't heard from her," Brooke said quietly. "Let's hope it stays that way."

"So you wouldn't testify?" Heidi pressed.

"I don't know. I don't think so," Brooke replied, spinning around the cup of her now-cold latte. "But if Dad wants to, I don't have a problem with it."

"You're sure? Because, honey, you know that we did like Clay. It's just . . ."

"He took all your money, Mom," Brooke said, still trying to wrap her head around the betrayal. "I more than understand that he needs to face the consequences of that."

Just leave me out of it.

"I know that your *brain* gets that. You're a smart girl. It's your heart I worry about."

"Mom," Brooke interrupted, trying to keep her voice gentle and patient. "This is why I moved to New York. So that I could get away from all of that."

Brooke heard footsteps behind her and turned to

see Alexis backing out of her office with an apologetic wave.

Sorry, Alexis mouthed.

Brooke waved her apology away. In fact, her boss's interruption made for the perfect excuse.

"Mom, I've got to go. Work calls."

"Okay, sweetie. Will you call me later? Your dad hasn't committed to testifying yet, so if you change your mind, it's really not a problem for either of us. We would completely understand."

"I'm not going to change my mind. Tell Daddy to go for it. Really."

"But, sweetie—"

"I love you, Mom. Tell Dad I love him, too."

Brooke hung up, knowing by now that it was literally the only way to end a phone call with her mother, who seemed physically incapable of saying the word *bye* to her only daughter.

"Come in," Brooke said in a bright tone to her boss. "Unless you'd prefer I come to your office?"

Alexis entered and sat down. "What is it you wanted to talk to me about?"

Well. So much for small talk.

"I'm sorry about the personal call," Brooke blurted out, knowing she was stalling big-time. "It's just . . . moms," Brooke mumbled as she dug around in her drawer for the emergency Hershey's Kisses she kept stashed.

"I understand. I've got one of those, too," Alexis said, her voice uncharacteristically kind.

"Yes, but do you have a criminal ex-fiancé for your mother to fret over?"

Alexis let out a sharp laugh that hinted at hidden pain. "No. But honestly, I think my mother would prefer me to have a con man than no man."

Brooke popped a Hershey's Kiss in her mouth and held one out to Alexis, who shook her head. Of course not. No chocolate for this one.

Still, Alexis's face looked happier than usual, her body language just a little more relaxed than Brooke was used to seeing. The result of spending time with a certain accountant, perhaps?

Excited to see another side of her boss, however slightly, Brooke smiled and kept up the small talk. "Is she one of those moms that sends you articles about freezing your eggs?"

"Oh, so you've met her?" Alexis said with a wry smile. She held out her hand, apparently having changed her mind about the candy. "My comfort food is usually Fritos, but I suppose this will work in a pinch."

Brooke tilted her head to the side, and tried to picture the delicate-featured, classy brunette eating salty, greasy corn chips. "Nope. Can't picture it."

Alexis chewed her Hershey's Kiss slowly and methodically, the way she did everything else. "Yes, well. Let's just say that my chip breakdowns are few and far between, and I ensure they happen in private."

"Do these breakdowns ever have anything to do with a certain sexy Brit?"

Alexis blinked. "What?"

Uh-oh. Too far.

Still, it was too late to backpedal.

"Oh, come on," Brooke said lightly. "You can't tell me you have private, early-morning meetings with your accountant and not notice that he's the sexiest thing since Mr. Darcy?"

Again with the clueless blink. "Are you referring to Logan?" Alexis asked.

You poor, oblivious creature. "Please don't tell me you've completely missed the fact that the man is gorgeous."

Alexis pursed her lips. "I don't know. I guess he's always just been . . . Logan. We're friends. And he's my accountant. Not exactly fantasy material."

"I'm pretty sure I'd forgive the pocket protector because, that accent though."

Alexis's smile faded as she chewed and swallowed the chocolate. "Is this what you wanted to speak of? My accountant?"

Brooke swallowed a sigh. Girl talk was apparently over before it even got started.

"Actually, no . . ." she admitted. "It's about the Tyler wedding."

Brooke took a deep breath. "I seem to be finding myself . . . attracted . . . to the bride's brother."

"Ah," Alexis said, not looking the least bit surprised.

"You don't seem . . . shocked," Brooke said.

"Well, I know him."

Brooke froze. "You know him."

"I know *of* him," Alexis amended. "I'm actually friendly with an ex-girlfriend of his."

"Nadia?"

Alexis's gaze sharpened. "He's mentioned her?"

Brooke bit her tongue, feeling oddly disloyal to Seth for even going there. "In passing," she said with a wave of her hand.

"Hmm, yes. They didn't end well," Alexis said.

Understatement.

"Well, regardless, I seem to find myself . . . attracted. I haven't crossed any major lines," Brooke said, deliberately omitting the fact that she'd crossed a minor one with that kiss, "but I'm embarrassed to say that I'm no longer certain I can be objective where he's concerned."

"I see," Alexis said slowly. "Is he planning the wedding?"

"Well, no, but he's financing it."

"And you're worried that you might comport yourself in a less-than-ideal manner because he's attractive?"

"No. But I'm worried *you* might worry that."

Alexis studied her for several long torturous moments that reminded Brooke uncomfortably of the time she'd brought home a particularly rough report card to her parents in the tenth grade when she'd been spending a whole lot more time on the cheerleading field than in the library.

"You're a professional, Brooke. It's why I hired you."

"I am," Brooke confirmed quickly. "It's why I'm coming to you now. Preemptively."

"Are you asking that the Tyler wedding be reassigned?"

"No." Brooke was emphatic. "I simply thought it might be prudent to let you know of the situation.

I'd love the opportunity to continue working with
the bride and groom directly, but because Seth—Mr.
Tyler—is very much involved, I was thinking that perhaps either you or Heather could take care of keeping
him apprised of the necessary details."

Alexis slowly reached out and helped herself to
another Hershey's Kiss. "No."

"Thanks—wait, what?" Brooke said as her boss's
response registered.

Alexis shook her head. "This is your wedding.
You need to handle all the parts, including Mr. Tyler.
I'm the one to sign off on all of the billing statements,
but that's as far as my involvement goes. I'm confident that there won't be a problem."

Brooke's head was spinning. "Okay, but—"

"May I speak out of turn?" Alexis said.

Brooke bit back a smile. "Do you even know
how?"

Alexis merely looked at her, waiting for a response.

"Sure," Brooke said, oddly eager to see what
might come out of her boss's mouth when the woman
didn't have her shields up.

"I think people make too big a deal about sex,"
Alexis said.

Not what Brooke had been expecting.

"It's just . . ."Alexis waved her hand impatiently.
"I know what the magazines and romance novels tell
us. That sex has to complicate everything, but that's
a myth. It only has to complicate things if you let it."

"And you don't . . . let it?" Brooke asked, trying to
follow along.

There was a brief flash of something across

Alexis's face—something Brooke might have called vulnerability if she didn't know the other woman better.

"Not anymore," Alexis said. "And if you're sitting there thinking that it's weird to be talking about sex with your boss, well . . . that's exactly what I'm talking about. Sex shouldn't be taboo."

Brooke reached for a Hershey's Kiss. And then another. Hell, she needed a whole bag for this conversation. And a vodka.

"I'll apologize for overstepping," Alexis said as she calmly stood. "Consider it food for thought."

"Wait, that's it?" Brooke asked, aghast. "I'm not . . . I'm not entirely sure what you're trying to tell me."

Alexis smiled. A real one, that reached her eyes. "Yes you do."

Brooke hesitated. "Are you telling me to sleep with Seth Tyler?"

Alexis shook her head. "I am not. I'm telling you to sleep with who you want to sleep with."

"Even if it's a client?"

"Admittedly, not my first choice, but then it's *not* my choice, is it? And you've read the Belles creed. It doesn't matter who's paying the bill because the real client is . . . ?"

"The bride," Brooke finished. It was no less than she'd been telling herself and Seth for days.

"All I'm saying is that it doesn't *have* to get complicated," Alexis said. "I've always managed to keep sex and the rest of my life separate, and I find I rather like it that way. In fact, sometimes—how did you put it?—*crossing that line* can actually ease the tension. Not add to it."

Brooke stuffed another candy in her mouth. "Respectfully, I can't believe we're having this conversation."

Alexis shrugged. "Respectfully . . . think about it."

Chapter Eighteen

∾

SETH KNEW THAT PEOPLE thought living in a hotel was lonely, but the truth was, it usually wasn't.

He liked the location. He liked the room service. Liked coming home to a freshly made bed and clean sink and never having to change a lightbulb.

But on Thursday evening as he wheeled his overnight bag into his set of suites after a long-ass, delayed flight back from Hong Kong, neck cramped, eyes gritty, and body tired down to his very bones, Seth paused in the foyer and looked at his home differently.

And for the first time in as long as he could remember, he wished for . . . something. Someone.

A dog. Even a godforsaken cat.

Or, maybe, a sassy-mouthed blond wedding planner.

He pushed this last thought aside as he dropped his keys on the console and flicked on the lights. Seth hadn't heard from Brooke since last Friday when she'd rejected his kiss. While he couldn't quite say he was over the sting of her rejection, at least he hadn't done damage to her working relationship with his sister. A couple of casual questions to Maya had reassured him that Brooke was still very much the wedding planner.

The whole thing was just as well, he thought as he entered the small but modern kitchen and opened the fridge door. Getting involved with any woman wasn't on the agenda right now. Not when every last drop of his energy went toward being a CEO worthy of filling his father's shoes.

But if he were to get involved with a woman, it sure as hell shouldn't be with one to whom he'd be writing a fat paycheck in a few months.

And unfortunately for Seth, he was increasingly worried that he *would* be writing a check. So far he'd turned up no tangible dirt on Neil, and his sister had given no indication that she regretted accepting the man's proposal.

There was, of course, still the chance that Brooke might turn something up during the course of wedding planning, but it had been a long shot that she'd sabotage her own paycheck in the first place. Now that he'd gone and made a move on her, he wasn't exactly betting the ranch that she was going to join his anti–Maya and Neil wedding campaign.

Which left him with the private investigator that Seth hadn't quite worked up the courage to call back.

Seth closed the refrigerator door upon realizing that it was mostly empty. Fine. He wasn't hungry so much as restless.

And not restless so much as horny.

"Shit," he muttered, bracing his hands on the granite counter, and debated a cold shower. But he'd been trying that for days, and so far it had been completely ineffective at banishing images of Brooke from his mind.

For the three days he'd been out of the country, he'd been telling himself that he'd call up one of his old flings the moment he got back to New York. As far as little black books went, his was underdeveloped compared to Grant's, but there were a handful of women who he'd consider friends with benefits. Women who, like him, were eager for companionship without expectation.

He picked up his phone with the intention of calling one of them, but the second he started scrolling through his contacts, he knew it was wrong. All wrong. Knew that there was only one woman who could assuage his lust.

Well, he'd be damned if he'd throw himself at her feet like a moron again, only for her to kick him when he was down. He'd shown her vulnerability and she'd all but laughed in his face. So no matter how much he still wanted her, he was just going to have to get over it.

Seth tossed his phone back on the counter and went to the old-fashioned bar cart along the window, pouring himself a couple of fingers of whisky as he stared absently out at the Manhattan skyline. Generally speaking, he wasn't a big fan of drinking his problems away, but unlike professional problems, this couldn't be solved with a bit of brainstorming, hard work, or strategizing.

He pinched the bridge of his nose and debated turning in early. It was barely nine, but he knew from experience that he was better off tackling the inevitable jet lag now before it walloped him in the ass in the days to come.

Maybe he'd get lucky. Maybe tomorrow he'd wake up and the first thought on his mind wouldn't be a kiss that had ended prematurely.

Seth's phone buzzed from the kitchen counter. He thought about ignoring it, figuring it was likely to be a business call that could wait until tomorrow, but then he glanced over.

It was the front desk of the hotel.

"Yeah."

"Mr. Tyler, there's a visitor here for you."

Probably Grant. The man had zero qualms about stopping by unannounced to raid Seth's booze collection, even though Grant's own whisky collection rivaled most of Manhattan's bars.

"Sure. Send him up."

There was a beat of silence. "Sir, it's a female visitor."

Seth's eyebrows lifted. "Maya?"

"No, not Ms. Tyler, sir. A Ms. Baldwin."

Seth's glass hit the counter with an awkward clank. *Brooke.*

He ran a hand through his plane-mussed hair. Frantically he ran through his calendar. Did they make an appointment he'd forgotten about? Had he missed a note from her about meeting to discuss the wedding?

"Sir? Shall I send her up?"

"Yeah." He cleared his throat. "Yes. Please send her up."

The wait for her to make it from the lobby up to his private residences should have gone quickly, considering the fact that he'd been waiting for days to hear from her, but it was quite possibly the longest three minutes of his life.

Remember. She rejected you. Play it cool, man.

There was a quiet knock, and he took another sip of whisky for courage before he straightened his tie and opened the door, prepared for . . .

Well, hell, he didn't know what he was prepared for.

The sight of her standing so close to his home nearly took his breath away. Her hair was pulled back in a ponytail, and just slightly messy, courtesy of the winter windstorm that was ripping through the city.

A blue wool coat was draped over her arm, and she wore a cable-knit white sweaterdress that fell just below her knees, stopping just short of her calf-high boots.

She was dressed stylishly but practically given the winter weather. Hardly the picture of a woman hell-bent on seduction, but Seth felt seduced all the same.

He inhaled, hoping that whatever she wanted would be quick, as he was rapidly changing his mind on the necessity of that cold shower.

"Ms. Baldwin," he said coolly, mentally applauding

himself for the detached tone his voice had taken on. "This is certainly a surprise. What can I—"

"Shut up," she said before he could finish his sentence. "Just shut up."

She stepped toward him, going up on her toes and pressing her mouth to his, and Seth's mind went blank with shock. With pleasure.

His hands lifted to her shoulders with the intention of pulling her back—of making her explain what had changed since the previous Friday night. But the way she clung to him, her lips moving against his with just a trace of desperation, gave him pause.

"Brooke, what's going on?"

"I want you," she said, pulling back just slightly. Her eyes made it only as far as his nose, as though she couldn't force herself to meet his eyes. "I know we don't want the same things, and you don't want complicated. I don't want complicated, either, and I was thinking . . . I was thinking maybe we get this out of our system."

Seth's fingers tightened on her shoulders as he jerked her toward him. "Just tonight?"

She bit her lip. Nodded.

"Thank God," he said roughly just seconds before he crushed his mouth against hers.

The kiss wasn't gentle. It had none of his usual finesse.

But he'd make up for it later. Now he needed her taste. Needed her moans and her softness. Needed to feel that she wanted him as much as he wanted her.

Seth backed them up so that she was all the way

in his apartment, fumbling behind her for the door as she dropped her coat and purse to the floor.

He slid his hands to her waist, dipping his knees slightly so he could move his mouth along the underside of her jaw before fusing their lips once more. As hungry as her kiss was, there was a shyness there, too—the faintest taste of hesitancy as though her brain hadn't quite caught up to her body.

Seth gentled the kiss, giving her time. He brushed his lips back and forth against hers in a soft coaxing motion, using his tongue only to flick teasingly at the corner of her mouth before taking it away again.

Again and again he kissed her gently, teased her, making them both wait as his hands roamed her sides, her back, until she gave a quiet desperate moan and said his name.

"*Seth.*"

Yes.

His hands moved upward until they cupped her face, and he expertly nudged her lips apart, sliding his tongue forward so that it tangled hotly with hers.

He heard another moan, and he wasn't entirely sure which of them made the noise. Sweet. *She tasted so damn sweet.*

"Off," she said, shoving at his suit jacket. "Get this off."

He pulled back slightly, breathing hard as he searched her face. "What changed your mind?"

"Hmm?" Her blue eyes were cloudy with desire as she ran her palms over his chest.

He caught her palms, held them flat against his

chest, and waited for her to meet his eyes. She did, shyly, and Seth felt something tighten inside him.

"The other day, when I tried—you didn't want me."

"Please don't think that," she said, licking her lips. "I did want you. You know that I did."

He did know that. He'd *seen* it. And yet . . . she'd walked away.

Brooke pulled her hands away as she stepped back. "Oh. God. You've changed *your* mind."

"Wait. What?"

She knelt to pick up her coat, her cheeks turning pink. "All of the reasons I said no before . . . the complications, the fact that I work for you . . . I should have left it at that, I should have left it alone. I just thought . . . God, I am so stupid."

He knelt down in front of her, capturing her wrist in his hand and pressing a thumb to her damp palm, stroking softly as he searched her face. "Don't run, Brooke."

She swallowed. "You haven't changed your mind?"

"About wanting you?" he said with a smile, pulling her to her feet. "Not even close."

"And you're okay that I don't want . . . more?"

His smile grew. "You *do* realize that a woman offering no-strings-attached sex is every bachelor's dream?"

"Yes, but is it *your* dream?" she asked directly. "And if we do this"—she gestured between them—"it won't impact my relationship with your sister? You won't think less of me for potentially having a conflict of interest?"

Seth reached forward, wrapping his palms around her hips and pulling her forward before resting his forehead against hers, needing to make her understand. "The only interest I care about right now is the interest I have in getting you out of that dress."

Chapter Nineteen

BROOKE HAD SPENT THE entire cab ride over to Seth's place trying to tell herself not to chicken out. Reminding herself that she was a modern twenty-something woman who was allowed to have a one-night stand with a man who she was attracted to.

As it turned out, chickening out wasn't the problem.

The second she'd gathered her courage and set her mouth against his, Brooke had realized the problem wouldn't be running away. It would be *stopping* at one night.

Now his large hands still rested on her hips, his thumbs pressing enticingly against her hip bones, and still he waited.

Of course he was waiting for her green light. Even though he was cocky and a bit stingy with his emotions, Seth Tyler had a thick layer of *gentleman* beneath all that swagger.

Tonight, though, Brooke didn't want gentle.

She wanted rough.

Her hands were resting on the hard planes of his chest, and she crept one hand up until her finger hooked under his tie as she tugged his face all the way down to hers, bringing his lips within millimeters of her own.

"Take me," she whispered.

This time when Seth's mouth crashed against hers, she knew there was no going back, and she relished it. Relished the need in his kiss, knowing that she echoed it with her own.

Brooke's hands tore at the knot in his tie as his slid beneath the hem of her dress and back up so that he cupped her backside. Leggings were a crucial, if not necessarily sexy, part of living through an East Coast winter, but Seth didn't seem to mind as he palmed her ass through the thin material with warm hands.

"I knew you would feel this good," he said against her mouth, his teeth nipping lightly against her upper lip as he squeezed her flesh.

"Skin on skin would feel better," she said, her head falling to the side so he could nuzzle her neck.

"Yeah?" he whispered against her throat. "You want my hands on you?"

He sucked at her skin, and Brooke whimpered.

Seth continued to knead her flesh through her leggings as she slid her hands down, tugging his shirt out of the waistband of his pants, sliding up under his undershirt until her palms met his bare skin.

He groaned softly, and Brooke smiled in victory. "You see? Better."

Seth's mouth slid back up to meet hers at the same time his hands slid even lower, scooping under her butt and hoisting her up. Brooke instinctively wrapped her legs around his waist, her arms winding around his neck.

"All right, Baldwin. You win," he said gruffly, kissing her before easily pivoting, supporting her weight as he carried her into the bedroom. "Skin on skin it is."

She expected him to deposit her on the bed, but he stopped just beside it, letting her body slide down his before he reached down and turned on the lamp on the nightstand.

"Um . . ." She gave the lamp a skeptical look. She was twenty-eight, not eighteen. Things were *mostly* firm, but not bright-light toned by any stretch of the imagination.

Seth's hands cupped her cheeks as his lips drifted across her temple. "I want to see you."

Brooke's eyes drifted closed as he kissed her slow and sweet, and she felt herself nod in agreement. Because she wanted to see him, too.

He nudged her back to the bed, and without speaking, they both went through the awkward, unsexy process of removing their shoes. Brooke peeled her leggings down her legs and tossed them aside as Seth shrugged out of his jacket, tossing it on a nearby chair.

Their eyes locked and Brooke swallowed nervously, but before nerves could take over, he stepped toward her, hooking his hands behind her knees and lifting her feet to the bed. His blue eyes stayed locked on hers as his palms slid up along her thighs, bunching her dress up around her hips.

His eyes drifted downward to the small triangle of her panties now exposed to his hot gaze.

He dragged the knuckle of his forefinger over her, feeling her wetness even through the fabric of her underwear, and her head fell backward, hitting a feather-soft pillow.

"You've been thinking about me. About this," he said, repeating the motion with his finger. "For how long?"

She didn't respond, and he withdrew his hand. She raised her head and glared in protest and he lifted his eyes. "How long, beautiful? How long have you been thinking about me touching you there?"

Brooke reached for his wrist, wanting to put his hand back between her legs, shocking herself with her boldness, but he resisted, dragging his fingers along her inner knee instead. "Something you want?"

"Damn you," she muttered, her head falling back on the pillow. "The whole time, okay? Since the day I first saw you. The first moment."

His eyes heated, but instead of replacing his hand, he hooked his fingers into the waistband of her panties, dropping to his knees as he dragged them down her legs.

"That's what I wanted to hear," he said roughly before grabbing her hips and dragging her toward the edge of the bed.

Seth shoved her dress upward, and then his face dropped between her legs before Brooke had the chance to register what he intended, and the soft slick of his tongue felt too good for her to do anything but lie there and enjoy it.

"Oh my God." Her fingers scratched helplessly against the comforter as he opened his mouth on her, licking her in long, hot strokes. "Seth."

He groaned in response, licking faster as he slid a hand down, one finger easing inside her. Her hips bucked at the invasion, and he looked up, his eyes holding hers as he slid the finger all the way in, stroking her once, twice, before adding a second finger.

His tongue never stopped its idle stroking as he pumped her with two fingers, and the orgasm built until all rational thought fled and instinct took over, her fingers tangling in Seth's hair as she held his face to her and went over the edge of bliss with an incoherent cry.

Seth stayed with her through every last shudder, pulling away only when every muscle in her body seemed to give up on her as she lay there bonelessly.

He wiped a hand across his mouth as he gave her a slow, sexy smile, and Brooke let out a husky laugh. "Looking pretty smug there, Tyler."

He peeled off his undershirt, and as he lowered himself over her, all traces of drowsiness fled.

"How do you work such long hours and still find the time to make your body look like this?" she said, pressing a kiss to his pec as she rolled him to his back and climbed on top of him.

"I get up at four a.m.," he said, easily adjusting his hips so that she straddled them.

She shook her head. "You and Alexis. Monsters."

"You sleep late?" he said, rubbing thumbs along the front of her thighs as he held her gaze.

"If I can," she said, feeling weird that it wasn't

weird that they were talking about this while they were half-naked.

"What about tomorrow?" he asked, the stroke of his thumbs against her legs changing direction so he now stroked toward her center instead of her knees.

"What about tomorrow?" she asked a little hoarsely. Talking was a lot harder when his fingers were so close to *there*.

The corner of his mouth quirked. "Can you sleep late tomorrow?"

"Um." Brooke struggled to concentrate. "I think so? I don't have my first meeting until ten, and it's in Midtown."

"Perfect," he said. "Because I plan to keep you up past your bedtime. Now, that dress. Off."

Brooke obeyed, but did so slowly, making him wait as her fingers drifted down over her sides, flirting with the hem of her dress before she very slowly eased it upward, over her head, and tossed it aside.

"That's better," he breathed, putting a palm to her back to steady her as he sat up suddenly.

His lips drifted over the curve of her breasts as his fingers unclasped the back of her bra before sliding it down over her shoulders and sending it in the general direction of the rest of her clothes.

"No fair," she said, feeling suddenly shy. "I'm all the way undressed, and you still have pants on, and . . ."

Seth closed a mouth around her nipple, and she forgot all about what she was going to say, instead wrapping her arms around his neck and grinding her hips down on his, releasing a guttural groan that should have embarrassed her but only made her even hotter for him.

He moved to the other breast as Brooke reached for his pants, grateful now for the light as she quickly managed to free him from the confines of his pants and briefs. She let out a satisfied whimper as she wrapped her palm around him, a sound that was quickly drowned out by his harsh groan.

"You like that?" she asked, pumping her palm against the silken firmness of his erection.

Seth's eyes were squeezed shut, his jaw tense as he nodded. Brooke slid forward slightly, rubbing the tip of him against her opening, and his eyes flew open and locked on hers.

"I'm on the pill," she whispered.

His fingers wrapped around her hips, lifting her up slightly and holding her still for a heartbeat before shifting them and pulling her down, easing her around him.

"Oh my God," she whispered at the delicious friction.

Her eyes started to close, but he dug his fingers into her hips. "Look at me."

She did, their eyes colliding as he sank all the way inside her. "This," he said. "*This* is what this is supposed to feel like, Brooke."

He was right. Brooke had always liked sex—*loved* sex—but while it always felt good, it had never felt like *this* before. This was like it was in the movies with both people wrapped up in each other, slow-motion, as some throbbing music wrapped around them.

Only there was no music. There was only the sound of their breathing, the slick slide of his body against hers, the way he whispered her name and the way she whispered his back.

He set both hands against her back, his mouth nudging her to lean back as he nipped at her breasts, alternating between teasing bites and slow, tender sucks.

Brooke's head fell back, eyes closing as her hips moved faster and faster, lost in the feel of him on her—in her.

"Oh God . . . oh God . . . yes, right there . . ."

She came with a low moan, her hips pressing even more firmly against his as she pitched forward again. Her teeth closed around the firm flesh of his shoulder, and Seth bucked under her, his fingers digging into her back as he exploded with a harsh roar that was a good more animalistic than she would have expected from a buttoned-up businessman.

She relished every moment of it.

Brooke didn't know how long they stayed there, his arms wrapped around her as she lay draped over his shoulder, panting against his neck as the heat of their bodies cooled to the self-satisfied postcoital bliss.

Later, she wouldn't remember how he maneuvered them down to the mattress, but she would remember the moment that he lay down beside her, pulling the covers over them, as his hand spread possessively over her belly, nudging her back against his chest.

She would remember that as good as the sex was—and it had been mind-blowingly good—the unexpected cuddling somehow seemed *better*.

Alexis said it was possible not to let things get complicated.

Belatedly Brooke realized that maybe she should have asked her boss *how*.

Chapter Twenty

IF THE NIGHT BEFORE Seth had been feeling regret about living in a hotel, he quickly reversed his opinion the next morning. There was something wonderfully convenient about being able to offer a woman a gourmet breakfast in bed without so much as turning on a stove.

Although, if any woman was worth slaving away in the kitchen for, it might just be the woman currently curled up in his bed.

After calling room service and asking them to send up five different breakfast options, Seth poured two cups of coffee, frowning when he realized he didn't know how Brooke took hers.

Which felt sort of strange, considering they'd spent a good deal of the last ten hours naked together.

It was an uncomfortable reminder that this wasn't like him. He'd had one-night stands before, mostly in his early twenties, but those had all been the sort of drunken hookups that ended with one of them leaving in the early-morning hours with a headache and regrets, not spending cozy mornings in bed.

And as for the women that had awoken in his bed, he *knew* them. He took them to dinner and did the flowers-and-expensive-wine routine before seeing them naked.

There'd been none of that with Brooke, and yet he *did* know her, he realized as he poured some milk into his coffee. It was strange, since she'd been a part of his life for only a few weeks and much of that had been spent with them at each other's throats, that she didn't feel like a stranger.

She didn't feel like a one-night stand, either, if he was being honest. *What a fucking mess.*

Seth gave a slight smile as he heard a rustling sound from the bedroom and, picking up the coffees, headed back to where Brooke was waking up. He leaned against the doorjamb as the lump that was Brooke's body was starting to stir—she was a burrower when she slept. When he'd awoken, she'd been curled into a tight little ball, only her long blond hair visible above the covers.

Now a slim arm appeared as she stretched, then another, and then finally her head as she rolled upward to a sitting position, unfortunately having the presence of mind to tuck the sheet beneath her armpits, covering up those gorgeous bare breasts.

She blinked sleepily as she tried to get her bearings.

"Morning," he said quietly as her gaze came to rest on him.

Brooke's hand immediately flew to her head, only to let it drop again with a sigh. "It's hopeless, huh?"

"Let's just say you look thoroughly bedded," he said, pushing away from the doorjamb.

"Translation. My hair's a mess?"

He smiled, wisely avoiding the question, and held up one of the mugs in his hand. "I didn't know how you like your coffee. This is black, but I've got sugar and some milk in the fridge."

"A spoonful of sugar would be great. No milk."

"I think I can handle that."

Seth headed back into the kitchen to add sugar to her mug. When he returned, he noticed that Brooke had done some sort of feminine witchcraft on her hair, turning the previous cloud of tangles into a tidy braid hooked over one shoulder.

"Is it bad to say I liked your hair better before?" he asked, handing her the mug before sitting on the side of the bed and shifting to face her.

She snorted into her coffee. "Why, because it reminded you of all your manly prowess last night?"

He smiled. "So you admit it was prowess."

Her eyes flicked to his. "Let's just say, last night was good. Very good."

Seth thought of himself as an evolved man, but he apparently wasn't that far beyond caveman, because the urge to puff out his chest at that moment was almost too strong to ignore.

Instead he took a sip of his coffee and held her gaze. "Yes. It was."

Brooke bit her lip as she cupped the large mug in two hands. "So, I feel like maybe we should have talked about . . . the after. And also, I didn't mean to sleep over. It was just—I thought—"

His hand found her knee. "Hey."

She took a deep breath.

"There was no way in hell I was letting you out of bed last night, much less out of my apartment," he said quietly.

Brooke took a deep breath and looked like she was about to protest, but they were interrupted by a knock at the door. Her eyes widened slightly in panic. "Someone's here?"

He reached out and flicked the edge of her braid before standing. "Room service. Stay."

A few moments later, he'd generously tipped the delivery woman after refusing to allow her to set up the table. Instead he wheeled the crowded cart into the bedroom himself.

Brooke blinked. "Um, how many people are you planning on feeding?"

"I wasn't sure what you liked to eat for breakfast," he said as he began to pull the silver tops off the various plates. "I got everything from a cheese omelet to pancakes to eggs Benedict."

Brooke bit her lip and eyed the room-service cart. "I'm normally a bowl-of-cereal kind of girl."

"It's just breakfast, Brooke."

She was already climbing out of bed. "Exactly. Breakfast. We said it was about one night. *Last* night. We agreed. Morning shenanigans didn't play into it."

"How do a couple of fucking pancakes and omelets equal shenanigans?"

"Don't play dumb," she said as she looked around

for her clothes. "This can't be anything. I work for you. Sort of."

"Brooke. Stop," he said, reaching for her. "Just because I'm offering you something to eat doesn't mean I'm going to start ring shopping."

She jerked away from his outstretched hand. "It starts with breakfast, but then what?"

He only stared at her.

"I don't want this," she said, gesturing at the breakfast cart. "Last night was great, but I don't want anything more."

Seth felt like he'd been poleaxed in the abdomen.

I don't want anything more.

Brooke couldn't have known, of course, that her softly uttered statement was an exact echo of what Nadia had said to him that night as she'd stared down at his pathetic self on bended knee.

I've liked spending time with you, Seth. But I don't want anything more.

Him. She hadn't wanted him.

And Brooke didn't want him, either. And objectively, rationally, he knew that was okay. But some long-silenced part of him was roaring in pain of a not-quite-forgotten memory.

"Got it," he snapped after the silence had stretched too long. "So next time, I just leave a fifty on the dresser, right?"

"Don't be a jerk," she said as she began pulling on her clothes.

"Yeah, *I'm* the asshole here," he said. "You're the one losing your shit over a few eggs."

She brushed past him. "I can't do this."

He grabbed her arm, pulling her back around. "Nobody's asking you to do anything. You're the one who came over here last night, remember? For someone who's so rah, rah happily ever afters, seems to me there's only one kind of happy ending you're after."

Her lips parted at his crassness, and she looked like she wanted to slap him. He almost wished she would.

"You know what I just realized?" she said, her voice low and vibrating with anger. "You're a lot like your hotels. Polished, attractive, efficient, and *cold*. Cold and soulless."

He said nothing. It was nothing he hadn't heard before. Nothing that wasn't true.

"Have a good day, Mr. Tyler. I can see myself out."

Seth didn't move. Not until he heard his front door close.

And then his arm lashed out, swiping several of the room-service plates off the cart and sending them crashing to the floor.

As he stared blindly down at the mess, he realized that only twice in his life had he really truly lost his temper to the point of lashing out. Once the other night with the fucking takeout in his office, and again just now with the damn room service.

Both could be owed to a certain Brooke Baldwin.

So much for not getting complicated.

Chapter Twenty-One

❧

I HANDLED IT BADLY. Do you think I handled it badly?" Brooke asked as she nibbled on a fingernail and followed Heather around City Winery as her friend placed a gold-wrapped chocolate truffle by each name tag set around the square table. Heather reached out to adjust the silver ribbon of the centerpiece so that it curled just-so around the base of the white pillar candle.

The bride had gone for a metallic theme, which Brooke had secretly wondered might be a bit cold, but she had to admit that the combination of sparkle and monochromatic tones of silver and gold was stunning. Especially given the oncoming February storm, which promised to be just enough to provide some picturesque snowflakes without being heavy enough to cause transportation issues.

"You're sure I can't help?" Brooke asked as she followed Heather to the next table, watching her friend repeat the same process with the favors, the fussing with the ribbon. Heather hesitated, and

Brooke had been part of the Belles just long enough to have a sense of what was going on.

"Hey," she said, touching Heather's arm. "It looks really good."

"Does it?" Heather asked, glancing around. "Are you sure the little snowflake lights aren't cheesy? They were my idea, but I've never seen Alexis use them, and maybe they're tacky."

Brooke snapped a finger in Heather's face, waiting for the usually confident blond girl's eyes to come back to hers. "None of that. Alexis trusts you."

"But—"

"Nope." Brooke held up a finger. "You're her assistant for a reason. She trusts you to make spectacular weddings."

Heather's wide green eyes flitted away nervously, still scanning the breathtakingly beautiful scene before her as though looking for flaws. "I know, it's just rare that I tackle the setup on my own."

The experienced wedding planner in Brooke knew that the wedding Heather was carefully crafting was sheer perfection. Brooke had met the bride of this particular wedding—a graphic designer for a major advertising agency—only once, but she knew that Heather had nailed her client's style. The reception hall was elegant and a little bit playful, classic, but with enough personality to keep it from being generic.

But the woman in Brooke had a sense of what Heather was going through. By Brooke's estimation, Heather was absolutely ready to be promoted to full-fledged wedding planner, and she expected Alexis would agree.

But *Heather* needed to know it. She needed to work through the pressure of having a wedding entirely on her shoulders, with no boss to deflect to or follow. It had taken Brooke nearly a dozen weddings before she stopped feeling queasy in the hours leading up to the ceremony, and even now she still got butterflies.

Heather needed to see that she could do it, that she could weather the stress.

And Brooke was absolutely confident that Heather could.

Brooke knew that she, Alexis, and Heather all felt equally passionate about weddings, but she suspected there was something more driving Heather. Something beyond Brooke's ambition or Alexis's perfectionism.

Being a wedding planner wasn't just a job goal for Heather. It was a life goal.

Brooke wound her arm around Heather's shoulder and squeezed. "So, I know you want to puke right now, but you're going to have to trust me on this, Fowler. This looks amazing. And this couple is going to have the best day of their life because of you. Now will you please hand over some of those gorgeously wrapped truffles and let me help you?"

Heather took a long breath before blowing it out. "There's another box by the front door. There might even be an extra or two, because one of the guys who works at the chocolate place thinks I'm cute."

"Because you are cute," Brooke said, heading toward the door to grab the box in question. "Is chocolate guy going to be a thing?"

"Oh God no," Heather said, resuming the process of placing the boxes alongside each plate. "I'm pretty sure he's, like, twenty."

"Because you're so old," Brooke said sarcastically, hoisting the box onto her hip and heading back toward Heather to begin placing the favors on a nearby table.

"Let's just say that this kid squeezes in shifts between classes at NYU, and I—" Heather broke off, fiddling unnecessarily with a candle. "College feels like a long time ago for me."

"You went to college near home?" Brooke asked, shamelessly fishing but doing so in what she hoped was a casual tone. "In Michigan?"

"Yup. Michigan State."

"Your family's still there?"

Heather nodded. "My mom."

Brooke waited for Heather to say more. The other woman wasn't chatty. Not like Jessie. But neither was she usually so one-word answers. Maybe Alexis was rubbing off on her.

The silence stretched on as the two of them silently resumed the process of placing gold boxes next to gorgeous little squares of ivory card stock embellished with a plain, typewriter-style font that perfectly offset the fussiness of the paper.

They finally reached the end of the room, and both turned to survey the finished setup. Even without the music that would eventually fill the space, and before the hundreds of candles had been lit, it was spectacular.

"You did good," Brooke said.

Heather gave a small nod, seeming to finally be satisfied with her work. "Thanks for your help."

"Thanks for letting me tag along."

Brooke's client roster was rapidly filling up, but she was still new enough to the New York wedding scene that she didn't yet have any weddings of her own apart from Maya Tyler's. As a result, a schedule that had once been nonstop from Friday morning through Sunday evening was a bit sparse.

Giving her far too much time to think.

About him.

"I think you handled it sort of badly," Heather said, out of nowhere.

Brooke glanced at her. "What?"

Heather gave her a half smile. "You asked me if I thought you handled the Seth thing badly. I was distracted and didn't respond, but I'm responding now, and it sounds like maybe both of you said things you didn't entirely mean."

Brooke sighed as she followed Heather toward the exit. "That's an understatement."

Heather glanced at her watch. "The ceremony won't start for another four hours. Want to grab a late lunch? I could use the opportunity to think about something other than all the things that could go wrong tonight."

"Absolutely," Brooke replied.

"Why does melty cheese always taste so good?" Brooke moaned around a bite of perfect sandwich. She and Heather were seated at a bustling little café right by the winery, nomming on delicious paninis stuffed with smoked turkey, Swiss cheese, and arugula.

"Is that how Seth Tyler got into your pants?" Heather asked with an eyebrow wiggle as she twisted the cap off her sparkling water. "By offering up grilled cheese?"

Brooke tapped a fist against her chest to help the bite of sandwich she'd started choking on go down a bit easier. "Going there, are we?"

"I may have been distracted earlier, but I don't think I missed the fact that you mentioned spending the night. Explain."

Brooke sighed and picked up the dill pickle that had come as a garnish on her plate, taking a bite even though she didn't even really like pickles. Stress eating at its finest. "It was just supposed to be a one-night thing. To scratch the itch and all that, you know?"

"And did he?" Heather asked. "Scratch your itch."

"Oh yes," Brooke said.

Heather cracked up. "Oh man. You are about two seconds away from purring."

Brooke felt her cheeks coloring and looked down at her plate. "It was, um . . . it was good."

"So why are you limiting it to one night?" Heather asked, taking a sip of her drink.

"One night of casual naked time is one thing, but multiple nights of naked time . . . that gets dangerous, you know?"

"Dangerous?"

"You know, with the whole heart and head getting involved with what was supposed to be the body's domain."

Heather bit her lip and leaned forward. "Okay, can I confess something?"

"Always."

"I have no idea what you're talking about."

Brooke blinked. "How do you mean?"

"I've never been in love," Heather said with a touch of irritability about the whole thing that was downright adorable.

"Never?"

"Nope." Heather took a moody bite of her sandwich. "I've had crushes. Even a couple of boyfriends who lasted a few months. But with every single one, I went into it eyes wide open, knowing that it would never turn into anything more than what it was. Sex. Companionship. Whatever."

"Trust me, love can be overrated," Brooke grumbled.

Heather tucked a curl behind her ear, but it popped right back out again. "You're talking about Clay?"

Brooke nodded. "They want my dad to testify at his trial."

"Oh God." Heather's eyes widened sympathetically. "But they don't want you to, right?"

"Not yet," Brooke said. "I'd probably be pretty useless. I was such an idiot, I didn't see any of the warning signs. I knew nothing about all his illegal crap until that day when they arrested him."

"I hate that that happened to you, Brooke."

Brooke forced a smile. "Me too. I've been trying so hard to put it behind me, to stop myself from feeling like a victim, but it's so much harder than I thought it would be."

"Because a person you cared about—the life you wanted—was ripped away. Getting past that is going to take time."

"I know." Brooke scratched at her neck, feeling suddenly restless in her skin. "Exactly. Which is why . . ."

"Which is why you're so confused by how much you like Seth Tyler?" Heather finished for her gently.

"Yes," Brooke breathed out, pushing her plate away. "I thought sleeping with him would help, you know? But instead . . ."

"Instead you want more."

"I don't know." Brooke put her elbows on the table, resting her fingertips to her temples. "Yes. Maybe. I said these horrible things to him, and I don't even know why."

"Sure you do," Heather said with a shrug. "You tried to build walls around yourself by swiping at him."

Brooke eyed the other woman suspiciously. "You're pretty damn wise for someone who's never been in love."

"I know, right?" Heather said, taking another bite of her sandwich. "But seriously, it's okay to make mistakes here. I'm guessing he hasn't been handling things very well himself."

"Definitely not," Brooke grumbled.

She hadn't heard from him at all since she'd stormed out that morning. Not that she was surprised. And it was no less than she deserved—she'd been a fool to think she could get Seth Tyler out of her system with one night of passion, and clearly he was grappling with the same demon.

But he'd just been so damn inaccessible. And even *that* would have been fine if he'd just shown her to the door, but he'd ordered her breakfast. And yes, she'd freaked out. Stupidly, admittedly.

But then he'd turned into such an *ass* that she couldn't figure out what the hell he wanted. To have breakfast with her or push her away?

Really, she could kill her boss for not explaining this uncomplicated-sex thing in more detail.

And more important, what did Brooke want? Did she want more than just a one-night stand, even if it meant risking things ending badly and ruining her first big professional break? Was any man worth possibly sacrificing a career opportunity for—even one with a touch that set her skin on fire?

"Any advice?" Brooke asked hopefully.

"Well," Heather said, licking a bit of grease off her thumb. "I'm no expert, obviously, but I'd say that this has less to do with romance nuance and everything to do with basic human interaction."

"Translate."

Heather gave her a sympathetic look. "I think you need to apologize. If for nothing else than for the sake of your conscience. And then you can either move on. Or move forward."

"But which one?" Brooke begged.

"No idea." Heather dabbed at her chin with the paper napkin. "But either way, might I suggest a sexy dress to help the apology go down easier?"

Chapter Twenty-Two

2∽

"I THOUGHT WE AGREED that you had free rein to make these decisions without me," Seth said, tapping his fingers against his leg as the car made the slow trek through Manhattan traffic.

"No, we agreed you'd back off your micro-management, not that you'd completely check out of the wedding altogether," Maya said. Her voice was gentle, but Seth felt the censure there, and it reminded him painfully of Brooke's parting words a week earlier.

You're a lot like your hotels. Polished, attractive, efficient, and cold. Cold and soulless.

He glanced across the car at his sister. "I'm sorry. I thought . . . I thought you wanted a bit more freedom without your brother breathing down your neck."

"Sure, when it comes to the embroidery pattern on my dress. Not when we're talking about the reception site," she said. "I just want you to see this place. It feels right, but I want your opinion."

Seth felt the tightness in his chest ease slightly at

Maya's words. He may not be up for Brother of the Year awards, but he couldn't be screwing up that badly if his sister cared about what he thought.

"What does Neil think?" he asked, glancing over at her.

His eyes narrowed as she immediately turned her head to look out the window. "He's been busy."

Seth's eyes narrowed even further. "He hasn't even seen the place?"

"He said he'd meet us there. He trusts me to make the decision. He wants it to be my dream wedding."

"Sure, but you shouldn't be having to do this all on your own," he said quietly.

Maya looked back, her smile genuine. "I'm not. Brooke has been . . . great."

"She's paid to be great."

Maya rolled her eyes. "Such a cynic. I mean she's been great as a friend. Neil's been busy, and you've been . . . you. Brooke's just been there."

Now it was Seth's turn to look out the window, avoiding Maya's prying gaze.

"She told me that you haven't responded to her emails," she said.

"Nothing to respond to," he said. "I asked her to keep me informed, and she has. Until she asks me a direct question or says something I don't like, I have no reason to respond."

"Sure you do. So you don't come across as a jerk."

He flinched, and Maya sighed before punching his shoulder in that light, pesky way only a little sister could. "What is going on with you guys?"

Nothing. Just that we fucked each other sideways,

*and then I found out the next morning that she
couldn't get away from me fast enough.*

He settled on something a little vaguer. "Nothing."

"Right," Maya said. "So you're telling me it's not
going to be super awkward when we see her in ten
minutes?"

His head jerked back around. "You said she
wasn't going to be there."

Maya smiled serenely. "I lied, obviously."

His head dropped back against the headrest. He
felt her studying his face. "Maya. Don't."

"Come on, don't be mad," Maya said. "I know
something is going on between you two, and I was
worried you'd say no if you thought she'd be there,
and I really need help making this decision."

Seth's eyes closed and he tried to focus on something—anything—other than seeing Brooke in the immediate future. "Okay, tell me about the place."

Maya gave the dreamy sigh he now thought of as
her "bridal" sigh. It happened whenever she talked
about rose petals or ribbons or potential locations.

"It's in this old office building that they're just
now finishing renovating. The entire building's been
vacant for years, but they're getting ready to reopen,
and Brooke got the inside track, found out that the
upper floors haven't yet been outfitted as offices, so
it's just this big open space with a view of the Brooklyn Bridge. It's prewar, and the crown molding is
just . . . gah . . . you're going to love it."

He gave her a look. "I'm going to love the crown
molding?"

"Yes. Yes you are. And the fireplaces, too. They're

not working, obviously, but Brooke has all these great ideas about how we can put up varying candle heights, create the illusion of a bursting flame—"

"Sounds like a fire hazard," he muttered.

"Whatever, we'll get flameless candles." Maya pointed a finger at him. "Don't try to take this away from me just because you have blue balls."

"I don't have blue balls. Also, I'm pretty sure that phrase goes against every sibling conversational code."

She pursed her lips and sat up straighter, looking out the window. "We're almost there. And Seth?" He looked at her, noticing the serious note in her voice. "You don't have to love this just because I do. I want your honest opinion. But just . . . if you could try to be . . . just act, like . . ."

"Like I have a soul."

Her nose scrunched. "I was going to say *agreeable*. Jesus, so morbid. Who gave you the idea you didn't have a soul?"

Your damned wedding planner, that's who.

Instead of answering, he jerked his chin the direction of her door. "Looks like we're here."

She clapped her hands in happiness as the driver opened her side. Before she got out into the frigid air, she reached across the car, touched his hand. "Thanks for doing this," she said.

"Maya, you know I'd do anything for you," he said quietly. "Seriously."

"I know. Likewise, and Seth . . . don't hate me, okay?"

He frowned. "For what?"

Maya was already out of the car, the door slamming shut on his question.

"Maya. What are you . . . damn it." Seth snatched up his gray scarf, hurrying out into the February-evening chill as he wound it around his neck and scanned the area for his sister.

Then he spotted her blond head immediately—getting into another car, which proceeded to speed away from the curb.

"Maya!" he shouted, but it was useless. She was long gone. He threw his hands up in the air. "What the hell is this all about?" he fumed.

His phone buzzed and he pulled it out of his pocket. A text from his interfering little sister. Talk to her. You're welcome! Love you.

"Damn it, Maya," he muttered again, this time with less heat.

"I think," said a soft voice from behind him, "that this might be sibling matchmaking at its very most devious."

Seth froze before he very slowly forced himself to turn around to look at the face that went along with that gorgeous voice.

Brooke.

Chapter Twenty-Three

JUST AN HOUR EARLIER, Brooke had been thinking that Maya Tyler might go down as her favorite client of all time.

But with Seth Tyler bearing down on her, his expression torn between disbelief and rage, she was definitely rethinking her warm feelings toward Maya.

The woman had thrown her to the wolves.

No, wolf.

And this wolf was *pissed*.

Maybe he had a right to be. His sister had just dragged him downtown during rush hour under the apparently false pretense of needing his approval on a wedding space, only to disappear into the back of what must have been a preplanned escape car.

And now he was stuck here with her, the woman who'd compared him to a *building*.

No wonder he hadn't responded to her emails. Not that her emails had been personal. Or even apologetic. They'd been entirely professional, more testing the waters to see if he even wanted to have contact with her.

Survey said *nope*. Not a single response or acknowledgment. It had now been a week since The Sex, and they hadn't exchanged a single word.

Judging from the murderous expression on his face, tonight wasn't going to change that.

Brooke blew out a breath. "If you want to get right back into your car, I won't take it personally."

Much.

His eyes narrowed. "You didn't know about this?"

Brooke rolled her eyes. "You mean did I bribe your sister into dragging you here so that I could trap you into talking to me? No. Like you, I thought Maya only wanted to see the venue once more before signing the contract."

His eyes flicked up to the building behind her. "So she really is considering doing it here?"

Even in spite of all the crap going on with her and Seth and her irritation at Maya's meddling, Brooke didn't bother to hide her excitement about the space behind her. "I think so. I hope so. It's not glamorous, by any means, but it's just, it's . . ."

How did she describe perfection? Brooke had fallen in love with spaces before, but never before had she had her breath taken away by a building. But the Hamilton House, with its stately exterior and charming interior, had hit her at the gut level. She was a sucker for any space that managed to preserve its history while stepping into the modern times with delicate class, and the people behind the Hamilton's restoration had gotten it exactly right.

Before she realized what she was doing, Brooke had hooked her arm in Seth's, turning so that they were both looking at the mid-rise building. It was unassuming, to be sure. The original brick had crumbled to the point of disuse, so the previously brick structure was now a more stable cement. But the original back had been repurposed to frame the doorway and windows. A strange-looking building, but all the lovelier for its quirkiness.

"Isn't it great?" she said.

She didn't expect him to respond, and he didn't. Instead she glanced over to find him studying her.

"Want to go in?" he asked.

Brooke blinked. "Really? You want to?"

He lifted a shoulder against the cold. "I'm assuming you have an appointment, or whatever. Shame to stand someone up."

"Actually, I have better than an appointment," she said, digging into her purse and coming up with keys. "Let's just say one of the property manager guys might have a little crush on me."

His eyes were unreadable. "Is that so."

Her breath caught a little at the unexpected possessiveness of his gaze and she blushed. "No, I just meant—"

He only shook his head and looked away. "I'd like to see inside. Maya, for all her manipulations, seemed genuinely excited about it."

"She was," Brooke said, grasping quickly at the subject change. "I think it's exactly what she's looking for."

Seth gestured something at his driver before they both moved toward the door. He waited silently as she unlocked it, her hands fumbling only slightly at the thought that she was once again spending time alone with Seth. It was strange, but as far as they'd come, as much as they knew each other—mentally, physically—all the tension of those early days came rushing back.

She wanted to beg him to tell her what he was thinking.

To know if he'd thought of her the way she thought of him.

If he could forgive her for the things she'd said but certainly hadn't meant.

Brooke pushed the door open and stepped inside. The building, for all its newness from the renovation, still held the feeling of a structure that hadn't been inhabited for a long, long time.

"The first tenants won't be moving in until early April," she said as they passed through a small but fancy marble foyer that would serve as the main reception area for the building. "It's fourteen floors, the bottom twelve all office space. But there was dispute over the top two floors, some wanting to lease it as executive offices, others thinking it would be a better investment to turn it into residential space."

"Who won?" he asked as she pushed the button on the lobby elevator.

She shrugged. "I'm not sure. Secretly, I'm hoping residential, because I can't imagine a better place to come home to at night—not that I could near afford it—but I'm not sure it's been decided yet. Whatever it is, it'll be a long-term investment. It's just open space right now. They'll need to figure out the floor plan, kitchen, appliances, blah, blah, blah."

Seth shook his head as they stepped into the small elevator. "Nightmare. All of this should have been planned from the very beginning. If this were one of my hotels—" He broke off, and she winced, wondering if he was remembering her callous words from before.

"Yes, well, there's a reason why the Tyler Hotel Group is one of the most successful in the world," she said quietly.

The elevator started upward, and they said nothing more until they reached the top floor. Seth reached out, setting a broad hand against the open elevator door and nodding her forward.

Brooke stepped out into the open space, the high heels of her suede boots clicking smartly against the dark hardwood.

"They should have done carpet," he muttered, glancing down. "More practical."

"Oh, no way," she gasped. "There is nothing better than hardwood."

His lips twitched. "I don't think you understand just how much I'm trying not to make a joke right now."

It took Brooke a moment to catch up, and she laughed when it clicked, grateful that she hadn't completely killed his already hard-to-find sense of humor.

Brooke spread her hands to the side. "So?"

He glanced around, and she tried to see the building through his more trained eyes.

Still, regardless what lens someone was viewing the room through, she couldn't imagine any fault. The dark floors contrasted perfectly with the white walls, the windows were plentiful, and delightful arches were sprinkled in among built-in enclaves for window seats, decor, or cozy cuddles.

She moved toward one of the windows in the middle of the wall. "This is the best view. The angle of the Brooklyn Bridge looks like something from a movie poster."

He moved behind her, not quite crowding her, but close enough that she could feel his warmth. Smell his scent.

"It's beautiful."

She swallowed, her brain knowing that he was talking about the scene before them, her heart—her stupid heart—wishing that he were talking about her.

Brooke moved aside before she could lean back. Or worse, put her hands on either side of that window, arch her back and beg him to take her from behind right there, right now. She hadn't gone with the sexy dress that Heather had recommended, but Seth had proven extremely adept at removing her clothing, and it would be oh so easy . . .

Damn it.

"So as you can see, there's plenty of space," she said, moving back toward the wall with the light switches. The romantic shadows were messing with her head. She pressed onward. "The lack of interior walls gives us amazing flexibility. Dance floor in the middle, dance floor in the corner. We could go with a circular layout, or more linear. We could even—" Brooke flicked the lights on with one hand, turning back to continue giving her sales pitch, but he was right there.

Right there.

She walked directly into his hard chest, having barely a moment to register surprise before his lips closed over hers.

The kiss was slow. Taunting. As though he knew exactly what she wanted, and what she wanted was this. *Him.*

Brooke kissed him back with everything, her tongue reaching for his as her fingers closed on his lapel, dragging him forward so they bumped awkwardly against the wall.

"You didn't email me back," she said, pulling her mouth away to dot kisses along his jawline. "Eight emails, you didn't respond."

He let out a low chuckle. "Someone's been counting."

"Someone's been ignoring," she countered.

He stilled for a moment, before his hands slid down from her shoulders to her waist. "Isn't that what a soulless man is supposed to do?"

Brooke sucked in a breath, not just at having her own tantrum thrown back in her face, but at the hurt in his face. At the pain in his eyes.

"Seth."

He didn't give her a chance to respond, instead slamming his mouth down on hers once more with even more force this time, the heels of his hands digging into her rib cage as he held her against the wall, his mouth bruising, punishing . . .

And she wanted it. She wanted it all.

Her tongue tangled against his, her fingers clawing at his shirt as her purse dropped to the floor with a messy thump, the keys in her hand falling with a noisy clank as they wrestled with each other's clothes, heating each other's skin even through the thick layers of their winter coats.

Brooke's hips tilted forward, needing to be closer, and Seth hissed out a curse as she rubbed against the bulge of his erection.

He slammed a palm against the wall behind her head before pulling back, groaning in frustration as he did so.

His breath was warm on her cheek, and Brooke kept her eyes closed, relishing the closeness, just for a moment.

"What are we doing here?" he asked.

Brooke could only shake her head. "I have no idea. I don't know how to think around you. I have things all planned out, and then . . ."

"And then what?" he asked huskily.

"And then you look at me, and I just, I just *want*."

"I take it this wasn't in your plans," he said, gently resting a thumb against her cheekbone.

"You mean Maya playing matchmaker? I had a hunch when she insisted you tag along, but I definitely didn't plan on her ditching us."

"I'll admit I'm having a hard time being pissed at her just now," Seth admitted.

Brooke opened her eyes to meet his. Their icy blue was unreadable. "I'm actually kind of glad she left. There are things I need to say, and I'm grateful not to have an audience for it."

He slowly pushed back from the wall, moving his warmth away from her, and her fingers clenched in a reflexive urge to tug him back. To tuck against his body and ask him to hold her. Or kiss her. Or take her against the wall, or . . .

"I'm listening," he said.

Seth crossed his arms, and the closed-off stance definitely didn't bode well for his reception of her apology. But she had to try.

Buying time, she knelt, picking up her purse, shoving the spilled lip balms and umbrella and hair bands back in. She picked up the keys in her other hand, jangling them in her palm nervously as she stood up once more and looked him in the eyes.

"I need to say that I'm sorry," she said, deciding on directness.

His eyebrows lifted. "For?"

"You brought me breakfast and I . . . freaked out. Unnecessarily so. And I said some nasty things when I left your place that morning. Things I didn't mean and that aren't even true."

He looked away, and Brooke's chest squeezed. She reached out a hand, her fingers touching his forearm. "They aren't true, Seth. I was feeling uncomfortable after the intimacy between us. I was embarrassed I stayed over when I didn't mean to, and the whole thing—it felt like too much."

"Can I ask you something?"

She nodded.

"Are you mad because I offered you breakfast? Or because you wanted to stay?"

She opened her mouth to deliver a safe, diverting quip about not being a morning person.

Then she saw the bleak look of vulnerability on

his face, and she realized that she wanted to be a little bit brave. For him.

"I freaked out because I realized I wanted more than the breakfast," she said. "I went in thinking I wanted only the sex, thinking I could be okay with that, but I ended up getting cuddling and breakfast, and then I wanted more. I wanted . . ."

"Lunch?" He supplied when she broke off.

Brooke let out her breath on a little laugh. "Yeah, maybe. But then what if I'd wanted lunch to become dinner, and then dinner had turned into more sex, and then more sleeping over, and then, you know, *repeat*."

"Would that be so bad?" he asked, taking a step closer to her. "Us spending more time together?"

Her heart knew exactly how it felt about that question. It jumped a little in excitement at the very suggestion of it. Her brain, however . . .

"Give me a chance, Brooke. I may be a bit ruthless, too ambitious for my own good, and cold as ice, but what you see is what you get. I can offer that much, at least."

"You're not cold," she whispered, moving closer to him, her eyes locked on the knot of his tie, which was just slightly less tidy than before, courtesy of their groping.

"No?" he asked huskily.

She shook her head. "I shouldn't have said that. And I definitely shouldn't have said that thing about you being soulless. It was cruel, and I'm not . . . that's not usually me. Know that. Please tell me you know that."

His blue eyes searched her face, and though she tried desperately to read through the mask, she had zero idea what he was thinking just then.

And then he pulled away. Slowly. Gently. But a rejection all the same.

"Show me the rest of the place," he said quietly, turning back to the large, empty space behind them.

"Right." Brooke blew out a breath. This was why they were here, after all.

So he hadn't accepted her apology, but he hadn't outright rejected it, either. She supposed that was something.

"You'll have to use your imagination," she said, putting her shoulders back and chin up and trying to get back into a professional headspace. "But as you can see, it's plenty big should Maya and Neil opt for the larger wedding, but if they decide to go more intimate, it'll be easy to partition off some of the space, give it a more intimate feel."

"How is Neil these days?" Seth asked as he clasped his hands behind his back and began walking around the perimeter of the room.

Brooke gave a little smile as she followed after him, the click of her heels echoing softly. "You mean has he tried to stuff your sister in the trunk of the car, or stolen money from her wallet, or shown up to a tux fitting with three other wives in tow?"

Seth gave her a look. "Your email reports have barely mentioned him, which, as you'll remember, is the entire reason I wanted the reports in the first place."

"Honestly," Brooke said, "I've barely seen the guy. Maya said he's been busy with work, and other than when we toured this particular facility for the first time, he's more or less left it up to us women."

"What did he think of this?" Seth asked, his eyes looking around, taking in every detail.

"He liked it, but then, as far as I can tell, Neil tends to like everything Maya likes. She could say she wanted to get married on a rowboat in the Hudson, and he'd think it was the best idea ever."

"Or at least he'd *say* he thought it was the best idea ever."

"Right," Brooke said patiently. "Because that's what fiancés do. I know you've still got your big brother cape on, but Neil's behavior is pretty standard for grooms. They walk a fine line. Even the sweetest, easiest of brides can get a bit touchy with the groom and his level of involvement in the planning. If he doesn't have any opinions, he's disinterested. If he has too many, he's difficult."

Seth stopped and turned toward one of the windows. "It still doesn't feel right."

"It may never feel right to see your sister get married," Brooke said quietly.

"You're probably right," he muttered.

"What I wouldn't give to have recorded that," she said lightly. "Is there anything else you want to see? I can show you the bathrooms. They're gorgeously remodeled, and there's this marble that's just, well, you'll have to see it."

He turned back toward her, and the gentle look on his face caught her off guard. "I'll take your word for it on the bathrooms."

"Fine, fine, miss out on the gorgeous faucets they selected. I mean, they're fabulous, but now you'll have something to look forward to when you come back for the actual wedding."

"So you think this is the place?"

"That's up to Maya," she hedged. "And Neil. But if it were my wedding, this would be my place."

"Why?"

Typical dude question, and Brooke didn't have an immediate answer. Instead she took her time, walking in idle circles before turning back.

"I have no idea."

Seth laughed. "At least you're honest."

"It's just like a feeling, you know? Like when you move to a new city or neighborhood and walk into a restaurant and know it's going to be your place. Or when you're house hunting, and you step through the front doors after seeing dozens of 'meh' and you just know."

"Is that how you picked your current apartment?" he asked.

"Eh. Not really. I mean, I like it, don't get me wrong, but I picked it out of practicality of needing a place to live more than anything else. It's not my forever home."

"At least it's more permanent than a hotel," he said, his gaze level.

Crap. Once more she was reminded of the fact that in the last conversation they'd had, she'd compared him to a hotel building. "I actually *didn't* criticize it, but you seem to think I should . . ." she said. "There's absolutely nothing wrong with where you live. And if it makes you happy—that's what counts, right?"

"If it makes me happy," he repeated slowly, precisely, as though this were a new concept. "Indeed."

They both fell silent, staring at each other for long seconds, although it wasn't awkward so much as necessary. As though they were trying to learn the other person, reading what they weren't saying.

But what had started as curious suddenly started to feel a bit heated. The air between them seemed to grow heavy, and Brooke's thoughts had wandered from what was going on inside his head to what he looked like under his clothes. She knew now, of course, but she wouldn't have minded a refresher course.

Time to retreat.

She lightly jiggled the keys in her hand. "Shall we get going?"

He nodded once, following her toward the door. Brooke lifted her hand to switch off the lights at the same time he did, his big hand covering hers, and she gasped at the contact, as though she were some pubescent girl touching the hand of a boy for the very first time.

She jerked her hand away, but he only flicked off the lights, slowly, purposefully, as though she weren't acting completely jumpy and weird.

The ride down the elevator was silent, and Brooke wondered if Maya would be pleased or disappointed with how her manipulation had turned out.

On the plus side, Seth hadn't refused to speak to her.

On the plus plus side, he'd kissed her.

On the negative side, he'd seemed to regret kissing her, even as it was happening.

And even worse, he seemed in no hurry to do it again.

Brooke locked up behind them, pulling her scarf out of her bag as they walked toward the sidewalk. Still silent. For a second she thought he might offer her a ride in his car out of that unwavering chivalry he seemed to carry about him, even when he didn't like someone.

He didn't. Instead he looked at her, nodded once as though he'd come to some conclusion in his head that she wasn't privy to, and turned toward his car.

Swallowing her disappointment, Brooke stepped toward the curb, her eyes scanning for an available taxi, knowing it was going to be a long shot on a Friday evening when everyone was eager to commence their Friday-night activities.

Which for her would likely involve a frozen dinner and another rerun binge of *Sex and the City*.

"Brooke."

She glanced over her shoulder. Seth was standing there, hands shoved in his pockets as he watched her. He stepped closer. "You said you were afraid you wanted more."

"Yeah?" she said, her hands slowly falling to her sides.

His jaw clenched. "You said . . . you said that after breakfast, you were afraid you'd want lunch. And that after lunch you'd want dinner."

"Right," she said nervously.

"Have dinner with me."

Oh. *Oh*.

He took another step closer, hands still shoved in his pockets, his shoulders hunched up around his ears like he was nervous. Nervous she might say no.

"I'm hungry, and I'm here, and if you don't have plans, I'd like to take you to dinner."

She swallowed. "To discuss wedding stuff?"

He shook his head once. "No. Because I want more, too."

Chapter Twenty-Four

❧

B ROOKE BIT OFF A piece of her steak, dragged it through the buttery sauce, and popped it in her mouth with a happy little sigh. "This place is *magical*. How'd you find it?"

Seth picked up his wineglass, debated a lie, then went with the truth. "It was my ex's favorite. We came here a lot."

"Ah," she said, picking up a fry and nibbling on the end. "*Nadia.*"

His eyebrow lifted. "You remember her name."

"Because I was jealous," she said point-blank.

He blinked. "You realize it's not typical to be so unabashed about these things, right?"

Brooke shrugged. "I never really understood the point in playing games. Seems like we'd all be a little happier and things would be a little less complicated if we all just said what we wanted, you know?"

"I do know."

"And it's what good businessmen and women do, right? They just put it out there. They know what they want. They go after it. Why can't personal life be that way?"

"And what is it that you want?" he said. "Other than to get me naked again, obviously."

"Obviously," she with a cheeky smile.

He noticed she didn't answer his question.

Brooke took a sip of her cocktail as she looked around. "Seriously, though, this place is great. Even if I am stuck picturing you gazing into Nadia's eyes."

"Do I look like the sort of man who gazes into someone's eyes?" he asked. He didn't want to talk about Nadia. Not here. Not now.

Brooke had a point though. The place *did* have its charm. It was a tiny, crowded little place on the corner of First and First, where the tables were too close together, the servers slightly frazzled, the food taking just a touch longer to come to the table than it should have. And yet nobody seemed to mind. Groups ranged from clusters of girlfriends chattering over wine to a business dinner in the corner to a rowdy celebration near the back to couples.

A lot of couples. Couples like . . . him and Brooke?

Hell, he had no idea what they were. Just thinking about it made his chest ache.

Apart from their rendezvous at his hotel last week, this was the first time when Seth didn't have to pretend—to himself, or to Brooke—that they were there for any reason other than being in each other's company.

He watched across the table as Brooke dug back into her steak, smiling at her enthusiasm before he tucked back into his own meal. They'd both opted for the steak frites. A caloric nightmare that was worth every single gram of fat.

"So what are you going to tell your sister about the success of her little matchmaking plan?" Brooke asked.

"I'm not," he grumbled.

"Oh, come on. You're not going to let her know that she was at least a little bit successful?"

"I've got you sitting across the dinner table from me giving me sexy eyes. I'd say that she was a *lot* successful," he said, holding her gaze.

Brooke's eyes narrowed playfully. "You're giving me sexy eyes back, Mr. Tyler."

"Because I want you," he said bluntly, setting his knife and fork on the plate and leaning forward slightly so he could lower his voice. "As much as I'm enjoying this steak, as perfect as this wine is, nothing tastes as good as you."

Her cheeks colored. "Seth."

"Tell me you haven't thought about it," he said, reaching out and prying her hand away from where it fiddled with her cocktail glass. He stroked his thumb along her palm. "Tell me you haven't thought about how we were together."

"Mostly I thought about after," she said a little glumly. "About how I took something pretty fantastic and turned it ugly."

"That morning wasn't all your fault," he said. "I could have handled things . . . better."

She smiled. "That's true. For a man who runs a billion-dollar business, you certainly don't have a way with words."

"No. I don't," he admitted. "But I'm trying."

You're worth trying for.

Fuck. The woman was turning him into a drippy mess.

"Well, you're doing quite well right now," she teased softly. "Although if you keep looking at me like that, we're never going to make it to dessert, and I've seen some chocolate decadence going around that looks really good."

Seth groaned. "Didn't anyone ever tell you not to tell a man that sex with him rates second to chocolate?"

Brooke opened her mouth to retort, but before she could (hopefully) contradict him, a shadow appeared over their table.

Seth glanced up, expecting to see their server.

"Nadia." Seth's hand jerked back so quickly from Brooke's that he nearly knocked her water glass over in the process.

Holy mother fucking *hell*. Had he somehow summoned her here?

It was his ex-girlfriend who reached out to calmly steady the teetering glass. "Hello, Seth," she said calmly. "It's nice to see you."

He forced himself to meet the familiar brown eyes of his ex. She was as exotically beautiful as he remembered. Her mother was Korean, her father Russian, and their only daughter was stunning.

And she knew it. She'd always known it.

A libel attorney, she was as smart and ambitious as she was gorgeous, and he'd found the combination intoxicating.

Hell, he'd found it a lot more than that. He'd been ready to put a ring on it.

But seeing her now, looking down at him in exactly the same way she had a year ago, her smile slightly mocking, her eyes completely cold, Seth realized for the first time that perhaps he'd dodged a bullet when she'd said no.

Would he have been content with Nadia as his wife?

Probably.

But happy . . . ? He studied her, from her shining dark hair down to her dark red manicure all the way down to the black Louboutin pumps she favored. No. He wouldn't have been happy.

And he was no longer interested in letting her look down on him.

He stood and pecked her cheek, feeling . . . nothing.

Not regret, or sadness, or relief. Only blankness.

She smiled her usual cool smile. It wasn't that Nadia didn't feel. It wasn't that she was an ice princess. He'd seen her get *wildly* passionate about some of her cases. It was just that she'd never been passionate about *him*.

Her eyes flicked over him. "You look good."

"You too," he said automatically.

Nadia turned toward Brooke and extended a hand. "Hi, I'm Nadia."

"Brooke Baldwin."

Nadia rarely bothered with small talk with people whose names she didn't recognize, and she turned back to Seth. "I thought you didn't like this place."

He frowned. "I like it."

"You always said that it was too far downtown."

"Doesn't mean that I didn't like it."

Nadia's brown eyes narrowed before she shrugged. "So how are you?"

"I'm good," he said.

Only after the words were out did he realize how inadequate they were.

He was better than good. He was better than he'd been in a long time, all because he was more alive than he'd ever felt. It was like some sort of damned movie where the character didn't even know he was half whole until he met that one person who completed him.

Or some shit like that.

"And you?" he asked politely.

Out of the corner of his eye, he could have sworn he saw Brooke pretending to fall asleep at the dull conversation.

"Also good," Nadia said. "My brother's in town. He was my date for the evening, actually. Just left to catch a cab back uptown to his hotel. And Maya? She's good?"

Seth's eyes flicked toward Brooke long enough to see her cracking up into her cocktail glass. He couldn't blame her. This was getting downright painful.

"She's—great," he said, catching himself before he could utter the word *good* again. "Getting married, actually."

"Ah, so Grant finally pulled his head out of his ass, huh? Gotta give him credit—he works fast."

Seth stared at her. "She's not marrying Grant."

"Oh!" Nadia's eyes went wide in the first bit of expression she'd shown since crashing his date. "I just assumed. He's always been so hung up on her."

"Told you," Brooke muttered.

Nadia glanced at Brooke, this time looking a bit closer. "You've met Grant? And Maya?"

"I'm Maya's wedding planner," Brooke explained with a smile.

"Oh. So this is a business dinner," Nadia said in a bored tone.

"No," Seth said, just as Brooke replied, "Yes."

He gave her a sharp look.

"Well, it was really nice seeing you," his ex said in the same tone he expected she gave her dentist when she told him she'd be back again in six months.

"Likewise." He kissed her cheek once more, registering how cool it felt, noting that her perfume was familiar and yet also completely unappealing to him.

Seth resumed his spot at the table just as Brooke reached across the table and picked up his glass of wine since her own drink was now empty.

"Well, that was *fun*," she said.

"Sorry about that. Shitty timing, seeing as we were just talking about Nadia, and how . . ."

Her eyebrows lifted. "How I sort of wanted to scratch her eyes out?"

Seth reached out, slowly taking the glass back from her, letting his fingers brush against hers, lingering against their softness.

"Feeling possessive, are we?" he said, his voice coming out as a low growl.

He noted the way she watched his mouth as he sipped his wine. The tip of her tongue flicked slowly across her lower lip, and he felt his cock stir. Goddamn, he wanted this woman.

"I may have changed my mind about dessert," she said, her voice lower than usual.

"Really?" he said, enjoying the game they were playing. "Because I was just starting to warm to the idea of watching you purr while you ate that chocolate soufflé."

She pursed her lips and leaned forward slightly, further lowering her voice. "How about you watch me purr with my lips wrapped around your cock instead?"

Seth gripped the glass so hard he was surprised it didn't shatter. "Yeah, okay. You win, Baldwin."

She grinned in victory, and two minutes later, they were out the door.

Chapter Twenty-Five

DEX HAD BARELY CLOSED the car door behind them before Seth reached for her. His fingers slid into her hair, his big hand palming her head as he drew her face to his.

Brooke closed her eyes, desperate for his kiss, but he paused, brushing his lips against her cheek. "I like you."

Her eyes flew open at the simple, unexpected admission, and she pulled back slightly to meet his gaze. "Why do you sound so surprised?"

The corner of his mouth turned up, his eyes locked on the spot where his thumb and forefinger rubbed against a strand of her hair. "I wasn't supposed to."

"You weren't supposed to like me?"

Blue eyes latched onto hers. "I wasn't even supposed to meet you. You weren't in my plans, and I like my plans."

"I'm shocked," she said teasingly. "Absolutely shocked."

Brooke placed both palms against his face and

drew him down to her, their lips meeting softly as they kissed sweet and slow.

His free arm wrapped around her back, pulling her close as his head tilted, deepening the kiss. She gave a small sigh, leaning all the way into the kiss. Every time he got closer to her, her breath caught, her pulse quickened, and she wanted. This kiss was no different. If anything it was even more dangerous to her. The passion was still there, hot and furious in the way their fingers clawed at each other, in the way they couldn't get close enough. But this time there was another layer to this kiss that made it all the more intoxicating.

I like you, he'd said.

She smiled into the kiss, her hands sliding up to his hair, even as her fingers longed for the moment that they were out of this car so she could tear off his ever-present tie, run her hands over his perfect chest . . .

Brooke pulled back and blinked up at him. "Where are we going?"

"My place?" he said, his lips sliding along her jaw.

Brooke's neck fell back helplessly as she struggled to hold on to her thoughts.

"Wait, no," she said, pushing him back slightly. "Can we go to my place?"

"Ah . . . sure? If you want."

"I do want," she said, feeling a little foolish. "It's just, last time we went to your place, it didn't end well, and I don't want all that bad energy to crash my horny, you know?"

"Crash your horny, huh? You're something else, Baldwin." He kissed the side of her head. "Okay."

Seth reached for the small button that controlled

the partition separating the driver section, and rolled it down just enough so that Dex's busy salt-and-pepper eyebrows were visible in the rearview mirror.

Brooke fought the urge to hide her face in Seth's shoulder. Groping in the back of a car, for God's sake.

"We'll be going to Brooke's place," Seth said in a matter-of-fact tone. "Eighty-Second and Second."

"Yes, sir," Dex said with a nod.

Brooke's head whipped around to stare at Seth's profile as he rolled the divider back up. "You know where I live?"

"Obviously."

She narrowed her eyes. "I've never told you."

"Nope."

She pinched his arm. "Don't be creepy. How do you know that?"

He caught her fingers before she could pinch him again, lifting her hand to his lips and kissing her knuckles. "Maya told me."

"But how would Maya know?"

Brooke thought back, remembered that Maya had given Brooke a crash course in the various Manhattan neighborhoods recently. They'd discussed Brooke's current neighborhood of Yorkville. But had she mentioned her specific address?

Possibly. Probably.

Maybe it wasn't so weird that he knew. It was just—

"What's wrong?" he asked, his lips still warm against her fingers as his mouth drifted down toward her wrist, his tongue flicking against the delicate pulse there.

"Nothing," she said. "Not really. It's just a little unnerving that you can be so . . ."

"Controlling," he said.

"I don't know that that's the right word," she said. But it wasn't the wrong word, either.

"I think you might find people appreciate you asking them directly if there's something you want to know rather than just deciding it's your right to know."

He met her gaze steadily. "This isn't really about your address, is it? It's that I'm still against the Maya/Neil thing."

"You have a right to your opinions and your hunches; I just think you should talk to your sister about it."

He turned his head slightly toward the window, his face looking bleak and hollow. "I'll consider it."

"Do. And to bring this back to us, I don't want to be one of your projects that needs fixing."

His head snapped back to look at her. "Why the hell would you need fixing?"

She lifted her shoulders. "Because of the thing with Clay."

Seth touched a knuckle softly to her cheek. "Thought you were over that."

"I am," she said automatically. "It's just important to me that you don't see me as that woman. The one that got ditched at the altar."

"All right," he said slowly. "Is it all right that I think of you as a woman though? Maybe *my* woman. For tonight."

She leaned forward slightly and brushed his lips with hers. "Yeah."

The car slowed to a stop, and Dex came around to open the door for them. Brooke accepted the chauffeur's hand, forcing herself to smile as though she wasn't horribly embarrassed, hoping that the dark night sky would hide her blush.

Seth muttered something to Dex along the lines of don't wait up, and a moment later the car pulled away, leaving them in the quiet of her neighborhood.

His hand rested on her back as he glanced up at the mid-rise where she lived on the fourth floor. "It's lovely."

She snorted. "It's not."

"It is," he insisted. "It's homey."

"I suppose," she said, trying to see the building through his eyes. Mostly she'd just been so darn glad to be out of California when she'd arrived that she hadn't paid much attention to the building that would be home.

She liked it well enough. The doormen were nice. The building was clean. Sure, the elevator was a little slow, and her door squeaked, and maybe the neighborhood was just a touch more secluded than she'd like. But she was determined to like it, therefore she did like it.

Seth linked his fingers in hers. "Take me home, Baldwin."

She laughed. "You know, for such a rich, savvy guy, you can be a total dork."

"I like to think it reveals my vulnerable side."

She glanced up at him suspiciously. "Do you have a vulnerable side?"

"I do. Her name is Brooke."

Her lips parted slightly as happiness washed over her. "You know I'm already going to sleep with you, right? You don't have to woo me with romance."

"No? In that case . . ." He lowered his mouth to her ear. "Take me upstairs so I can fuck you. Hard."

Brooke's thighs clenched in want, but she didn't have to be told twice.

On autopilot she made it through the front door, said hello to Christian, the nighttime doorman, and managed to get Seth into the elevator before dragging him against her.

He shoved her against the wall of the elevator, gripping her chin with one hand as the other slid down her hip, kneading the soft flesh as he nipped at her mouth.

Seth let out a low growl when the elevator jerked to a stop a second later. "Seriously?"

Brooke giggled, the sound happy and girlish. "This isn't a Tyler high-rise. There are only six floors, and I'm the fourth."

"Just as well," he said, against her neck. "Now I won't have to get you naked in the elevator."

His hand shot out, opening the elevator door before it could shut again, and he tugged her forward and out into the hallway with such sexy authority, that for a moment Brooke thought she might want to be stripped down and seduced in the elevator, spectators be damned.

"Which way?"

Brooke's apartment was the first door on the right, and though she expected him to pull her close the second they stepped inside, he surprised her by stopping to look around first, keeping a tight grip on her hand.

Not that there was much to see. Her condo in LA had been nearly three times the size of her apartment here, and the furniture she'd had shipped from California looked horribly out of place, the light wood and white linens of her West Coast lifestyle clashing with the old walls and dark flooring of her New York place.

"It's nice," he said.

Brooke shrugged, seeing it through his eyes and realizing how horribly temporary it looked. She wanted to settle in. She'd tried. But everything looked sort of mismatched, and not in the quirky, eclectic way. It was more the disorganized mess of someone with an identity crisis.

"You okay?" he asked.

She glanced up, surprised to find him looking at her instead of the apartment. The question was so simple, so no-bullshit that she felt herself nearly crumbling in the face of his basic, direct question.

She didn't even know that she wanted to crumble.

But being here in a home that wasn't yet fully home, with a man who liked her, she felt a strange sense of pain and happiness at the same time, and she felt . . .

Confused.

Something that felt suspiciously like tears pricked at the corner of her eyes and she frowned. *Oh no*. Not now. She hadn't cried once. Not in the days after Clay went to jail, not when every single client had left.

It made no sense that *this* would be the moment where she felt the most fragile.

She blinked rapidly and did the only thing she could think of to ward off whatever unfounded breakdown was on the horizon.

She threw herself at Seth.

He grunted in surprise but caught her easily, his arms going around her as she grabbed a handful of his hair and pulled his mouth down to hers.

She raked her teeth against his lip just a bit harder than was nice, and he pulled back slightly, his eyes puzzled. Searching.

Brooke shook her head. "Please."

For a second, she thought he wouldn't understand what she was saying. Wouldn't understand that she was begging him to help her forget.

But then he pulled her to him, kissing her roughly as his palms molded possessively over her back, and she smiled.

He got it. He definitely got it.

Seth's hands weren't gentle as he tore at her clothes, and hers were greedy right back, shoving his coat to the floor and tugging at his shirt so hard a button flew off.

He growled against her neck. "You'll pay for that."

"Yeah?" she said a little breathless. "Charge it to the Belles."

"Not the type of payment I had in mind."

And then his hands were undoing the buttons of her pants, his hand sliding inward until he rubbed against the front of her panties.

Seth drew in a hiss of air. "You're so wet."

"Seems to be a constant state with you," she said, her voice breathless.

His hand slipped down further, one finger easing under the elastic and stroking against her damp flesh.

Seth's groan mingled with her own as he caressed her sensitive skin with light, teasing strokes.

She arched against his hand, trying to get more contact, and instead of torturing her further, a finger slid into her with one slick satisfying thrust.

"Oh God," she said, her head falling against his shoulder. "Oh God, that feels good."

He slipped another finger inside of her and began pumping them into her steadily, and without even thinking about it, she began to ride his hand, shamelessly, wantonly. Seth kissed the sensitive skin of her neck as he rubbed his thumb roughly against her clit, and she pivoted her hips onto his hand in desperate, aching need.

She wanted the dirty, unabashed moment to last forever, but he found her rhythm almost immediately, and suddenly her orgasm was tearing out of her in a harsh cry that seemed to echo off the walls.

Brooke's body immediately went into recovery mode, her knees buckling.

Seth slid his free arm around her, his mouth moving to her ear. "I've got you."

Brooke slumped against him, letting him absorb her, giving in, just for a moment, to the boneless pleasure of losing one's mind.

Seth adjusted his hand slightly, pulling out of her panties, but resting there against the vee of her thighs. She had the fleeting thought that she should be embarrassed, but instead she felt satiated.

Wanted.

Beautiful.

When her breathing returned to normal, she kissed his shoulder in an absentminded thank-you before pushing back and looking up at him.

He gave her a quiet, private smile that made her tummy flip before dipping his head and capturing her lips in a sweet, pulling kiss that was just the right amount of tender and hot. Brooke's hand wandered downward, her palm cupping him through the expensive fabric of his suit pants. She smiled against his mouth when she found him rock hard.

Seth groaned. "Find something you like?"

"I'm not sure yet," she said, pulling his bottom lip between her teeth and nipping lightly. "I think I'm going to need a closer look."

His breath caught as she slowly lowered to her knees in front of him, holding his gaze as she very slowly unfastened his pants.

Brooke licked her lips as she pulled down the zipper, and Seth muttered a harsh oath before one hand tentatively came up to the side of her head as though he might need to hold on for balance.

And she was firmly committed to making sure that he did.

Brooke greedily shoved his pants and briefs over his lean hips, making a little breathy sigh of pleasure when his cock sprang free.

"Update," she said, glancing up his body and finding him watching her once more. "I definitely like what I see."

"Show me how much you like it," he said on a

husky rasp, his hips hilting forward so he brushed against her parted lips.

Happy to.

She extended her tongue, swirling it around his head before parting her lips and taking him all the way inside her mouth.

"Ah. That's it," he said, the fingers on her hair becoming a bit rougher. "That's it, baby. Oh God."

Brooke loved him with her mouth, alternating between slow, savoring sucks and teasing flicks of her tongue. She laved the underside of his steel-hard cock with her tongue and coddled his balls with one hand, which caused him to emit a low growl. He had her head with both hands now, and sensing that he wanted to take control, Brooke stilled so that he was using her mouth, his hips doing all the work as he plunged in and out.

"Damn it, Brooke. I can't—I'm going to—"

She nodded, wanting it. Wanting the taste of him.

But even as he swore, he was tugging her to her feet, capturing her chin with his thumb and forefinger and stamping a hard kiss across her lips.

"I need to be inside you. Now."

Brooke didn't have to be told twice. She took his hand and led him to the couch, holding his gaze as she walked backward.

"Here?" he asked, lifting his eyebrows.

In response, Brooke quickly kicked off her shoes, stripped off her pants and underwear, and then very slowly knelt on the couch so that she was facing the window, her forearms resting on the padded couch arm as she looked back at him over her shoulder.

Seth needed no further invitation. His eyes traveled the line of her bare ass and hips before his hand reached out and followed the same motion, palming her butt as he knelt behind her.

"You need to be taken on the couch, baby?" he murmured, running a palm down her spine before resting it in the small of her back and pushing down slightly so that her ass tilted up to him.

Her only response was to circle her hips so that her butt pressed against him suggestively, and he groaned, sliding a hand between her legs and stroking her clit as he lined up against her opening.

"You better be holding on," he said roughly.

And then he plunged forward in one hot, firm stroke.

Yes. Yes, this is what she wanted. Needed.

Seth's hands found either side of her hips, holding her still as he withdrew slowly, only to push forward hard and fast, just the way she wanted it.

"Harder," she said, her head dipping forward, her hair falling in her face. "Take me harder."

Over and over he slammed into her. He wasn't gentle, and she didn't want him to be. She rolled her hips, arching back to meet his every thrust.

And though it was good—damn good—she couldn't resist taking more. Her hand slid down between her legs, stroking herself in tiny circles.

"I'm going to come," he ground out, his pace quickening. "I wish you could see yourself like this. Watching you in the reflection of the window . . . I thought nothing could beat your mouth, but this is better."

Brooke snuck a glance over her shoulder, and the savage look on his face was all she needed to explode, this orgasm even more intense than the last one.

"Fuck," he said as she began to clench around him. "*Fuck*."

She felt him jerk, felt his fingers dig in hard to the soft flesh of her hips as he came inside her in a heart-stoppingly perfect moment of intimacy.

Brooke collapsed face-first onto the couch, and Seth fell with her, carefully maneuvering them so that her back was to his front.

It should have been awkward. Her with her shirt and no pants, him with his pants around his ankles and his shirt half-unbuttoned.

But neither seemed to care as he slid an arm beneath her head before the other came around her and pulled her even closer.

She opened her mouth, desperate for something witty to say. A casual little quip like the women of *Sex and the City* always had at the ready.

But she didn't want a quip. Wasn't sure she wanted casual, either.

Hell, Brooke wasn't sure what she wanted.

All she knew was that she didn't want him to leave.

Chapter Twenty-Six

SETH WASN'T ENTIRELY SURE what he was expecting from a private investigator.

A Hawaiian shirt, maybe. Or perhaps a cheap leather jacket and sunglasses worn indoors. An off-the-rack brown suit that was too big in the shoulders.

But whatever it was he was expecting, it certainly wasn't Tommy Franklin.

The PI Seth was a heartbeat away from hiring to do some digging on Neil Garrett was . . . normal.

Tommy was slightly taller than average and had the broad, bulky frame of a man who liked his carbs but tried to combat that affection with plenty of time at the gym. There was no bad suit or Hawaiian shirt in sight, just a black sweater, dark jeans, and loafers. With his dark blond hair, blue eyes, and even features, the PI had the type of face that was attractive enough to be pleasant but not so attractive you'd remember him.

In other words, exactly the sort of person who could blend into the crowd, asking questions that wouldn't get a second look.

"Thanks for coming," Seth said, extending a hand toward the guest chair and inviting Tommy to sit.

"Not a problem," the other man said affably, sitting down. "Lots of fakers out there. Always happy to give my clients whatever validation they need to feel comfortable."

Seth had contacted the PI by email a few weeks earlier, but had held back on actually making the move. Hell, even now he still wasn't sure it was the right thing to do, but he was losing sleep over the thought of his sister marrying this asshole, and he didn't know what else to do.

Still, *comfortable* was a bit of a stretch.

Seth wasn't sure any man would feel comfortable with the fact that he was about to hire someone to spy on his sister. Well, not his sister so much as the man she'd decided on.

But wasn't that just as bad?

Hell, maybe even worse. It was flat-out saying that he didn't trust Maya's judgment.

Or Brooke's, for that matter.

Which on paper made Seth a complete asshole.

And yet, no matter how hard he tried, and Seth had tried, he couldn't shake the pervading sense low and dark in his gut that Neil Garrett was not the right man for his sister.

There were plenty of areas in life where his sister bested him. Charm. Wit. Likability. She was better at tennis, golf, and chess. She was a better cook and could negotiate like nobody's business.

But when it came to reading people, Maya was too trusting. Giving people the benefit of the doubt they didn't deserve. That was where he came in.

"So your email said your sister's gotten in with a bad guy," Tommy said as both men settled in their respective seats and studied each other.

Seth gave a curt nod. He'd gotten Tommy's name from Dennis, an old college buddy, who'd hired the man to follow a cheating now ex-wife. Cliché, yes, but then the twenty-two-year-old ex had been a bit of a cliché, too, carrying on with a half dozen of Dennis's wealthier friends, likely to hedge her bets when he eventually dumped her.

Which he had.

Point was, Dennis had trusted Tommy, and Seth trusted Dennis.

"You mind if I take notes?" Tommy asked, pulling an iPad out of his briefcase.

Seth waved his permission.

"So this boyfriend—"

"Fiancé," Seth corrected curtly.

Tommy nodded and tapped something. "Name?"

"Neil Garrett."

"And you don't like him."

"I do not."

Tommy continued to tap. "Gut reaction? Or something specific?"

"Gut reaction," Seth said, grateful that he didn't have to explain it. Grateful that he didn't have to say out loud that he was having his sister's choices researched without so much as a shred of evidence that the man she was marrying was anything less than smitten with her.

"The gut often knows best," Tommy said with a nod. "How long's Garrett been in the picture?"

"They got engaged after dating for three months. Casually, apparently, as I wasn't even aware of the guy. They've been engaged for about a month now. So, four months altogether," Seth said.

Saying aloud that Neil and Maya had been engaged for a month made Seth realize that he'd only known Brooke for a little under a month.

Which seemed strange.

Strange, because she'd managed to wiggle more determinedly into his life and under his skin in the span of thirty days than Nadia had in three years.

The realization was unsettling, although not entirely unwelcome.

"Your sister is wealthy?" Tommy said, his tone matter-of-fact.

Seth nodded once.

"And Garrett. Employed?"

Seth shrugged. "Apparently he's starting up his own business. But whenever I've pressed for details, I can't get so much as a name, much less a sense of when he starts to plan making money from it."

"'Investment mode'?" Tommy said with a little smile, making air quotes around the words.

Seth snorted. "Exactly."

"Anything else I need to know?" Tommy asked. "Where the guy's from, what his schedule's like?"

Seth shook his head. "I'm not entirely sure. He and I aren't exactly cozy. I know he's been out of town on work lately. Investment opportunities or some bullshit. Seems to be more often than not, but I don't have a sense on specifics."

Tommy nodded, tapped something else on his iPad. "That's where I come in. My job is to get the specifics and get them to you so you can make an informed decision about the next steps you need to take."

Seth swallowed. He was doing this. He was really going to hire this man.

Tommy slid his iPad back into his bag and then leaned forward, the alert sharpness of his expression telling Seth that there was a shrewdness hiding behind the easy smiles.

"All you have to do is say the word, and I'm on it," Tommy said.

Seth gave a half smile. "Why do I get the feeling there's a warning in there somewhere?"

Tommy didn't smile back. "I'm discreet. Your sister and Garrett will never know I've looked into him unless you want them to."

"But?"

"But, the toll of these things often isn't paid by the person I'm following."

"Believe me, I'm very aware who's paying for this," Seth replied wryly. Tommy Franklin was not cheap.

"That's not what I mean," Tommy said, looking a little grimmer. "I'm saying that invading the privacy of a loved one, even if it's in their best interest as it is here, can wreak emotional havoc."

The PI's words struck a chord, but Seth kept his voice impassive. "I'd rather lose sleep over my own guilt than worry over my sister's future."

Tommy studied him a bit longer, but he seemed

to see the resolve on Seth's face, because he nodded, clapped his hands against his legs, and then stood, hand outstretched. "We're in business, then."

Seth hesitated only briefly before shaking Tommy Franklin's hand.

The moment he did, Seth became horribly aware he'd made a deal with the devil.

Only in this case, the devil wasn't the private detective so much as it was the cold chunk of ice that lived in Seth's heart.

Tommy had already explained his payment terms over email, but Seth listened as the other man explained them once more. Half up front. A quarter more with the first report, due in a month or shorter. The last quarter when the job was done.

The men shook hands once more, and Seth showed Tommy to the door. Seth's hand was just reaching for the door handle when the door burst open from the other side.

"Yo, Tyler. Take me to lunch, and tell me every detail about what's going on with your wedding planner hottie," Grant said, striding into the office with the confidence of a man who'd done so a hundred times before without knocking.

Seth's best friend halted when he saw that Seth wasn't alone. "Ah. Shit. Shit. Sorry, man. Etta said you didn't have anything on your calendar when I called earlier this morning."

Fuck.

Seth didn't have anything on his calendar. He'd purposely asked Etta to keep his lunch hour free so he could catch up on email, and then insisted Etta take her dopey intern to some overpriced lunch so he could meet with the private detective in peace.

A peace that was shot to hell now that Grant was studying the other man curiously.

Tommy Franklin was no slob, but he also wasn't wearing the usual Tyler Hotel Group business uniform that other men wore. There was no suit, no monochromatic tie. Grant would know immediately that this wasn't a standard business meeting.

Double fuck.

Tommy gave a polite but bland smile and slipped out the door with little more than a nod to Seth and Grant. It was nicely done. A subtle way of escaping without introductions, and yet there was no sense of rudeness or awkwardness. Just a simple straightforward exit.

Any other acquaintance of Seth's would have dropped it without a second thought.

Unfortunately for Seth, Grant was not any acquaintance.

"Who was that?" Grant asked, curiosity shining through his brown eyes.

"Nobody," Seth muttered, shutting the door and heading back toward his desk.

It was the wrong thing to say. Not only was Grant annoyingly inquisitive by nature, he also knew Seth too damned well. Knew when he was lying.

"You would have put *nobody* on your calendar," Grant said. "And *nobody* wouldn't have required you sending Etta out to lunch when it's not her birthday."

"Not true," Seth muttered. "I send her out in the week before Christmas sometimes. She likes to go see the tree at Rockefeller."

"Right," Grant said, crossing his arms. "You keep telling yourself whatever you need to, to avoid the guilt that's written all over your ugly face right now."

"I don't know what you're talking about," Seth replied as he turned his attention toward his computer screen, even though his brain refused to register any of the hundreds of emails in his inbox.

Grant ambled closer to the desk, his easy lope a contradiction to the ire on his face.

"Tell me that man wasn't who I think he was," Grant demanded.

Seth spread his hands to the side. "Hard to say. You're the only aspiring mind reader in this room. Am I supposed to know what you're rambling on about?"

Grant's light brown eyes glinted angrily. "Don't bullshit me, Seth."

It was the seriousness in his usually lighthearted friend's face that had Seth coming clean.

He met Grant's eye steadily. "That was Tommy Franklin. He's a private investigator I hired to look into Maya's fiancé."

"You son of a bitch," Grant said, almost before Seth finished his sentence.

"I told you I was going to do it," Seth said, hating the note of defensiveness in his tone.

"And I told you not to."

"Well, then it's a good thing you're not the boss," Seth said pointedly.

"I'm not talking to you as one of your subordinates right now, and you fucking know it. I'm talking to you as a friend, although right now I'm seriously debating whether you're worthy of the word."

Seth withheld the flinch, but barely.

There were very few people in this world capable of wounding him, but Grant Miller was definitely one of them. And because pain was an unfamiliar sensation he'd never quite learned how to deal with, Seth lashed back.

"This really isn't any of your business, Grant."

"The hell it isn't." Grant slammed his palms on the desk. "This isn't right, and you know it. Maya deserves our trust."

"There's no 'our,' here, Grant. She's my sister. You made your opinion clear and I noted it, but this is up to me. I'm the one that will have to call this man brother-in-law. I'm the one who will have to pick up the pieces if he hurts her. I'm the one who will have to sort out the financial aftermath if he's after her money."

"That's what this is all about," Grant said coldly. "The money."

Okay, that was enough.

Seth slammed his own hands on the desk, standing and glaring up at his slightly taller friend. "That's not fucking fair. I care about Maya more than anything in the world, and you know that."

"Well, your brand of brotherly love sucks," Grant snarled.

"Back off," Seth said, taking a breath and trying to cool his temper. "This isn't your call."

"Well, it damn well should be."

"Why, because you're in love with her?" Seth challenged, the words out of his mouth before he could think better of them.

Grant's chin knocked back as though Seth had dealt him a physical blow, and because Seth knew Grant every bit as well as Grant knew him, he knew what that reaction meant.

It meant that Brooke had been right. Grant was in love with Maya.

Seth swore softly, his head dipping forward. "You should have told me."

"It wasn't yours to know," Grant said, his tone rougher than Seth had ever heard it.

"She's my sister. You're my best friend."

"Exactly. You would have tried to fix it. You'd have gotten all up in there," Grant said.

"And that would have been a bad thing?"

Grant's laugh held no humor. "This may come as a shock to you, but there are some things you can't control, Seth. Your sister's heart is one of them."

Seth met his friend's eyes, hurting for him, even with the anger between them. "Does she know?"

Grant shook his head miserably.

"You know that my finding dirt on Garrett will work in your favor," Seth said slowly. "If the man's a fraud and she breaks up with him—"

Grant was already shaking his head. "My love for her isn't like that."

Seth's eyes narrowed. "Meaning what?"

"Meaning that that's not how I love," his friend said. "I don't risk other people's happiness for my own peace of mind."

The quietly uttered statement was a direct hit, and this time it was Seth's head that knocked back as though struck.

"Seth." Grant rubbed a hand over his face. "I know it was hard for you when Hank died. I know it was hard learning that he kept his heart condition a secret from you."

"Which he didn't from you," Seth said bitterly.

"You know I would have told you if he hadn't made me promise to keep it quiet," Grant replied. "And in the same way I begged him to tell you, to just be honest, I'm begging you now. Don't do this to Maya. Don't be dishonest with her."

"You don't get it," Seth said a little desperately. "If I have a chance to help someone I care about, I have to take it. If my dad would have told me, I could have done something. I could have saved him."

"Don't do that, man," Grant said. "Is that what's driving you? You couldn't save your dad, so now you're thinking you're saving Maya?"

"I have to try," Seth said.

"That's not love, Seth. Sticking your head into someone else's business, not trusting them to do their life their way . . . that's not love."

"It's my kind of love," Seth snarled.

Grant made a disgusted sound and shook his head. "And that, my friend, is why you're so goddamn alone."

The tightness in Seth's chest constricted horribly, and for a moment he felt like he couldn't breathe.

"Get out," Seth snapped. "Get the hell out."

"Happily," Grant snapped back.

It was the last word his best friend said before he stormed out of Seth's office, the door slamming shut behind him.

Leaving Seth as he'd always been.

Alone.

Chapter Twenty-Seven

ᴖ

"Ugh. Valentine's Day is the worst," Jessie huffed as she carefully arranged fancy Levain Bomboloncini, the trendy bakery's signature go-to snack, hand wrapped with pale pink paper, on a tray. It was four o'clock on a Friday, and a rare moment of calm in the Belles, with all four women in the same place, as Alexis had asked them to block off a couple of hours to add some classy Valentine's Day decorations around headquarters.

"Nuh-uh," Heather said, helping herself to one of the miniature powder-dusted doughnuts and earning a glare from Alexis. "You don't get to say that, what with your boyfriend and all."

"Um, I can *totally* have a boyfriend and still hate Valentine's Day," Jessie said.

"Nope." Heather's mouth was full of raspberry jam. "That's reserved for us single girls."

"Hear, hear," Alexis muttered as she carefully placed handblown hearts into one of the hurricane vases on the reception table.

Brooke glanced over at the Wedding Belles' owner. "You too, Alexis? You hate Valentine's Day?"

"Not professionally," Alexis said, stepping back to admire her handiwork. "It gets people feeling all dreamy and spendy, which is good for business. But personally . . ." She shrugged. "Not my favorite."

"I take it from your scandalized expression that you do like the holiday, Brooke," Heather said, reaching for a miniature Godiva from the small crystal bowl on the table and getting her hand slapped by Jessie.

Brooke paused in the process of stuffing vellum valentines into fancy envelopes. All of their previous clients received handwritten notes from the Belles, unless, of course, they were on Alexis's carefully maintained Divorce List That Wasn't Spoken Of.

"I do like Valentine's Day," she admitted, running a finger over the cupid stamp on the envelope.

"That's because she's taken a luv-er," Heather said in a singsong tone.

Brooke's insides warmed as she thought about Seth. Not that he was the romantic type. She certainly wasn't holding her breath for flowers and candy when Valentine's Day rolled around in another week. More likely he'd forget about the day altogether, and then make it up to her with his hands and mouth and sexy words late into the night . . .

"Are you blushing?" Alexis asked, giving her a suspicious look.

Jessie laughed. "No, that's just good old-fashioned overheating. Her mind's gone to The Gutter."

True. Super True.

"Okay, but seriously," Brooke said, changing the subject away from her sex life. "Even if I didn't have a luv-er, I'd still love Valentine's Day."

Heather pointed at her own face. "See this? Skepticism."

"Big surprise," Alexis said. "You remind us almost daily that you doubt all things men and romance."

"As do you, dear," Brooke heard herself say mildly.

Her boss shot her a surprised look. "Excuse me?"

Brooke's eyes widened as she glanced around at the group of women. "Oh, I'm sorry. Were we not supposed to talk about the fact that you keep all men at a safe distance?"

Heather let out a surprised laugh, and Jessie pointed toward the kitchen. "I'm just gonna go ahead and get us some wine."

The receptionist glanced at Alexis in question as she said this, and Alexis glanced at her watch, then shrugged at seeing the late afternoon hour. "Nobody has any last-minute appointments?"

"Nope," Heather and Brooke chorused.

"Then what the hell," Alexis muttered, going to the front door and pulling the silver Closed plaque from the door and carefully hanging it over the doorbell.

Brooke silently cheered. If girl time, plentiful chocolate, and pretty pink hearts didn't call for wine, she didn't know what did.

"I'm thinking champagne," Jessie said, coming back with a bottle and four flutes. "The cheap stuff, so don't freak, Alexis."

Alexis scoffed. "I never freak."

"'Tis true," Heather said, flopping back onto a white love seat and patting the spot next to her for Brooke to come join. "I mean, I maybe saw her almost freak once when she found out that a bride was having an affair with the groom's father and wanted to announce it at the rehearsal dinner, but even then she didn't have a hair out of place."

"Of course not," Alexis said primly, sitting in a chair and smoothing a hand over her dove-gray slacks as she accepted a glass of champagne from Jessie. "Because I'm not a complete heathen."

It was said jokingly, but as Brooke studied her boss in all her put-together glory, she realized that Heather was right. Alexis wasn't just cool under pressure; she was downright rigid at times. Not in the cold, emotionless kind of way; it was just that the woman seemed to operate 100 percent from her head, and almost zero percent from her heart.

Brooke, on the other hand, was a bundle of messy emotions.

Always had been, probably always would be.

But only the happy emotions. That was very important. If one was going to wear one's heart on her sleeve, as Brooke tried to, it was important to keep sadness and anger at bay, giving in only to the giddy, good stuff in life.

It was how she survived.

Once all the women had champagne in hand, Jessie lifted a glass. "To Valentine's Day."

"Which isn't for another week," Heather argued. "Plus, no way am I toasting to that. It's not even a real holiday."

Jessie rolled her eyes. "Well, what would you toast to?"

Heather slid a sly glance toward Brooke. "How about to the newest addition to the Wedding Belles?"

"We've already toasted to me," Brooke said. "That first lunch at MOMA when you took me under your collective wing and were just . . . wonderful."

"Okay, don't get weepy," Heather said. "And I was thinking more like toasting to your new man."

"Oh, it's a little early for that," Brooke rushed to say. "We're just . . . playing."

Alexis caught her eye and winked before lifting her glass. "Okay, then. To playing."

They all clinked glasses and took a sip of the delicious bubbly. It might have been "the cheap stuff" by Alexis's shopping standards, but it was still darn yummy.

"So things are going well, then?" Alexis asked. "With you and Seth?"

"I guess so," Brooke said, running a fingernail over the stem of her glass. "I mean, he's not sending me texts by the hour confessing his love or anything, but we do dinner a couple times a week. Sometimes to discuss Maya's wedding stuff, sometimes not, and it's . . . I don't know. It's nice."

"Old-fashioned dating," Heather said wistfully. "God, I miss that."

"Do you think it's too soon?" Brooke blurted out.

All three women looked at her in surprise. "Too soon for what?"

Brooke twisted a lock of hair around her finger anxiously. "You know, to be seeing someone. I just got out of an engagement a few months ago, and I've only known Seth for a few weeks. I feel like I'm supposed to take time to heal, or something."

"If you feel ready, then you're ready," Jessie said confidently.

Brooke noticed that Alexis avoided her gaze and didn't chime in, and she sat up straighter, pointing at her friend. "There. That. What is that?"

"What is what?" Alexis said, still not meeting her eyes.

"You think it's too soon!" Brooke accused. "You think I was supposed to wait longer to recover from Clay."

Alexis rolled her eyes, finally glancing at Brooke. "Not true. I'm the one who encouraged you to go to Seth that first night, remember?"

"Oh. That's true," Brooke mused. "So what was with the Thinking Face?"

"Uh-oh," Heather said. "Alexis's Thinking Face is never a good thing."

"I don't have a thinking face," Alexis said. "I just . . . I am happy for you, Brooke, of course. And I don't believe that there's any minimum amount of time required for the heart to heal. But—"

Brooke sighed. "I knew there was going to be a *but*."

"I just want to make sure that you've *let* yourself heal," Alexis finished, her voice gentle.

"Of course I have," Brooke said automatically. "That's why I came out to New York instead of staying in LA licking my wounds."

"Running away isn't the same thing as healing."

"Alexis!" Jessie said.

"No, it's okay," Brooke said, her eyes never leaving Alexis's. "I asked for her opinion."

"And it is *just* an opinion," Alexis clarified. "But while I was all for you acting on instinct with Seth, owning your womanhood, or whatever, I just want to make sure you've had a chance to sort out what happened with Clay. Your heart suffered a pretty big shock."

"Yes, I'm aware," Brooke said, unable to keep the slight edge out of her voice.

Alexis reached out, resting her fingers against Brooke's knee. "It's just that you never talk about it. Not really. I mean, you talk in general terms about what happened, but there's a distance to the way you tell the story. As though it happened to someone else."

Brooke opened her mouth to argue that she was very aware who it had happened to, only . . .

Alexis's words started to get under her skin.

As in, *the other woman might be right.*

"Have you talked to Clay since the day of your wedding?" Heather asked quietly.

Brooke shook her head, somewhat surprised and peeved by Heather's apparent siding with Alexis. She had been all gung ho on Seth and Brooke getting together until this point, but now she seemed to be changing her tune. What was up with that? "No. I thought it would be . . . too painful."

And Brooke avoided pain at all costs. Because really, it was just the smart thing to do, right? Why dwell on something that hurt when you could shift your attention toward something that made you feel good?

But was she blurring the line? Was she confusing positive thinking with avoidance?

She frowned and took a sip of champagne.

"Now look what you've done," Jessie scolded the other two women. "You stole her happy!"

"I'm still happy," Brooke said, but it sounded false even to her own ears.

"I shouldn't have said anything," Alexis said, apparently having a rare moment of self-doubt. "I just see you putting on this happy face every single day, and I admire it, but I worry that you're going to shatter one time."

Brooke swallowed. "I'm okay. I'm really okay."

"Of course you are," Heather said, putting an arm around her. "You have us now."

Brooke forced a smile, except . . . now she was *aware* that it was forced.

"Do you think I should talk to him?" she asked. "To Clay?"

"Only if you want to," Alexis said. "Only if it feels right."

Brooke sat forward, rubbing her temples against a sudden headache. She didn't know if it felt right. And yet, now that this was all out there, she was realizing just how forcefully she'd been putting these thoughts at bay. It wasn't that she didn't think about what happened . . .

It was that she didn't let herself.

"Maybe you could start by talking to your parents," Jessie said in a bright voice. "Baby steps, you know. Find out what's going on with all that so you can get closure without actually having to talk to the scumbag."

At the mention of her parents, Brooke's head shot up. "What day is it? Oh my God. I totally forgot!"

"Forgot what?"

Brooke stood, going to the reception desk where she'd dropped her bag to get her phone. "The trial. It was supposed to start today."

"Wow, really?" Alexis said. "I hadn't heard anything about it."

"You've been following Clay's case?" Brooke asked.

"Just monitoring the situation," Alexis said in a mild voice. "But there hasn't been much."

"They wanted to keep it a closed courtroom," Brooke said, pulling her phone out. Her stomach dropped as she realized it had been on silent all day, evidenced by the multiple missed calls and text messages she was seeing now pop up on the screen. "To keep the media out, or whatever."

"Your dad decided to testify?" Jessie asked quietly. Brooke nodded. "I told him to."

And she told herself that it didn't bother her.

But the truth was, she wasn't at all sure how she felt about it. On the other hand, her parents not testifying because of her . . . no good. Not when Clay had taken and lost their retirement fund. It still made her sick to even think about it.

And yet, there was this part of her that still thought of Clay as the man she loved. The man she was going to marry.

She swallowed against the strange lump in her throat. What was this?

Messy emotions, that was what. This was why she

avoided letting her thoughts go in this direction. This was why she didn't let herself think about Clay.

This was why . . .

Oh God.

She read and reread her text from her mom. Call me as soon as you get this.

There were four missed calls.

Even as she held her phone, it buzzed again with a message from her dad. Hang in there, sweetie. We know it's hard. Call us.

What was hard?

What was she supposed to be hanging in there for?

She rapidly began scrolling through her other unread text messages. She had a handful from her LA friends. Friends she'd more or less been avoiding since she'd moved out to New York, because they made her think of Clay.

Hang in there, babe. Karma will get him.

This is bullshit. Thinking of you.

Are you okay? Call me.

Brooke let out a silent scream. What were they all talking about? What was wrong with people that they'd deliver the platitudes before the freaking news itself?

She dropped into Jessie's chair behind the reception desk, her hand fumbling for the computer mouse and keyboard, knowing it would be faster than typing on her phone.

Brooke brought up Google News and typed in Clay Battaglia.

Dozens of stories popped up, all within the last hour.

She didn't click into any of them, because she didn't have to.

The headlines said it all.

AMERICA'S FAVORITE CON MAN DODGES
JAIL TIME IN A LAST-MINUTE, UNEXPECTED
PLEA BARGAIN.

Clay had taken a plea deal.

Clay wasn't going to jail.

Oh God.

Oh. *God.*

It's okay, she told herself. *It's okay, it's okay, it's okay.*

But it wasn't okay.

Just like that, all of the pain, all of the anger of the past five months came roaring over her fast and furious.

And after a lifetime of looking on the bright side, Brooke realized she had no idea how to deal with the darkness.

She only knew that she felt like it would break her.

Chapter Twenty-Eight

WHEN CELL PHONES FIRST came on the scene decades earlier, Seth's father had not been a fan.

Convinced that mobile devices would be the end of family life and business productivity as he knew it, Hank Tyler had tried to banish cell phones wherever he could.

At home, that had meant Seth and Maya were allowed use of their cell phones only in the after-school hours to communicate their whereabouts, and in the evening after all homework was complete. Never at the dinner table, never on family outings.

It was trickier at the office.

In the early days, there'd been a no-personal-cell-use policy. But as smartphones became more ubiquitous, Hank had realized that smartphones made his people more available—not less.

Eventually, the policy had been relaxed so that there were just no cell phones allowed in meetings, from the junior business analysts all the way up to the CEO himself. It was a policy that Seth had never minded. It focused everyone's attention on the agenda items at hand, and with no distractions, meetings were more focused and efficient.

Case in point, Seth's budget meeting wrapped up in record time, and with a rare few minutes to spare, he headed back toward his office with the intention of hitting up Google and researching if there was some new "it" gift for Valentine's Day. Were flowers in? Out? Was chocolate too cliché?

Then again, even if chocolate *was* cliché, he didn't think Brooke would say no. He was rapidly learning the woman had a serious weakness for the stuff. Dark chocolate, milk chocolate, even white chocolate—all were fair game.

In the elevator, he pulled his phone out of his pocket to make a note to ask Maya for a list of the best chocolate stores in the city—his sister shared Brooke's sweet tooth, although she was an equal opportunity sugar eater and knew her way around every overpriced macaroon, truffle, and cupcake in Manhattan.

Six missed calls. Seth frowned, since few people had his personal cell phone number, and those who did were more inclined to text than call.

His stomach dropped when he saw that four of the calls had come from Brooke.

The other two were from Etta. Etta, who of all people knew that he wouldn't have his cell on in the meeting. Then again, Etta also would have known how to reach him if it were a true emergency, so he relaxed. Slightly.

But Brooke didn't seem the type of woman to call him multiple times in an hour unless it was urgent. The second he stepped off the elevator, he dialed her back, cursing under his breath when it went straight to voice mail. He chose not to leave a message and clicked off the call, striding toward his office.

"Where's Etta?" he barked at Jared, noting that his assistant was nowhere to be seen.

Jared spun around in his chair, and Seth saw that the man had a phone affixed to his ear. The younger man's eyes went wide with panic, and Seth could practically hear him thinking about how to listen to whomever was on the other end *and* answer Seth's question.

"Never mind," Seth muttered, heading into his office even as he started to text Brooke.

Hey, everything okay?

He skidded to a halt when he realized his office was not empty.

There was Etta sitting on his couch.

With Brooke.

Who was crying on his assistant's shoulder.

If Seth's gut had tightened earlier when he'd seen the missed calls, it twisted into a full-on knot now at the sight of tears running down her face.

Seth went to Brooke immediately, dropping his iPhone to the coffee table with a careless clatter as he went to his knees in front of her. "Sweetheart."

She gave him a watery smile and ran the back of her hand against her runny nose in a childlike gesture as she sniffled. "I'm so sorry. I shouldn't have come here. It was just, you didn't answer, and I thought I could just wait, and then—I just—I—"

Brooke started crying all over again, and Etta wrapped her arms more firmly around the younger woman, rubbing her back in small circles.

Seth was torn between being grateful for Etta's maternal instincts and barking at his assistant to back off so that he could be the one holding her.

Etta met his eyes and shook her head slightly, giving the barest of shrugs.

Whatever Brooke was crying about, she hadn't told Etta.

"Poor thing's been sobbing too hard to get many words out," she said quietly to Seth as though Brooke weren't there. And she might not be wrong. Brooke was shaking, her sobs nearly drowning out his and Etta's side conversation.

"Brooke," Seth said, taking her hands in his. "What's wrong?"

She only cried harder, and Seth glanced back at Etta, giving her a silent command, which she instantly understood.

Etta gave one last pet to Brooke's mussed blond hair, making soothing noises, before easing her away from her shoulder and shifting to the side.

Seth was already there, taking Etta's place the second she stood.

His heart both warmed and twisted at the way Brooke instinctively curled into him, one hand fisting against his lapel as she buried her damp face in his neck.

The businessman in Seth—the *doer*—wanted

answers, and wanted them now. Wanted to know who or what had hurt her so that he could crush it. But the man in Seth—the one he hadn't realized was there until he met Brooke—was content simply to hold her. To absorb her pain as his own, and he *was* in pain. Every hoarse cry, every tear that dripped down Brooke's face felt like a jab to his own heart.

"I'll be outside if you need anything," Etta said quietly. He nodded, barely registering as she left, closing the door quietly behind her.

Brooke's fingers clenched in a choppy, uneven rhythm against his lapel, and he pulled her even closer, turning his lips to her hair. "I've got you," he whispered quietly. "Whatever it is, I've got you and we'll fix it."

He meant it, too.

Objectively, he was aware that he'd known this woman for a little over a month. It was far too soon to start thinking of them as a unit—to start thinking of her as *his*. And yet, he also knew down to the quietest, most secret part of his soul that she was his. And he was hers.

And that they would fix whatever had broken inside her.

For a few long minutes, he did nothing but stroke her back in long soothing motions, his cheek resting on the top of her head.

He didn't know how long they sat there, but eventually, he noticed her crying start to slow. From a sob to a cry, a cry to a sniffle.

And then . . .

Silence.

She slumped against him, her face still buried in his neck as she let out a shuddering sigh.

"All cried out?" he asked softly.

Brooke nodded.

He waited.

Several more moments passed before she finally moved, pulling back from him, her fingers brushing uselessly at the wrinkled fabric of his suit.

"I'm sorry," she said again, her voice husky from crying. "I knew you'd be working. I should have waited until later."

His hand cupped her cheek. "I'm glad you came."

I'm glad it was me you wanted to see.

"So you're done for the day?" she asked hopefully.

He wasn't. He had another half dozen meetings, not counting the new technology company that wanted to take him to cocktails tonight to convince him to install their waterproof televisions into Tyler Hotel showers.

He also knew that Etta would take care of re-arranging all that for him. He'd seen the way she'd looked between him and Brooke. Seen that she'd understood.

"I'm here," he said, dodging her question slightly.

She gave a grateful smile, and he was relieved to see that it was a real smile, and even with her red eyes and pink nose and messy hair, she looked beautiful.

Seth resumed stroking her back, and Brooke rested her cheek against his chest as she draped over him, one arm wrapping around his waist as though using him as an anchor. He figured he'd have to wait awhile before she told him whatever it was that had taken away her sparkle.

But Brooke surprised him by getting right to it.

"Clay," she said hoarsely.

He jolted. "Your ex."

Brooke nodded. "I never really . . . I never told you what happened between us. Not really. I mean, you know the headlines, but you don't know"—she took a deep, shuddering breath—"the full story."

"So tell me now," he said quietly, sensing that she needed to share. He waited patiently as she kicked off her shoes, pulling her feet up on the couch and wrapping her arms around her legs, before resting her chin against her upraised knees.

"I met Clay at a bar. Cheesy, right? I was out celebrating a girlfriend's birthday. I showed up late, since I had a wedding beforehand, and by the time I got there, my girlfriends were a bit past buzzed. The bar didn't have a dance floor, but the shots of tequila had motivated them to make their own, and since I wasn't quite to the drunken dancing phase, I found myself alone at the bar sipping a cocktail."

"Dirty Belvedere martini?" he asked, his fingers finding the ends of her hair as he listened.

She tapped her nose to indicate he'd gotten it right. "Anyway, this guy comes up on my right side, and it sounds lame, but I felt him before I saw him, you know? Like I was *aware* of him."

Seth nodded in understanding even as he silently hated another man for capturing her attention in that way.

"He, however, wasn't aware of me. He didn't even

glance at me as he waited patiently to catch the bartender's attention, and then his drink order . . . same as mine."

Brooke's eyes closed as she broke off and she shook her head. "Anyway, I wasn't drunk enough to be out swaying with my girlfriends, but I was just buzzy enough to be brave, and so when the bartender set down the guy's martini, I sort of clinked my glass against his and said something like, 'Cheers to dirty Belvederes,' or something completely horrible and awkward like that."

"I take it he noticed you *then*?"

She gave a sad smile. "Yeah. He looked over, gave me this small smile, and I was just, like, done, you know? *Boom*. It was all over for me. He had these warm brown eyes, dark blond hair, tan skin . . . totally like cliché California surfer dude, but in the hottest way possible. And well, I've always had a type, and Clay was it.

"We started dating," she continued. "I'd always been sort of romantically inclined. Convinced that when I met *the* guy, the one I was supposed to be with forever, I'd know, and that that would be it. We'd get married and live happily ever after. And by the third date with Clay, I knew. Or at least I thought I did."

"So was it a fast engagement?"

"No, actually," she said. "I'm a little embarrassed to say that had he proposed earlier I would have leapt in with two feet, but we dated for a couple years. Moved in together. He got to know my family. My parents thought of him like a son." She rubbed her forehead as though this last part hurt the worst.

"Then it was ring shopping, the sunset proposal, the whole bit."

Seth said nothing. He waited, his body tensed, knowing the story didn't have a happy ending.

"I planned the *crap* out of my wedding," Brooke said. "I mean, not all that surprising, right, given my career, but I'd like to think that I also did it for all the right reasons. Because I wanted it to be the most special day of my life, not because I wanted it to be the most spectacular wedding of all time. I kept it traditional. I didn't go bridezilla. Clay and I made the decisions together, we talked about everything from the flowers to the first-dance song."

Brooke let out a choked laugh. "Here I thought we had the best communication ever, because we could talk about colors and tackle the most stressful parts of wedding planning without so much as the slightest argument. But he was playing me. He was playing me so hard."

Her sad eyes looked over at him, and his heart twisted at the turmoil swirling in the blue depths. Seth's fingers clenched into a fist, and his breathing grew ragged with anger. Brooke kept going. "The FBI took him away in handcuffs at the altar. Because *that's* how I thought my wedding would go. I always thought Ponzi schemes and money laundering and identity fraud were phrases dreamed up by Hollywood screenwriters. But I heard all of those and about a dozen more that day. My *wedding* day."

"Ah, Brooke," he breathed out, feeling completely at a loss about what to do or what to say. He'd read the story online, of course, but hearing it all from Brooke's perspective, the woman whose life this asshole had shattered, made it so much more heart-wrenching and real.

"I thought he'd get put away and be in jail for a long, long time, you know? And I thought that as long as he was in jail, I wouldn't have to think about it. Or him. I wouldn't have to deal with it, you know?"

Seth nodded, although in truth, he wasn't sure he entirely did know. Avoidance wasn't really in his makeup. He was more of a take-control-of-every-detail-and-then-tighten-the-reins type.

Not that it had served him particularly well over the years.

But Brooke's method hadn't served *her* well, either. He was no shrink, but he was pretty sure he was witnessing the culmination of months' worth of trying to pretend like a seriously shitty event hadn't gone down.

And yet, Seth was impressed, too.

Impressed that this woman who had had her heart and dream publicly smashed to smithereens had still managed to keep her overall bright and sunny out-look on life. Brooke still managed to put her heart and soul into planning weddings because she refused to give up on the happily ever after.

"Well, he's not going to jail. He pled out, and now I'm . . . I'm worried he'll contact me," Brooke whispered.

Seth stiffened. He hadn't considered that. Hell, he hadn't let himself consider that. But it made sense. A man didn't lose a woman like Brooke Baldwin and not try to get her back. Even if he was a white-collar criminal.

"How do you feel about that?" he asked, trying to keep the tension out of his voice.

She sighed. "I . . . I don't know. That's terrible, huh?"

"Maybe not," he said, reaching for her hand and rubbing a thumb over the soft skin of her inner wrist. "It's a complicated situation."

"You must think I'm an idiot," she mumbled, looking down at her hands. "For not seeing it. For not knowing who and what he was."

"Hey now," Seth said quietly, turning her face toward him and meeting her still-puffy eyes. "Don't do that. Clay Battaglia was damn good at what he did. He fooled plenty of people, many of whom I consider friends."

Seth knew people to whom Clay had been a colleague, a comrade, even a mentor. People had trusted him, and the sting of betrayal had caused a ripple.

But it was more than a ripple to Brooke.

It was a damned earthquake.

Seth disdained the man for giving business a bad name, but he *hated* him for what he'd done to the woman in front of him.

And even as he leaned forward to capture her lips in a comforting kiss, Seth couldn't stop his brain from churning with ways to ensure Clay could never hurt her again.

Brooke kissed him back, and the slight edge of

desperation in the way she clung to him broke his heart, even as he was relieved that he was the one that she'd come to.

They pulled back minutes later, slightly breathless.

Brooke very gently set her fingers against his cheek. "Thank you. For being here when I broke."

"You didn't break," Seth said. "You just cracked a little."

Brooke smiled weakly. "I was just so sure I was okay, you know? I don't know which is more foolish, the fact that I didn't see Clay for what he was, or the fact that I didn't think it would impact me."

Seth turned his head slightly, kissing her fingers. "Just a little paper cut. This isn't going to leave lasting scars."

I'll make sure of it.

"I don't want to see him," she said, more to herself than to him. "Maybe that's still me avoiding, but I just . . . I don't know what he can say other than sorry, and weird as this sounds, I don't think *sorry* is what I need from him. I need for him to leave me alone."

"Well, the good news is that he's still a couple time zones over," Seth said. "And from what you're saying, I'm sure his plea bargain involves probation, plus hours of whatever testimony he must have agreed to hand over to the feds to avoid jail time."

She rubbed tiredly at her forehead. "I suppose. The whole thing just makes me feel tired."

The need to care for her was fierce. "Let me take you home. To my hotel," he clarified.

Please say yes.

Brooke dropped her hand back to her lap, giving him a small, tired smile. "I'd really like that."

Seth smiled in victory before standing and holding out a hand to her.

The moment when her palm touched his felt like . . . everything.

Hours later, Brooke had taken a bubble bath, eaten a mountain of homemade macaroni and cheese, made by Seth himself, courtesy of Manhattan grocery delivery and some guidance from the Food Network, and consumed just enough wine to have dropped into sleep the second her head hit the pillow.

Seth smiled as he tugged the blankets up mostly over her head, knowing by now that she preferred to be nestled as deeply as possible under the covers.

He had every intention of going to clean up the kitchen before booting up his laptop and figuring out just how much he'd missed in his unexpected time off this afternoon.

Instead, he found himself sitting on the edge of the bed, hands clasped between his legs as he stared blankly at the closet door and took in the shock of the day.

Brooke's con-man ex had managed to wiggle his way out of prison time.

Seth swore softly, his head falling forward.

For all his reassurances to Brooke that Clay would be held up on the West Coast, the truth was, Seth couldn't count on any of that.

And even if Clay was stuck in California, the man

had access to the Internet and phones. Even if he couldn't see Brooke, he could make contact.

A man who'd betrayed her trust in the most blatant, violating way possible could hurt her again with minimal effort.

Damn it. It wasn't right.

Seth couldn't stop Clay from calling her, or texting her. It's not as though he could monitor Brooke's phone, and even if he could, he wouldn't.

He was controlling, not psycho.

Brooke made a sleepy sound, and Seth turned his head slightly, watching as she shifted under the covers, pulling more tightly into a ball.

Seth's chest tightened. There was no way he could sit back and do nothing. No way he would let someone else he cared about be blindsided by fate.

For long minutes, Seth sat at her bedside, thinking. Planning.

Seth couldn't control Clay Battaglia's actions.

However, he could *monitor* them.

The question was . . . *should* he?

Seth closed his eyes, wishing that he could call Grant. His friend would likely have some zero-bullshit advice. But other than curt exchanges about work, the two men hadn't spoken since their argument a week earlier. Even if Grant picked up his call, Seth had a good idea what his friend would say. *Don't do it, man.*

Brooke stirred again, rolling closer to him. Her knees hit his hip, and her face emerged from under the covers, apparently wanting to see who was blocking her space.

She gave him a sleepy smile. "Hi."

He smiled back.

"You know watching women sleep fits into the creepy category, right?"

"I thought it was fair game as long as I didn't have a camera."

She giggled, a happy sound that was at odds with her ragged sobbing from earlier.

Those giggles were everything, and he knew then.

Knew that he would do anything to keep her from crying again.

He waited until her breathing had resumed the slow regularity of sleep before he quietly went back into the kitchen.

But instead of tackling the dishes, Seth unplugged his cell phone from his charger, taking it into the small den off the living room and closing the door behind him.

And made the call.

Tommy Franklin picked up on the first ring. "Mr. Tyler, how can I help you?"

"Franklin. How are you?" Seth forced himself to keep his voice steady and cool, as though this were a normal business arrangement. He didn't bother with small talk.

"Fine. Although, if you're checking on my progress, I already told you I'll reach out when I have something concrete."

"I'm calling about something else, actually."

"Ah."

Seth took a deep breath, gave himself a chance to back out. Then he remembered Brooke's tears.

"I'm wondering if you do business on the West Coast," Seth said gruffly. "Or if you have any colleagues you recommend."

"Absolutely. What do you have in mind?"

Last chance to back out . . .

Seth rubbed his forehead, bowed his head. And pressed forward.

"I need you to check out someone for me. Have you heard of Clay Battaglia?"

Chapter Twenty-Nine

In her several years of experience, Brooke had learned that there were two types of wedding planners.

Those that you hired for their vision—the firecrackers who gave you their opinions, like it or not, but in the end were worth it, because their vision was probably better than yours anyway.

Then there were the wedding planners you hired to implement *your* vision—the ones who listened to what you wanted and found a way to make it work.

Brooke was the latter. She was a people pleaser, and nothing made her happier than when she could make a bride's dream come true, securing that perfect venue or quaint little church, or even that moment when you could matchmake her with her ideal dress.

But that said, Brooke wasn't above having private little celebrations when her vision and the bride's vision aligned.

Such was the case in Maya Tyler's wedding.

Even if Brooke and Seth weren't doing . . . well,

whatever it was that they were doing, Maya and Neil's wedding would go down in the books as one of Brooke's favorites.

Maya had chosen Hamilton House for her reception. They'd just put the deposit for the gorgeous space Brooke had shown Seth just a couple weeks earlier, and Brooke wasn't sure who was more excited, her or Maya.

Even Seth seemed more or less on board. Brooke wouldn't go so far as to say he was excited about the wedding, but he'd quieted his objections.

So far they'd even managed to compartmentalize her work from their personal life. As previously agreed, Brooke ensured he signed off on any big expenses, but beyond those weekly check-ins, they rarely talked about the wedding.

It wasn't ideal. The woman in Brooke was more than a little curious about how he was dealing with his sister marrying a man he didn't approve of, but the wedding planner in her knew that boundaries were important.

Her other in-progress weddings made for occasional pillow talk, but never Maya's.

Speaking of Maya . . . Brooke checked her watch. The other woman was fifteen minutes late. Which wasn't totally unusual. Maya was late more often than not, although she typically texted.

Still, it gave Brooke an extra few minutes alone with her favorite spot. Maya was meeting her here today to discuss layout. Brooke already knew what she'd do. A skinny stage set up along the far wall for a live band. A dance floor in front of that, big enough to feel festive, but not so big that it was intimidating. She'd put the bar in the opposite corner, along the windows, so that when people waited for their champagne or martini, they'd have a view of the Brooklyn Bridge.

Maya and Neil had settled on an early December wedding, and though Maya was still debating on color scheme, Brooke had her fingers crossed for a gold-and-white holiday theme. Twinkle lights everywhere, flocked trees with glittery gold ornaments, delicate flutes of sparkling champagne with delicate gold wine charms with the couple's initials, or perhaps even a little touch of edible gold glitter . . .

Brooke's daydreams were interrupted by the slam of the door, and she turned, expecting to see Maya and Neil, and instead seeing . . . Maya and Grant?

"Hi, guys," she said, carefully hiding her surprise.

It wasn't the first time Grant had tagged along. Whatever tension had been between Grant and Maya at the announcement of her engagement seemed to have faded. Or at least Grant managed to put on a serious happy face, because he'd been nothing but smiles and jokes when they went cake tasting, or flower browsing, or sampling meatballs from a dozen different caterers. It seemed Maya had replaced Seth with Grant as the male voice of reason in the group, what with Neil being so absent from the planning. She kept insisting that it was worthwhile to have a male perspective along with them for input, but Brooke suspected the woman simply enjoyed Grant's company.

So Brooke wasn't shocked to see Grant. But Maya had specifically said *Neil* would be here today—that he'd regretted having to travel so much and wanted to be actively involved in more of the planning. Oh well. If Brooke were totally honest, she felt more comfortable around Grant than Neil.

She smiled as she crossed the cavernous space toward the two friends, although her smile froze just a touch when she got close enough to see their expressions.

Something wasn't right.

Maya was smiling, but it was too wide, and her eyes had a slightly wild look about them. And her ponytail looked like it had been hastily styled rather than gathered and teased into its usual classy perfection.

Grant gave Brooke a dark look before bending his long body to give her a brief peck in greeting. "Hi, Brookey," he said quietly. It was his usual greeting, but it lacked his normally warm, jocular tone. There was no sign of the playful Grant she'd grown so accustomed to. He looked every bit as brittle as Maya.

"What's wrong?" Brooke asked, not bothering to pretend that everything was okay when it so clearly wasn't.

Brooke wouldn't have thought it possible, but Maya's smile seemed to grow even wider. Even more false. "I have news!"

Out of the corner of her eye, Brooke saw Grant's jaw clench as though he was gritting his teeth. Whatever Maya's news was, he didn't like it.

"Oh yeah?" Brooke asked, using her best soothe-the-bride voice.

What she wouldn't give for a piece of furniture right now to plop said bride onto, because Maya looked ready to snap in half.

"We changed the wedding date!" Maya said, her voice too loud. The announcement echoed throughout the room, and though Brooke registered surprise, there was also relief—because based on their facial expressions, she'd thought it was much worse.

"Well, that's no problem," she said, reaching out to touch Maya's hand. "People move dates all the time. Did you guys decide December's just too hectic after all? Because we could just as easily transition to a late-autumn wedding, or even January if you wanted to stick with the winter theme."

Grant's tongue pushed out his cheek as he rolled his eyes toward the ceiling. Maya just continued to stare blankly at her, and Brooke's surprise turned to panic.

"What am I missing?"

This time Maya's eyes darted away as Grant met Brooke's gaze. "March. They want to move the wedding up to March," he said plainly, his voice sounding oddly flat and devoid of emotion.

"March!" Brooke burst out, before she could think better of it. "As in . . . next month?"

Maya nodded, and her horrible forced smile finally collapsed. "Neil and I . . . talked. Everything was just taking so long, and he thought—we thought—do we really want to wait that long to be married?"

Brooke's mind was spinning. This was not good. Not that she hadn't worked under these kinds of conditions before. Changing the date was uncommon, but not unheard of. Unplanned pregnancies and ailing parents could often change the timeline. Sometimes it was a couple deciding that they didn't want the fuss, or a change in financial situation calling for a simpler-than-planned wedding.

But instinct told her that something else was at work here.

Plus that meant the wedding was a month away.

That was too fast. Granted, speed could be achieved with money, and the Tylers weren't hurting for it, but . . .

Uh-oh.

Seth was holding the purse strings. And although he'd seemed more or less resigned to the wedding, something told her he wasn't going to deal well with this new timeline.

She itched to ask Maya if she'd told her brother, but right now wasn't about Seth and his issues with Neil. Right now was about Maya and the fact that the woman looked moments away from tears.

"We can make a March wedding work," Brooke said soothingly, rubbing a hand over Maya's arm. "But, sweetie, you know I have to ask . . . are you sure this is what you want?"

Maya's hand shook just a little as she lifted it to brush a wisp of hair away from her temple. "Neil said that if I loved him, it shouldn't be about the wedding, but about the marriage."

Brooke thought she heard Grant growl, and silently, she echoed his sentiments. While true that some couples fell prey to the trap, becoming so wrapped up in the wedding that they lost sight of the relationship, Maya was far from being a wedding-obsessed diva. She cared, yes, but she had her head on straight. She seemed to be in it for the right reason.

Because she wanted to marry Neil.

And yet it was *Grant* who was here.

Hmm.

"Where is Neil?" Brooke asked gently.

"Traveling," Maya said. "I think Dallas. Or Houston. Maybe Atlanta. I can't—he's been busy."

Grant moved closer, setting a hand on Maya's back. Maya didn't glance up, or even smile, but Brooke thought she saw some of the tension leave the other woman's body.

"You don't have to do this, you know," Grant said softly.

Just like that, the tension was back in Maya's shoulders, and she stepped away from Grant. Her eyes narrowed slightly. "I want to."

"Maya, you've been wanting your dream wedding since you were a little girl. You really want it thrown together in one month?"

"Brooke can make it nice," Maya said, shifting her gaze to Brooke. "Can't you?"

The pleading quality in Maya's voice chafed at Brooke's heart. "Of course I can."

There would be trade-offs, of course, but now wasn't the time to mention that.

"Can we still do it here?" Maya asked hopefully, gesturing around the space.

"I'll definitely find out," Brooke said, already taking out her planner and making notes. "This place is new enough that I doubt they're booked up."

Maya's shoulders slumped in relief, although there was no easing of the tension around her mouth or the desolate look in her eyes.

This was bad. Really bad.

"There's one other thing I was hoping you could help with," Maya said.

"Anything," Brooke said, jotting down a couple of other notes in her planner without looking up.

"Could you tell my brother for me?" Maya said, her voice a pleading whisper.

And just like that, it went from bad to worse.

Chapter Thirty

❧

SETH STOPPED BY ETTA'S desk in between meetings, waiting impatiently for her to finish up her phone call with the office supplier.

She crossed her arms and leaned forward. "You know, with a girlfriend as cute as yours, you'd think you'd smile a bit more."

"Well, if my girlfriend were here, I'd smile," he muttered. "But when I have a headache and eight more hours of meetings ahead of me, I scowl."

Etta rolled her eyes and opened her desk drawer, rummaging around until she came up with three different bottles. "Tension headache, migraine, or sinus?" she said, gesturing at the options.

"Give me one of each," he grumbled.

"Tension," she said, reaching for the middle bottle. "Definitely a tension headache."

She dropped two oblong pills into his outstretched palm before nudging her own water glass at him. The pounding in his head was severe enough that he accepted the water rather than fetch his own. He washed the pills down before rubbing at his neck. "Thanks, Etta."

"So she *is* your girlfriend," Etta said with a smug grin.

"What?"

"I called Brooke your girlfriend. You didn't contradict me."

"If I wanted to play weird word games with women, I would have stayed in high school," he said, heading toward his office.

"Did you send her something for Valentine's Day?" Etta called.

In response, he slammed the door behind him.

Yes, he'd bought Brooke something for Valentine's Day a week earlier.

He'd sent flowers and chocolates to the Wedding Belles, and made dinner reservations at Eleven Madison Park.

None of that was the alarming part.

The alarming part was that he'd *wanted* to do it. He'd wanted to do each and every over-the-top step, and her smiles had been well worth it.

So had the rather epic sex that had followed.

There was no way to avoid the fact that he was dangerously close to being smitten with Brooke Baldwin.

Seth dropped into his chair, dropping his head back and closing his eyes, praying that the pills would do quick work so that he could tackle a couple of overdue emails.

But the damn headache was still going strong when his cell rang a few minutes later. He pulled it out of the inside pocket of his suit jacket, intending to reject the call. Until he saw who it was.

Tommy Franklin.

His private investigator.

Seth's pulse jumped with something he hoped was nervousness but worried was fear.

"Tyler," he said, answering the call.

"Mr. Tyler, Tommy Franklin here. Is now a good time? I know we didn't have anything booked, but you said to call when I had something concrete."

Seth's heart began to hammer. He swallowed. "Yeah. Now's fine."

"All right," Tommy said, his tone having the same businesslike clip Seth was accustomed to hearing during the workday. It somehow made the whole thing easier. Slightly.

"I'll of course send the complete report electronically as well, complete with password-protected documents, but I find it's sometimes easier to explain the high-level findings over the phone. And of course, if there are questions—"

"Franklin," Seth interrupted, rubbing at his forehead that hadn't ceased aching. "Just spit it out. I'm not a besotted husband waiting to hear if the love of his life's been sleeping with the milkman."

"Who do you want me to start with?" Franklin asked.

"Garrett."

"Is actually not Garrett. Or Neil for that matter. The man's real name is Ned Alonzo. Mother is a Katherine Alonzo, a hairdresser in Albuquerque. Father listed as a Jorge Alonzo, died in a car accident when Ned was a teen, although wasn't in the picture even before that."

Seth inhaled deeply. He'd been right. Neil Garrett wasn't who he said he was.

Of course, there were worse things than changing one's name. Perhaps the man had just wanted a fresh start, or—

"Garrett, or Alonzo, whatever we want to call him, is nearly eight hundred thousand dollars in debt."

Just like that, Seth ceased to be aware of the pain in his head, because his chest suddenly hurt too much. "Sorry. Eight hundred thousand? As in, nearly a million dollars in the hole?"

"Gambling addiction. The man did okay playing small tables in casinos across the country, likely starting as a hobby. Thought he could make it in the big leagues in Vegas. He started out legit. Charmed the right people, got access to the big tables at the big resorts. Lost big money fast, and tried to make it up underground."

"And he didn't."

"Nope," Franklin said.

"How long ago?"

"That he lost the money? He started to go under about eight months ago, but it escalated rapidly. He headed to New York not too long after getting roughed up by one of his bookie's juice men."

"Where he met my sister."

"Right. Here's the part you may want to take a deep breath for," Franklin warned.

"It gets worse?"

"I was able to access some of the security video footage of some of Ms. Tyler's favorite places from that list you sent me. Her local Starbucks, favorite wine bar, the restaurants she prefers to meet her girlfriends for lunch. He made an appearance at all the same places she did for nearly two weeks before he first approached her in line at that Starbucks."

"Christ."

"Without any kind of audio coverage, I don't have verbal confirmation, so I feel duty-bound to inform you that it could be a coincidence, but in my professional opinion . . ."

"It wasn't a coincidence," Seth finished grimly.

"I don't believe so, no. This man needed money in a hurry, your sister has money, and Garrett played her rather perfectly. Also, I looked into some of the more expensive gifts he bought her. The jewelry, the lavish dinners, the designer accessories . . . it appears that they were all charged to one of Ms. Tyler's credit cards."

"Wait, Maya paid for her own gifts?"

"I suspect she's unaware. The card hadn't been used for several months prior to her meeting Neil. My guess, he swiped it from her wallet, her dresser, maybe an old handbag."

Seth dragged a hand over his face. He'd known this was coming. In his gut, he'd known. But damn, he would have been happy to be wrong.

"He's planning to use her money to settle his debt."

"Yes, and there is one more bit of bad news."

Seth gave a mirthless laugh. Of course there was. "Hit me."

"Those dates you sent me, with Garrett's travel for work."

"Yeah."

"Definitely not traveling for work. He's bought

tickets to every location he's claimed, trying to create some credibility, but he's bought tickets to Vegas for those exact same dates, every time. Guess which flight he got on. Every time."

"Shit."

"Exactly."

There were several moments of silence as Franklin seemed to sense his client needed a chance for everything to sink in.

"Anything you'd like me to dig further into?" Franklin asked. "I haven't seen any signs of other women, if that's a consolation."

"It's not," Seth replied flatly.

The PI snorted. "Thought as much."

"This is good stuff," Seth said quietly. "Not what I wanted to hear, but . . . thank you."

"Just doing my job," Franklin said matter-of-factly.

"I don't suppose part of your job might include telling my sister all these bits of good news?"

Franklin gave a polite courtesy laugh. "Trust me, you're not the first person to ask. I suspect I could make a killing delivering other people's bad news."

"No doubt," Seth said, his head pounding even harder as he tried to figure out how the hell to break this kind of news to his sister.

"Ready to hear about the other job?" Franklin asked.

The other . . . ?

Ah, fuck.

Seth was so busy reeling from news about Garrett—no, Alonzo—that he'd nearly forgotten that he'd also hired Franklin to check into Clay Battaglia's whereabouts.

"Sure," he managed.

"Unfortunately, I wasn't able to get as much on this one. There's plenty on his arrest and crimes, of course, but the details of his plea bargain are locked up pretty tight, courtesy of the feds. What I could figure out was that he's on house arrest for the next six months, which means he's not going to be making his way out to New York anytime soon. He's got probation a year after that. All of his phone calls are monitored, as are his texts, his tweets, and pretty much any time he takes a shit is recorded."

"Doesn't sound that different from prison," Seth muttered.

"I have no way of knowing for sure whether he'll get in touch with Ms. Baldwin," Franklin continued, "but I'm inclined to think no."

"Why's that?" Seth asked, grateful that the man was passing along at least one piece of semi-good news.

"Because he's engaged."

Seth's head snapped up. "Say that again?"

"A jail bunny named Julia Sharna. Visited him in jail every day. He proposed the day he was granted the plea bargain. Incredibly, the press hasn't gotten ahold of it yet, but it's only a matter of time. She's got a fat rock on her finger, and she's been seen coming and going between her apartment and his place with moving boxes."

Seth sat back in his chair with a slump. The pulsing in his head had receded just slightly, courtesy of the pills Etta had given him, but he had a whole other kind of pain now.

For his sister.

For Brooke.

And right on the heels of the hurt was anger at these two shitheaded men that had messed with women he lov—

Cared about, he mentally corrected. He couldn't love Brooke.

Could he?

Right now, the semantics didn't matter. What mattered was, instead of feeling relieved that her ex would be keeping his distance, there was no way that news of his whiplash engagement to another woman wouldn't hurt her.

He definitely wouldn't have minded being off base in this case. Seth said a curt good-bye to the private investigator, promising him the final payment installment and thanking him for his work.

He'd barely dropped the phone on the desk, trying to get a grip on his next move, when there was a knock at the door.

Seth propped his elbows on the desk, his head in his hands as he hollered for his assistant to come in. At least he hoped it was Etta. If it was that pipsqueak Jared . . .

"Bad time?"

Seth's head snapped up. It was neither Etta nor Jared.

It was Brooke.

"Hey," he said, wincing when he realized his voice sounded slightly hoarse.

"Etta said you weren't feeling well?" she asked, closing the door and coming into the room. She was wearing jeans today that outlined her every perfect curve, tucked into knee-high brown boots with a soft-looking blue sweater that made her eyes seem even brighter than usual.

Damn, she was beautiful.

"Just a headache," he said, standing and going around the desk to kiss her cheek.

She placed a hand on his cheek before he could pull away, searching his features with narrowed eyes. "Seems like more than just a headache. What's wrong?"

Everything.

Everything was wrong.

His sister was marrying an imposter with a gambling addition, and Brooke was about to find out that the man she was supposed to marry had opted to marry someone else rather than contact her with a motherfucking apology.

"Just a long day is all," he said, looking away from her.

Brooke bit her lip, and for the first time, he registered that he wasn't the only one who wasn't himself. Brooke also seemed more tense than usual.

For a moment he wondered if Tommy Franklin had been wrong, and if news of Clay's engagement to the jail bunny had already broken.

But no. She didn't look broken so much as nervous.

"Come sit with me a sec," she said, taking his hand and tugging him toward the couch that was strangely sort of becoming their place. For a piece of furniture he'd barely touched since moving into this space, it was getting plenty of use these days.

Seth glanced at his watch regretfully. "I can't. I'm supposed to be at a meeting in four minutes."

"Etta's rescheduling it."

He blinked. "She's what? Why?"

Brooke took a visibly deep breath. "Because I told her what I was here to tell you."

The weariness that had been threatening to choke him receded as Seth's body went on high alert. "Tell me."

She gave a nervous smile and moved around to the couch to sit. "Let's at least sit down."

Seth didn't budge. The pulsing in his temples was back full force, the medicine completely inadequate against the pure shit that was this day.

"Tell me," he repeated.

"You're impossible," she muttered as she stood back up. She kept the coffee table between them, and he didn't register that he'd crossed his arms until he watched her mimic his stance.

He had the vague sense that he was being an ass, but for the life of him, he couldn't figure out how to unwind. How to ease the tension, or stifle the sense of dread, or even how to wipe the wariness off her face. Seth just needed to have all the facts, needed people to stop hiding stuff from him and tiptoeing around, and fucking lying.

"Brooke, for God's sake, just say—"

"Maya and Neil moved up the wedding."

Seth didn't move. "They what?"

Brooke licked her lips nervously but didn't look away from his glare. "The wedding's going to be in March."

"March?" His voice came out as a roar. "It's the fucking end of February."

"Yes, I'm aware of the date," she said coolly.

"Shit," he grumbled. "That fucking bastard is behind this. Did she flip when you told her no? She'll calm down, just give her a bit of time. I can't believe this."

"I didn't tell her no, Seth."

His eyes narrowed. "What do you mean? You can't pull off a wedding in a few weeks."

"Of course I can."

"Well, you shouldn't! Not when it's this wedding."

"That's not your call."

"It sure as hell is. Did you forget who's paying for this?"

"No," she snapped. "Not for one minute, because you can barely go that long without reminding me. But as I've told you a million times, my first commitment is to the couple getting married, and if they want to get married in March, it's my job to give them their happily ever after, on whatever timeline they want."

He groaned and dropped his arms to his sides before lifting them to link behind his head, turning in a circle as he tried to rein in his spitting emotions. "Are you fucking kidding me with that? The happily ever after shit? Still?"

A little flicker of hurt passed over her face, but it was quickly masked by irritation. "Yes, that shit, *still*. I know you're determined to think that all people are crap on the inside, but you're wrong. People are good, and happy endings are possible."

"Says the woman who walked down the aisle toward a con man," he muttered under his breath.

But not all the way under his breath, unfortunately. Brook gasped, flinching as though he'd struck her.

"Shit. Brooke, I'm sorry, I didn't mean it."

"Yes, you did," she said, straightening her spine and resuming her defensive posture, which was now infused with a healthy dose of anger. "You did mean it. Just let it out now, Seth. Get it out of your system. You think that because I made a mistake with Clay that your sister must be making the same mistake with Neil, right? Is that how the cynic's mind works?"

"Yes!" he exploded. "Yes, that's exactly how the cynic's mind works, and damn it, Brooke, this cynic was right."

She rolled her eyes. "Not this again."

He took a deep breath and strove for calm. "Look, I know you don't want to hear this, but I *am* right on this one, Brooke. Neil Garrett's real name is Ned Alonzo. He's got a gambling addiction that has him nearly a million dollars in debt. Maya's nothing to him but a cushy way to pay off his debts."

Her lips parted in shock. "How can you know that? Did he confide in you?"

Seth snorted. "That'd be hard, right? Seeing as he's been hitting the tables in Vegas while you and my sister run all over the city trying on dresses and tasting cakes."

Her eyes narrowed in warning. "Is that really what you wanted to say to me?"

He sighed. "No. I'm sorry. I just found all this out

seconds before you walked in, and I'm still dealing with it."

"What do you mean you found out? How?"

Well, here went nothing.

"I hired someone," he said, refusing to let the statement come out as guilty. "I hired someone to look into Neil. Ned. Whatever."

Brooke's mouth fell open. "You have got to be kidding me."

He shook his head and shoved his hands in his pockets.

"Okay," she said, seeming to take this in. "Okay, at least tell me Maya knows. That you didn't go *behind her back* to research her fiancé."

He stared at her silently.

"Oh my God, Seth," Brooke breathed. "You know, for all your talk about how clueless Maya and I are, you're clueless on a whole other level."

He ignored this. "I did it to protect her. And it's a damn good thing, because if I hadn't found this out, she'd have married a man who didn't love her, who'd have taken all her money and made her miserable."

"And that would have been her mistake to make," Brooke said quietly.

"But—"

"No *but*," Brooke said, coming around the table so they were face-to-face. "You were right about Neil, apparently, and I'll give you that. But what you did was wrong on every level. Going behind her back? You're not God, Seth."

"And what was the better alternative?" he snapped. "Letting her get hurt?"

"I don't know," Brooke said tiredly. "Maybe? I mean, I guess now that we know, we can't actually let her marry him without knowing the facts, but you interfered in the worst kind of way."

"Because I love her," he argued.

Brooke shook her head. "That's not love."

Seth froze. Her words were a carbon copy of what Grant had said to him a couple of weeks earlier. Two of the people he cared about most were telling him verbatim that he didn't know how to love.

That he didn't even know what love was.

And damn it . . . damn it, but it *hurt*. It tore at his soul like a savage beast out for blood. Because right now he didn't feel like a man who couldn't love.

He felt like a man whose every fiber was filled with love for a person who was standing there looking at him with disdain and pity.

Well, screw this. Screw her. Brooke thought he was heartless? He'd show her what stone-cold really looked like.

"And I suppose you do know what love is," he struck out. "You've experienced it in all its lovey-dovey glory?"

She lifted her chin, refusing to be embarrassed or ashamed. Good for her. "Yes. I did."

"With Clay," he said, stepping forward.

Brook hesitated just a second too long before nodding. "Yes. He and I didn't end well for obvious reasons, and he was . . . he was not a good person. I don't doubt for one second that he did care about me. He did know how to love, because I felt it."

"Yeah?" Seth asked cruelly. "Then maybe you can tell me why he's engaged to another woman."

Brooke didn't move. Not even to blink. "What?" Her voice wobbled, and she cleared her throat. "What?" she asked again, more clearly this time.

For a moment, Seth panicked, wanting to take his words back more than anything he'd ever wanted in his life. To go back thirty seconds, hell, go back thirty minutes, and quit acting like an idiotic defensive animal in pain, lashing out like a moron. He was more evolved than this, surely.

But the words were out there now, and he couldn't take them back. Wasn't even sure he wanted to, because he'd need to confess sometime, and it might as well be now, when she was already hating his guts. Maybe if he ripped off the Band-Aid all at once, he'd still have a chance.

"How the hell would you know . . . oh my God." Brooke was staring at him in miserable understanding. "Your private investigator. You had him look into Clay, too."

Seth nodded.

"Unbelievable," she spat out. "You really think you can control people the way you do your business. You really equate your power trips with affection."

"I won't apologize for trying to protect you," he said woodenly.

"What about Maya? Are you going to apologize to her?"

"Yes," he said gruffly. "And she'll be mad for a while, but at least she won't marry the guy."

"So you get everything you want," Brooke said

quietly. "Everything's exactly as you want it, all tidy and in order as it should be, according to Seth."

"Not everything." Seth was swift to correct, reaching toward her and dropping his hand when she stepped back. "I won't have everything I want if you walk out that door, Brooke."

He held her eyes, begging her to understand, and for a second he saw something flicker, and he felt hope swell hot and potent through his veins.

"You don't get it, Seth," she said, her voice rising. "You really don't get it. You understand, right, that what you did is no different from what Clay did? More legal, maybe, but you hid the truth from me just like he did. You let me believe you were something you're not. You hurt me, Seth. Just like he did. Maybe worse."

His heart felt like it was being ripped in two. "Brooke, no, it wasn't like that. I just wanted . . . needed to know that you were okay."

"It's not always about what you need!" she shouted. "You tell yourself that you're acting for the sake of those you care about, but you're only out to protect yourself. This is about you and your selfish compulsion to control everything around you, so don't for one minute expect me to believe you actually care."

"I do care," he said, his voice cracking a little. "You've made me believe that the happy endings do exist, and I wanted—"

"Stop," she interrupted. "Stop right there. Happily ever after does exist. I won't let you take that belief away from me. But Seth, my happily ever after is not with you. Let's be very clear on that. "

She turned away, and his eyes closed in silent misery.

She was halfway to the door before he could find any more words. "Would it help if I told you why I did it?" he asked desperately to her retreating back. "If I told you why I asked the detective to look into Clay?"

Brooke paused but didn't turn around. Waiting.

It was because I love you.

But by the time he finally uttered the words out loud to his cavernous office, Brooke was long gone.

Chapter Thirty-One

❦

Brooke? You're still here?"

"Yep," Brooke called out in response, not glancing up from her computer screen as she perused Pinterest for ideas on her latest client's vision for a wine-and-cheese-tasting-themed bridal shower party.

Sounded right up her alley.

Especially the wine part. Especially these days.

Heather came into Brooke's office, plopping in her chair and helping herself to some of Brooke's Hershey's Kisses. Not that there were many left—she'd been going through them at twice the normal rate lately. Between the chocolate, the cabernet, and Seth Tyler, Brooke was well on her way to an early death.

"Looks like I'm not the only one being super lame tonight," Heather observed.

"I don't think working late is lame. I love my job."

"Honey, it's eight thirty. On a Friday," Heather said pointedly.

Brooke sighed. Okay. So it was kind of lame. But

for the past two weeks, work had been the only thing holding the fragile parts of her heart together.

It turned out that Seth's spy had been dead-on about Clay being engaged. To a woman he'd met in prison, of all things.

Not only that. They'd eloped. Or whatever you called it when two people who barely knew each other went down to a courthouse and made it legal. The story had broken online in the hours after Brooke had stormed out of Seth's office, prompting a barrage of well-meaning but painful texts and calls from her parents and friends out in California.

Not that Brooke had issues with courthouse weddings. She respected that for some couples they were the right thing. She just hated that one half of one of those couples was the man she had been a stone's throw from marrying.

And yet, Clay's shotgun wedding wasn't what was bothering her. Her pride, yes, but not her heart.

Her heartache was courtesy of a man she'd known for a small fraction of the time she'd known Clay, and yet somehow had fallen for twice as hard.

And to give Seth credit, he had called. Several times. In the first days after she'd walked out, she'd missed calls and texts and flowers.

But after those few dogged days of silence on her part, there'd been . . . nothing.

He'd given up.

Brooke wasn't entirely sure how she felt about that. And yes, she knew that made her seem like a game player. As though she wasn't sure she wanted him but also wasn't okay with him not wanting her.

It was all just damn confusing.

"Do you want to go out?" Heather asked. "Grab a drink?"

Brooke gave her an apologetic look. "I kind of . . . don't."

"Excellent," Heather chirped, tucking a blond curl behind her ear only to have it pop right back out again. "Me neither."

With that, Heather bent down to the oversized tote between her feet and came up with a half-full bottle of wine and two plastic cups.

Brooke watched as Heather poured them two glasses and then acting on impulse, reached out and gave the other woman a hug.

Heather hugged her back, smoothing her hair. "I'm sorry, babe."

"Me too," Brooke whispered. "He was supposed to be one of the good ones. Crotchety, but good."

"Maybe he still is," Heather said as they pulled back. "I mean, it was lame what he did. So lame. But I think we can give him at least a little teeny tiny point for his heart being in the right place, you know? He didn't want his sister to marry a shithead. He didn't want you to be dragged down by *your* shithead."

"I guess," Brooke said, swirling her wine. "I just can't shake off the sting of betrayal. Two men in a row who don't come clean. And if he didn't tell me about his creepy little spying plan, who knows what else he didn't tell me about?"

"True that," Heather said, sighing and taking a large gulp of wine.

Brooke bit her lip. "Have you heard how things are going with the Tyler wedding?"

Heather shook her head. "Sorry, no. That's all Alexis, and she doesn't really mention it."

After her fallout with Seth, Brooke had reluctantly abdicated her role as wedding planner for Maya's nuptials. She felt terrible, but there was no way she could have faced Maya, knowing what she knew about Neil, or whatever his name was, and not saying anything. She kept expecting to hear that the wedding had been called off, but so far it looked like everything was moving forward as planned, though she couldn't imagine that Seth would hold his tongue and actually let Maya go through with marrying that jerk.

She stifled another surge of anger at Seth. This was why you didn't go meddling in other people's business. Finding out things you weren't supposed to know, knowing secrets that weren't yours . . . it messed everything up.

"Has he called lately?" Heather asked over the top of her plastic wine cup.

Brooke shook her head. "Nope."

"How do we feel about that?"

"Terrible," Brooke muttered. "But seeing him would also be terrible, you know?"

"Sort of. Actually, no, not really."

Brooke reached for a piece of chocolate and held it up for Heather to see. "It's a bit like this piece of candy. It's so good. And also so *not* good for you. You know?"

"Super eloquent," Heather said, patting her knee before leaning back once more. "And don't hate me for saying this, but are you sure that maybe you don't need closure with Mr. Hotel Trillionaire? I mean, you didn't get it with Clay, and look what happened with that. Breakdown city."

Brooke laughed as she unwrapped the Hershey's Kiss and popped it in her mouth. "I so love these little chats of ours. I have you to dole out the snarky straight talk, and Alexis to dole out the practical straight talk. Even Jessie is a straight shooter, she just coats it in sugar. Where's the friend who tells me what I want to hear?"

"I think you're that friend," Heather said. "So when I fall in love and want to hear that I did the right thing by dumping a hot rich dude half in love with me, you come to my office and have one of these pep talks, 'kay?"

"Seth wasn't half in love with me," Brooke rushed to say.

Heather blew out a breath. "Okay, I know you don't want to hear this, but if he didn't care, he wouldn't have done what he did. He was high-handed, yes. A little sketchy with his forthcomingness, yes. But did he tell you why?"

"No," Brooke admitted. "I think he tried to, but his tongue got tied, and . . ."

"And . . . ?"

"I walked away. And ignored all of his calls."

Heather's expression was kind but direct as she nudged the Hershey's Kiss bowl in Brooke's direction. "What do you think he was about to say?"

"I don't know," Brooke whispered.

Except Brooke was terrified that she did know,

and it filled her with a strange swirl of elation and dread.

What Seth had done was wrong. Instead of talking to his sister about his concerns, instead of trusting her, he'd assumed that he knew best. Because he loved her. Which didn't make his actions okay. That kind of love could be stifling and do a hell of a lot more harm than good.

And yet . . .

And yet, Brooke was certain that Maya and Seth would come through it. That Seth could learn how to love and respect boundaries.

Which begged the question: Had he had Clay investigated for the same reason?

Because he loved Brooke?

And if he did . . .

Just what the hell was she going to do about it?

Chapter Thirty-Two

～

ETTA HAD GOTTEN SO sick of Seth interrupting her, asking for medicine, that she'd started leaving the pill bottles on Seth's desk as a preemptive measure. They both pretended they were for tension headaches, but they both knew better. His head hurt, yes. But the main source of tension was in his chest.

And not in the "oh shit, call 911" type of chest pain. After his father's death, Seth had gotten acquainted real fast with his cardiologist, and so far, his ticker looked exactly as it should for a man in his early thirties.

No, Seth's chest hurt from something even more timeless than clogged arteries.

It was women.

Women made his chest hurt.

Specifically, a blond wedding planner who was no longer *his* wedding planner. Or his sister's wedding planner, if one wanted to get specific about it.

Seth understood why Brooke had passed off Maya's wedding to Alexis. He respected the choice, even, because Brooke was a consummate professional, and the conflict of interest would have killed her.

But it didn't make him miss her any less.

The emails he received from Alexis Morgan at the end of every business day were perfectly fine. Professional, to the point, and loaded with details of his sister's wedding that he didn't give a crap about. Bows. Blooms. Even the decision to use ivory candles instead of pure white, as though Seth gave a fuck.

Because yes, the wedding was still happening. Maya was still marrying a man she thought to be Neil Garrett.

Seth hadn't told her the truth.

He wasn't sure he'd ever experienced such acute agony as knowing something that his baby sister needed to know but also knowing that he'd come about the information in the entirely wrong way.

Seth had two options, to tell her or not to tell her, and both seemed unbearably selfish.

If he didn't tell her, she'd enter into a relationship with an imposter, but at least she wouldn't blame Seth when it went sideways. To Brooke's point, he'd be letting Maya lead her own life, her way.

If he did tell her, she'd hate his guts for not telling her about the investigation he'd launched, but at least she'd be free of the dirtbag. Because much as Seth was realizing that he shouldn't know what he knew, he couldn't unlearn it.

Hell.

Seth reached for one of the pill bottles. Maybe he did have the ol' tension headache after all.

It was the end of the workday, and he'd turned

down all business dinner obligations, so at the very least he was spared the company of other people.

The downside?

Yet another night at home. Alone. In his hotel suite.

With no sister, since she was in bridezilla panic mode.

No best friend, since he and Grant were still chilly as all hell.

And no Brooke.

At this point, Seth was about five minutes from asking Jared the Sniveling Intern out for a beer.

Luckily, he was saved from such acts of desperation by a knock at the door and his sister's familiar face.

"Hey," she said quietly. "You got a minute?"

Seth swallowed and nodded, gesturing awkwardly for her to come in, feeling uncomfortably emotional that she'd come to see him. It seemed a long-ass time since she'd sought him out.

Maybe not even since that day when she'd first told him she was getting married.

Seth was on his feet, moving toward her and scooping her into a hug before his confused brain could even register his intentions. Seth was not a hugger, but as he pulled his sister close, tucking her head against his chest, whether she liked it or not, he realized just how desperately he needed her.

He'd always assumed it was the other way around. That she needed him. That Maya needed Seth to guide her and guard her and, hell, double-check her shit taste in men. And perhaps there was still a little bit of that at work. The woman had apparently lost her credit card to a gambling-addicted imposter and still didn't know he was racking up charges. There were things he would and could do to increase Maya's independence and awareness of the world around her.

But that wasn't what this moment was about.

It was about *him* needing *her*. Needing to learn how to love her the right way, because he did love her. Fiercely.

"Hey there," she said with a little laugh as she patted his back. "Okay?"

"Yeah," he muttered, clearing his throat and forcing himself to release her. "Okay."

She gave him a knowing look. "You don't look okay. You look terrible."

"Stop. I'm blushing," he said sarcastically, returning to his desk chair.

"I'm serious. I don't know what you did that made Brooke dump you, but you need to undo it. You're miserable. She's miserable."

His head shot up. "You've seen her?"

"Well, no," she admitted.

"Talked to her? Have you talked to her?"

She gave him a little smile. "Oh man. You are adorable right now."

"Maya."

His voice was close to pleading, and her smile slipped. "No, sorry, big bro. I haven't talked to her."

He slumped back. It was no less than he'd expected, but it picked at the not-yet-healed wound all the same.

"Much as I'm dying to interrogate you about your

love life," Maya said as she sat across from him and crossed her legs, "I'm actually here to talk about mine."

Seth forced his face to remain impassive. To let her lead the conversation where she wanted it to go, not where his control-freak tendencies thought it should. "Sure. What's up?"

Maya waited until he met her eyes before she spoke again. "I'm in love with Grant."

Seth opened his mouth, but nothing came out. He was suddenly very grateful he was already sitting. Maya gave him a little smile. "I know. Trust me, I know. You don't have to say anything, I just . . . I wanted you to be the first to know. Well, second," she corrected.

"You told Grant this already?" he asked, finding his words.

She shook her head, her eyes clouding over. "No. I told Neil."

Well . . .

Hell.

This was not how he'd expected things to play out.

Seth cleared his throat. "Just so I'm understanding. You told the man you're going to marry that you're in love with another man?"

Maya held up a hand. "Small correction. I told the man I *was* going to marry that I'm in love with another man."

Seth felt a stab of relief so intense it nearly blinded him for a moment. "You're not marrying Neil?"

Maya shook her head. "No. And actually, his name isn't Neil."

Seth froze.

"It's Ned Alonzo," Maya said with a little sigh. "He's not an entrepreneur; he's a two-bit poker player and sports bettor, and I don't even know what else."

In all of his troubleshooting mental exercises in trying to figure out how to deal with this mess of a situation, this had not been one of Seth's scenarios.

He cleared his throat. "Oh?"

She gave him a look. "Please. Don't pretend you haven't been awkwardly sitting on this information for weeks trying to figure out how to break it to me. I know you, Seth. I knew when I hired my own private investigator that you were likely doing the same thing."

Well, knock him over with a feather. "Maya, I—"

She shook her head and stood. "I know you love me, Seth. I know it's why you did that. I know that. I'm not going to say I'm not a tiny bit pissed, but honestly . . ." Her eyes filled just for a second. "I want to say thank you. For caring, even if you do so in a horribly invasive way."

Damn. Now his eyes felt suspiciously close to spilling over with . . . something.

"I want to talk more about this, but there's someone else I need to talk to first," she said quietly. "And that conversation's going to be a hell of a lot more difficult than this one."

"Grant?" Seth asked.

Maya nodded, and for the first time since she walked into his office, she looked less than 100 percent self-assured. Maybe a tiny bit scared.

Seth opened his mouth to tell her that maybe the

conversation wouldn't be as hard as she thought. That maybe Grant felt the same way.

But then he remembered what Brooke had said. That Maya needed to live her own life, make her own choices . . . and her own mistakes. Although he didn't think this thing with Grant and Maya, whatever one might call it, was a mistake, still, he kept his mouth shut and decided to go a different route.

Maya shook her head in disbelief as he rounded the desk and wrapped his arms around her once more, although briefer this time.

"Two hugs in one day?" she said when she pulled back. "I don't know what the heck Brooke Baldwin did to you, but I think I like it."

Seth's good mood faded slightly at the mention of Brooke, knowing that he wasn't likely to get the second chance with her that he had apparently gotten with Maya. He and Maya were blood, with close to three decades of history behind them. Brooke had known him for all of two months and had no reason to give him a second chance. Hell, he wasn't entirely sure he deserved one.

Maya went on her toes and kissed his cheek. "I love you. You know that, yeah?"

"I know. I love you, too."

"And Brooke. You love her, too?"

Seth waited for the familiar stab of panic at the thought—at the uncomfortable sense of unpredictability that came from losing one's heart to someone spontaneously, without knowing whether they loved you back. Of the wild, terrifying abandon of caring about someone so deeply that they could turn you inside out.

He felt none of that. There was only sureness. Rightness.

"Yes," he said simply. "I love her."

Maya's smile was wide and beaming. "You know how you're always throwing out advice at me, even when I don't ask for it?"

His eyes narrowed. "Yes."

She patted his chest playfully. "Well, here's some unsolicited advice for you. If you want to win her back, go big. Throw your whole heart into it. Because I think she's worth it."

Seth watched his sister stroll out of his office, all sassy confidence as she went to get her man.

Just like Seth was about to get his woman.

Because unlike Maya, Seth didn't think Brooke was worth it.

He *knew* she was.

Chapter Thirty-Three

J UST THINK, MAN, BY this time tomorrow night you could be getting laid," Grant said, picking up an ugly vase off Seth's bookshelf as though he intended to pack it and instead going to the fridge to help himself to a beer.

Such had been the entire afternoon.

His best friend's idea of "helping him pack" seemed to be limited to the refrigerator and pantry, and instead of anything making it into the boxes, it all went directly into Grant's stomach.

Seth ignored his friend as he picked up an ugly metal figurine, studying it for a half second, realizing he'd never even noticed it before, and chucking it in the Goodwill pile that was considerably larger than his keep pile.

Goal number one of new life, get shit I actually like.

Actually, no, that wasn't the first goal.

First he was going to win back Brooke.

Then he'd figure out how to hire a designer that

didn't have a strange fascination with humanoid figures crafted from various types of metal.

"I'm just saying, you'd be a lot less grumpy if you got laid," Grant said, pointing the beer bottle at him.

"Great. I'll be sure to call you in the aftermath so that you can reap the benefits of my postcoital glow," Seth replied.

Grant winced. "Dude. Don't."

"You don't get to *don't* me. You're sleeping with my sister."

"Hell yes, I am," Grant said with a cocky smile. "And it's—"

"No," Seth said. "No fucking way. Don't finish that sentence. For Chrissake, get me a beer. No, never mind, I need whisky."

It had been six weeks since Maya had called off her wedding and told Grant how she felt about him. Seth wasn't exactly sure how everything had played out, and wasn't at all sure he wanted the details, but they were both the happiest he'd ever seen them, and that was enough for him.

He and Grant had mended things, too, in the way that men not entirely comfortable with emotion tended to do. Seth had shown up at Grant's door with a bottle of Pappy and invited himself inside. Grant had nodded, stepped aside to let him in.

And just like that, they were back to normal.

Simple. Basic. Easy.

Fixing things with Brooke? Not nearly so easy.

Even the reappearance of Grant in Seth's life wasn't helping his nerves right about now. For close to two months he'd been working tirelessly on what

Etta had started calling The Project, and although he'd never felt so solid about something in his life, he couldn't deny that the undercurrent of the unknown was starting to eat at him.

"What do you think she'll do?" he asked, pouring a liberal amount of bourbon into his tumbler.

Grant's expression turned considering as he studied his beer bottle. "Honestly, man? I don't know. If I've learned anything in the past couple months, it's that I'm not nearly as good at reading women as I thought I was. And if that's true of me, the certified chick whisperer, then there's really no hope for you, my friend."

"Helpful." Seth lifted his glass. "Thanks."

"Well, what do you want me to do, man, stop by the wedding shop with pinot grigio and marshmallows and see if she's been doodling your name in that planner she always carries around with her?"

"I don't know why she uses the paper planner," Seth said, mostly to himself. "It'd be far more efficient to use an iPad or an electronic alternative."

Grant barked out a laugh before letting his head fall forward in defeat. "Do me a favor and keep that bit to yourself tomorrow, 'kay? Say the *good* stuff."

"That's the plan," Seth said, taking a last sip of his drink before setting it aside and forcing himself to pack at least one more box before the pizza and baseball game he'd promised Grant. Pretty lame way to be spending your last night in a place you'd spent the better part of a year, but then this hotel suite had never really felt much like home in the first place. He figured a nice cheesy slice of pepperoni and the Yankees were a good enough send-off for a place where he was just now noticing the pictures on the wall.

"You're sure she's going to show up tomorrow?" Grant asked, halfheartedly opening a kitchen cupboard and dropping a salt container into the open box of pantry items that would be transiting over to the new place.

Seth gave him an exaggerated glance. "Not helpful."

"I'm a details guy," Grant said.

"No you're not," Seth said. "*I* am. You're the big-picture, no-clue-on-execution guy."

"Fine," his friend said with an easy shrug. "Looking at the big picture . . . do you think she's going to show up tomorrow?"

"*Jesus,*" Seth muttered, giving up on the boxes and lowering himself slowly to the uncomfortable metal bar stool. If the place wasn't packed by tomorrow, it was no big deal. He owned the fucking hotel—he could move out next month or next year if he wanted.

"So that's a no," Grant said. "We're not sure?"

No. He wasn't even a tiny bit sure that all of his efforts over the past few weeks were going to do shit to win her back, but he felt good about the plan.

Sort of.

"Alexis said everything was going according to plan," Seth replied. "And if anyone can make a plan come to fruition, it's that woman."

"True," Grant said. "I only met her once, but she's sort of like a hot robot, no?"

Seth gave a rueful smile. "I always thought Alexis was a bit like a female version of me."

"Yeah, that's what I said," Grant replied. "A robot. But you're not as hot."

Seth gave his friend the finger before reaching out and idly twisting his glass on the counter. "Do *you* think she'll come?"

"You mean, does my big-picture genius think the love of your life is going to fall into your arms and maybe swoon a little at your grand gesture?" Grant asked with a sly grin, leaning back against the fridge and crossing his feet at the ankles.

Seth's heart soared a little at the picture his friend painted. To have Brooke within arm's reach again, much less in *his* arms . . .

Grant's expression turned sympathetic. "Yeah, man. I think she's going to be there. And if not, she's an idiot. Okay?"

Seth nodded, appreciating his friend's vote of confidence.

And yet he really, *really* hoped she'd be there.

Chapter Thirty-Four

Brooke was just coming out of a bridal shop down in Tribeca when she got a text from Alexis.

You still downtown? Any chance I can ask a huge favor?

Absolutely, **Brooke typed back.** What's up?

Larabee Bride is having second thoughts about the Plaza. Looking for something a bit less high profile, more amenable to customization. Any chance you could show her the Hamilton House? I'm all the way uptown, and it'll take me forever at this time of day.

Brooke swallowed, wishing the favor was anything but that.

She hadn't been inside the Hamilton since planning Maya's wedding.

Well, Maya's *almost* wedding.

Alexis had had a hell of a time trying to figure out how to back out of a wedding that had already been put on a rush schedule, but even with all the hassle the non-wedding had caused the Belles, Brooke was glad for it. Glad that Maya wouldn't be marrying Neil who wasn't really Neil.

Still, she tensed in dread at the thought of going to that space again. Not because it reminded her of Maya. Maya and she were actually on good terms, even having grabbed lunch a couple of times recently so Maya could fill her in on what had happened with Neil and about finally getting together with Grant. Brooke was thrilled that those two had finally owned up to how they felt about each other.

But she didn't want to go to the Hamilton House.

It reminded her of Seth.

Seth, from whom she hadn't heard in nearly two months. Seth, whose name everyone seemed to be reluctant to mention around her, as though she might break.

She wouldn't break.

Not because she was avoiding what happened. She'd learned her lesson after holding in her feelings about Clay and nearly letting it destroy her.

This she'd faced head-on in the form of twice-weekly therapy. Not to talk about Seth specifically, although he was certainly a frequent topic of conversation. But after the train wreck of the past months, Brooke had had the epiphany that a happy life didn't come from constantly shoving anger and pain to the side and pretending they didn't exist.

They did exist.

Anger and pain were real, and some people were just lame (see: Clay and Neil/Ned), and the world wasn't always going to be sunshine and rainbows.

She knew that now. And interestingly, the more she let in the not-so-great things, the greater the good things became.

Almost as though she was becoming happier by allowing herself to be unhappy sometimes.

Crazy, but true.

It was this realization that made her decide what she needed to do. She needed to go to Hamilton House. Needed to face all of the memories, both good and bad, that would come with it.

It would be one step closer to being able to think of Seth with just a *little* bit of pain, instead of the ripping, gut-clenching pain that still kept her awake at night sometimes.

No problem, **Brooke texted.** Now?

Bride's on her way, **Alexis texted back.** Maybe ten minutes or so?

On it.

Brooke hailed a taxi and made it in twelve minutes flat.

She hesitated only briefly before entering the building, faltering when she saw a middle-aged man in a basic black suit standing behind the previously deserted reception desk.

Somehow she hadn't thought about the building

being populated, but of course it would be. The lower office floors would have started to fill up by now, and they'd need some sort of security.

"Hi there," she said, approaching with a smile. "I'm Brooke Baldwin, here to meet a Ms. Larabee to tour the top floor for a possible event."

"Of course," the man said with a formal nod. "Ms. Morgan said you'd be needing these."

He held out a modern key fob. An upgrade from the old-fashioned key she remembered.

"Ms. Larabee's not here yet?"

"Not yet, miss. I can send her up when she arrives?"

"Sure, that'd be great," Brooke said, suddenly anxious to have the space to herself again, just for a few minutes.

Maybe if the Larabee bride did choose the space, Alexis would be open to tag-teaming on the reception. The wedding planner in her was still simmering a little that she hadn't had a chance to work her magic in that space to realize its full potential.

Brooke let herself into the elevator, juggling the plastic fob lightly in her palm as she ascended. When the doors opened, she stepped out onto the wood floor and promptly skidded to a stop, taking a step backward.

Whoops. Wrong floor.

But a glance back at the floor number engraved on the elevator door showed her she was on the right floor.

And yet, it was different. Everything was different. It was still bright and open, but someone was clearly in the process of dividing the space into separate rooms. And doing a fine job of it, too, Brooke realized, as she took a step forward, her heels echoing with that lovely clicking sound she remembered.

Everything was exactly as she would have done. The new drywall running along the center of the space ensured that the main living area still had plenty of daylight, with two separate sitting areas, one centered around the fireplace with what appeared to be the early stages of a small built-in bar. There was no physical separation between that and the next area, which had a circular sectional couch centered around a television that begged for cozy movie nights or curling up with a good book.

Whoever had designed it had wisely understood that you didn't need walls in between rooms when you could use space, and that seating area flowed into a dining room, which was bordered by a new kitchen, clearly under construction, and . . .

It was somebody's home, Brooke realized.

The space was as beautiful as Brooke remembered it—more so, now that it had a purpose—but it was no longer set up to be a versatile wedding reception site. Someone was intending to live here.

"Oh man," she said, realizing there'd been a super awkward, horrible mistake. Brooke pulled out her phone to text Alexis about what seemed to be a major misunderstanding.

Thank God whatever richer-than-God person who had bought the property hadn't moved in yet. Crazy awkward to walk into someone's home uninvited.

Brooke heard a loud clang, as though someone had dropped a tool, and her head snapped up and looked in the direction of the wall that led to what must be the bedrooms of the house.

Crap. Definitely not alone. A construction worker, maybe?

Brook turned, slowly creeping toward the elevator, her gait made slow and clunky in an effort not to let her heels click on the floor as she made her escape.

Then she heard the sound of a door opening and closing and heavy footsteps as someone entered the main space where she was currently tiptoeing around like an overdressed cat burglar.

Keeping her fingers crossed that it really was a worker and not the owner of the house, Brooke turned on her heel, fully prepared to be at her most charming and apologetic for the confusion.

The apology froze on her lips. Heck, all rational thought froze in her brain.

Seth was here.

Seth was *here*.

Standing in the not-quite-finished kitchen, wearing . . .

Jeans.

And a T-shirt . . . and work boots?

Brooke blinked, half-terrified that her mind had gone and given up the ghost and quit on her. Seth Tyler might wear jeans, sometimes, but only when paired with a cashmere sweater or tailored dress shirt. Definitely not a basic white T-shirt that clung just a little bit snugly to the sculpted muscles of his upper body.

"Is that dirt on your face?" Brooke blurted out.

Yeah. Okay. Not exactly what she'd always imagined saying upon seeing him again, but really, he was wearing *work* boots. And there was a hammer in his hand.

Her ovaries would be fainting if they weren't so confused by what was happening right now.

He lifted a self-conscious hand to his cheek before dropping it with a shrug. "The shelves I'm installing must have had some dust on them."

"The—" Brooke cleared her throat. "The shelves you're installing?"

Her voice was far too high, and he gave her a crooked smile and tilted his head in the direction of the other room. "Want to see?"

Brooke had about a billion questions for him, none of them about shelves, but since the important questions seemed far too complicated to possibly make it from her brain to her mouth, she went with the simpler option. "Okay."

He stood still as she walked toward him, and for a brief moment, she thought his eyes might be appearing slightly hungry as they looked her over, but then all expression disappeared between the impassive mask. It was like they were going back to that first day at the Belles, when he'd been cool and unapproachable and impossible to read.

But no, that wasn't quite right.

He wasn't that man at all. He was different. Not

just because of the jeans and the boots and that seriously sexy hammer. *He* was different. Seth the person had changed. She just wasn't sure how.

Or why.

For a foolish moment, she thought he might extend a hand to her and lead her to these mysterious shelves, but instead he turned away and walked ahead of her, leaving her to follow him.

She swallowed her disappointment and trailed after him, finding a long hallway on the other side of the wall. It had wisely been kept from being too narrow; instead, the second half of the floor had been divided into a T-shaped hallway to allow in natural light, with a handful of doors leading into separate rooms.

Brooke curiously glanced into a couple of them as they walked by, but not much had been done. A card table had been set up in one with a laptop, as though it was serving as a temporary office.

Another held building supplies, another was empty, and one was a bathroom.

Finally, they made it to the last door, and Seth turned back, gesturing for her to enter first.

She gave him a wary look before she stepped into the room.

"Oh," she breathed.

It was a bedroom.

A gorgeous, enormous master bedroom.

At the center was a king platform bed with dark gray bedding and puffy white pillows. There were two chaise lounges along the windows with a view of the city. She pivoted, taking in the newly constructed walk-in closet that was bigger than her current bed-room twice over. Through an open door she could make out a marble bathroom with a walk-in shower and separate tub.

Wordlessly she turned toward Seth, waiting for an explanation.

He gestured with his chin toward a pile of wood in the far corner that she'd missed. "Most everything here was delivered and built for me, but I wanted to do something myself. I thought, 'How hard can a bookshelf be?' Hard, it turns out. Although I'm inclined to blame the directions."

"Seth," she said, halting his uncharacteristic babbling. "What's going on?"

"I bought it," he said, as though those three little words were a normal thing to say about property in downtown Manhattan.

"The building?" she asked.

He shrugged.

"Good Lord," she said, running a hand over her hair. "You bought the building?"

"Well, I tried to buy just one floor, but this way was just . . . easier."

She let out an incredulous laugh. "Of course it was. You're Seth Tyler."

He said nothing.

"There's no bride coming by tonight, is there? You and Alexis set this up."

He nodded. "Yes."

Well, at least he wasn't lying to her. That was something.

Seth blew out a breath, tapping the hammer lightly against his thigh in agitation. "There are five bedrooms. Three and a half baths. A study. You already saw the beginnings of the main living area, but I'm also planning to put a piano in. Did you know I play? And since I own the whole damn building, I'm thinking of installing some sort of doggy area on the rooftop so I don't have to go as far to let him or her out when the weather sucks."

"A dog?" Brooke interrupted his strange monologue. "What dog?"

"I don't know. The one I'm going to get," he said, his words tumbling over one another in his obvious excitement. "And I'm dividing one of the lower floors into apartment units, and I'm giving one to Dex to make it easier for both of us when I need to get uptown for work. And there's no room service, but that's not going to be a problem, because I've hired this crazy French dude to teach me some cooking basics. And I told Maya she could decorate, but only if she runs everything by me, because I want this place to be *mine*. To feel like *me*. I'm not exactly sure what that looks like yet, but I'm working on it. A little every day."

His words were getting closer and closer together, coming out in a bit of a nervous rush, and Brooke's eyes started to burn at the corners as she felt tears threaten.

"Don't cry," he whispered. "I die when you cry."

"I don't understand what's going on here," she said.

"Yes you do," he said quickly. "You know exactly

what's going on here." He tossed the hammer to the side, and she winced as it clattered to the gorgeous hardwood floor. He moved closer; his fingers wrapped around her stiff upper arms, drawing her forward.

"I know this is a risk," he said quietly. "Setting this up like this, doing this all behind your back, tricking you into coming here. I know you're thinking that I'm controlling everything, and I'll admit that I am. I've controlled every single detail of this right down to this ugly T-shirt in hopes that it would help make me seem more approachable. Although, that was actually Grant's idea."

"Grant's in on this?" she asked, trying to keep up.

"He likes to think so," Seth said with a wry smile. "Anyway, I know I'm being controlling. I know that it's a problem of mine, and it will probably always be a problem of mine, but I'm working on it. I swear that I am. If you want to walk away right now, I'll let you, but I had to try. You see that, right? I had to try to be more, because you *make* me want to be more. More than a scared little boy who tried too desperately to direct all of the pieces and people of his life because he was terrified of losing them."

Brooke's eyes closed as her emotions wavered between happiness and confusion. "This is a hell of a speech, Tyler."

"I'm sorry," he said in a rush. "I'm so sorry about the thing with Maya, the thing with Clay. It was all badly done. So badly done, and I'd give anything to take it back, and since I can't . . . I need to tell you why. I tried to tell you that day, but . . ."

He took a deep breath. "I did it because I love you. And that's not an excuse, but it is the truth. I know it's soon, I know it's crazy, but my feelings for you are the most real thing I've ever known."

Her emotions weren't wavering anymore. They tipped firmly in the direction of ecstatic, overjoyed, elated, and she opened her eyes.

"You decided not to live in a hotel anymore."

His mouth drooped a little in disappointment at her words, but she had to do this her way.

"I want a place of my own," he said. "A home."

"And you're, like, the richest man in New York, which means you can pick literally any place," she said slowly.

He shrugged. "Sure."

"But you chose *this* place."

"Obviously, Brooke," he said, with just the slightest edge of impatience that made her grin, because it was so wonderfully, beautifully Seth.

"You chose it because you knew I loved it."

"Yes," he said quietly.

Brooke lifted her eyebrows.

"I'm not asking you to move in, if that's what you're thinking," he said, releasing her arms and shoving his hands into his back pockets. "Not today, anyway."

"Then what *are* you asking?" she said, taking a step closer, loving the way his cool blue eyes warmed when she got near.

"Anything," he said, his voice slightly desperate. "I'll take whatever you're giving. A drink. Dinner. A walk. Maybe a movie. Joint custody of the dog. Keys to the same home—this home. A wedding. Babies. Things like that."

Brooke laughed as she lifted her hands to his shoulders and pressed her body into his. "Easy there, big guy. I'm still trying to adjust to the fact that you're wearing jeans and carrying a hammer around."

His arms gingerly went around her, resting lightly against her back as though he thought she might run at any time and was prepared to let her go even though he didn't want to. "The shirt and hammer did it for you, huh? Grant will be pleased."

"Yeah, I'm definitely not thinking about Grant right now," she said, her eyes dropping purposely to his mouth.

"No?"

She shook her head and slowly pulled his head down to hers, pouring her entire heart into the kiss. His arms tightened around her, no longer tentative as their mouths met again and again in the sweet elation of rediscovery.

"I'd thought you'd forgotten about me," she said softly, pulling back slightly and running her fingers along the silken hair around his ears.

He shook his head. "Never. Not for one second. I just went underground for a bit to up my game."

"You did good," she said, brushing her lips against his and inviting another kiss.

Instead of taking her up on the invitation, he leaned back slightly, eyes narrowed. "Did you miss me?"

"I did," she said slowly. "But I think it was good

to have a little distance. To figure things out and find myself in the aftermath of everything, you know?"

His eyes clouded, and she rushed to reassure him. "You know what I figured out?"

Seth said nothing.

Her hand slid down to his lips, her fingertips tracing his firm, unsmiling mouth. "I figured out that I don't want a relationship that's easy the way it was when I was with Clay, before it all went to hell."

"No?" His voice was rough.

"No," she whispered. "I want a relationship that might be hard sometimes but is worth it. And you, Seth Tyler, are most definitely worth it."

His slow smile was just about the best thing she'd ever seen in her life, and his former wariness gave way to cocky seduction.

"Is that so?"

"I'm pretty sure," she teased. "There are some things I'll need to consider, first."

"Like?"

"Like how ugly that bookshelf is if and when you ever finish it."

"What else?" he growled, maneuvering her back toward the bed.

"Like exactly how long we're supposed to wait before you let me move in with you."

"Five minutes. Next?"

Brooke smiled. "Just one more thing . . . I'll need to consider how much I love you."

He froze in the process of sliding a hand under her shirt and searched her eyes. "Yeah? How much are you thinking?"

"All the way, Mr. Tyler. I'm thinking I love you all the way."

Seth pushed her back onto the bed with a wicked, happy grin. "Prove it."

And Brooke did. She *definitely* did.

Acknowledgments

THANKS SO MUCH TO everyone who used their precious reading time and book dollars to meet the Wedding Belles! It's always so much fun for an author to delve into a brand-new world with brand-new characters, and the idea for a wedding planner–centric series is one that's been on my writer's bucket list for a long time.

I can't think of a better "home" for the Wedding Belles than the fantastic team at Pocket, who've helped see my writing dream into reality, with amazing covers, marketing support, and editing.

First shout-out goes to Elana Cohen, who had faith in this book from the very beginning and worked her butt off to ensure that it lived up to its potential. I owe so much to her, as do Seth and Brooke, whose romance sparkles all the more because of her guidance.

To the rest of the fantastic team at Pocket, you guys are absolutely exceptional and deserve a long slow-clap. From the breathtaking cover to the precise editing and proofreading, you guys are absolutely responsible for turning a writing dream into a beautiful book.

I also need to say a huge public thank-you to my dear friend, Kristi Yanta, for her exceptional beta-reading services. Nobody knows my writing and understands my vision for each book quite like Kristi, and I'm so lucky to have her stick by my side through multiple publishers and multiple series, ensuring that each LL story is the best it can be.

And finally, to my "behind the scenes" crew: my amazing assistant, Lisa; my Twitter guru, Kristina; and my daily (online) writing companions, Jessica Lemmon and Rachel Van Dyken—you guys make my job easier and more fun.

Turn the page for an exclusive sneak peek of

FOR BETTER OR WORSE

BOOK TWO IN THE WEDDING BELLES SERIES

Available September 2016 from Pocket Books!

Chapter One

For as long as Heather Fowler could remember, living in Manhattan had been The Dream.

The one she'd talked about as a precocious eight-year-old when her mom's best friend, turned chatty by one too many glasses of the Franzia she chugged like water, asked her what she wanted to be when she grew up.

At eight, Heather hadn't been exactly sure about the *what* in her future, but she absolutely knew the *where*.

New York City.

Manhattan, specifically.

The obsession had started with *Friends* reruns, and had only grown as she'd moved on to her mother's *Sex and the City* DVD collection, which she'd watched covertly while her mother had worked double shifts at the diner.

People in New York were vibrant, sparkling. They were *doing* something. Important things. Fun things.

She wanted to be one of them.

By the time Heather was in high school, The Dream was still going strong.

While the overachievers had dreams of going to Mars, and the smaller-thinking ones had aspirations of getting to the mall, for Heather it had always and *only* been NYC.

Her mother had never pretended to understand Heather's dream. Joan Fowler had lived her entire life in Merryville, Michigan, with only two addresses: her lower-middle-class parents' split-level and the trailer she'd rented when, at four months pregnant, her parents had kicked her out.

And while Heather had wanted something more for her mother—and something more for *herself*—than hand-me-down clothes and a two-bedroom trailer that smelled constantly like peroxide (courtesy of her mother's hairdressing side job), Joan had always seemed content.

But to Heather's mother's credit, Joan had never been anything less than encouraging.

If you want New York, you do New York. Simple as that.

And so Heather had.

Though it hadn't been simple. There had been detours. College at Michigan State. A tiny apartment in Brooklyn Heights with four roommates that, while *technically* located in New York City, wasn't quite the urbane sophistication she'd pictured.

But Heather's resolve had never wavered. In one of her college internships, a mentor had told Heather to dress for the job she wanted, not the one she had.

Heather did that, but she'd also broadened the idiom: *Live the life you want, not the one you have.*

In this case, that meant saving up enough to cover rent that was more expensive than she could comfortably afford. *Yet.* More than she could afford *yet.* Because Heather was close to a promotion from assistant wedding planner to actual wedding planner. She could feel it.

The apartment was going to help her get there.

An apartment in zip code 10128, just to the east of Central Park.

She'd done it. She'd achieved the dream, or at least part of it.

And it was . . .

Terrible.

It was two a.m., and she wasn't even close to anything resembling asleep. Heather's eyes snapped open after yet another failed sleep attempt. Her nostrils flared in an unsuccessful bid for patience before she turned and banged her palm against the wall over her Ikea headboard.

She'd purposely left the walls of her bedroom white because she'd read it was soothing. The curtains were also white, as were the area rug at the foot of the bed, the flowers on her table, and the lamp shades.

White is soothing, white is soothing, white is soothing . . .

She waited. And waited. There was a pause and Heather held her breath.

Then: *Bum ba-dum bum bum bum . . .*

White wasn't soothing enough for this shit.

Heather fought the urge to scream. Was the music actually getting louder? Was that even possible?

Apparently. Because whoever lived on the other side of her bedroom wall either couldn't hear her banging or straight-up didn't care.

Heather closed her eyes and tried to tell herself that it was soothing. Tried to pretend that the mediocre pounding of the drums and the squeal of some sort of guitar was a lullaby.

Her eyes snapped open again. Nope.

Heather threw back the covers—a fancy new white duvet for her fancy new place—and shoved her feet into her slippers, pulling a hair band off the nightstand and dragging her messy, dark blond curls into a knot on top of her head. She slid on her glasses, threw on a gray hoodie that she didn't bother to zip, opened the front door of her apartment, and made the short journey to the door of 4A.

The building was old, hence the thin walls, but it was also recently renovated, hence the modern-style doorbell, which Heather pressed firmly with one manicured finger.

And again, when there was no answer.

And again and again and again.

She pressed it until her finger started to cramp, and until—

Whoa.

The door jerked open, and Heather was suddenly face-to-face with a male chest. A *shirtless* male chest, replete with rippling abs and pectoral muscles that she'd seen the likes of only in magazine ads or on billboards. An upper body so spectacularly shaped that it was downright tacky.

Yes, tacky was definitely what it was.

Not hot. Not hot at all.

Heather ordered her gaze upward and found it meeting the greenish-blue eyes of a dude who looked *highly* amused for someone who'd nearly had his doorbell torn off.

The guy leaned one forearm—every bit as tackily muscular as the chest—against the doorjamb as the other scratched idly at his six-pack.

"Hi there," he said, giving her a crooked smile. It was a good smile. It was a good voice, too, but Heather was *sooooo* not in the mood to be charmed.

"Let me guess," she said, gifting him with a wide fake smile. "You're in the midst of a quarter-life crisis, maybe it's taking a little longer to get the corner office than you'd hoped, and you decided to scratch the itch by, wait for it . . . starting a band."

Seemingly oblivious to her sleep-deprived bitchiness, his smile only grew wider. "You're the new neighbor."

She pointed at her front door just a few feet away. "4C."

"Nice," he said appreciatively.

For a second she could have sworn his eyes drifted down toward her chest, but when she narrowed her eyes back up at him, he was all innocent smiles.

"So that's a yes on the new band, then?"

Instead of answering her question, he extended his hand. "Josh Tanner."

"Pretty manners for someone with no neighborly

consideration," she muttered as she reluctantly put her hand in his. "Heather Fowler."

"Heather Fowler," he repeated slowly, as though trying to decide whether or not her name fit and coming up undecided.

Before she could respond, he reached out, his thumb and forefinger tugging at a curl that had come loose from her messy bun. "Pretty."

"Okay, enough," she snapped. "Are you going to stop with the music or not?"

"Well now, that's hard to say." He crossed his arms over his impressive chest. "I'm very volatile, what with the . . . what was it? Quarter-life crisis?"

"Just keep it down," she said wearily, rubbing at her forehead.

"Mrs. Calvin never used to mind," he said.

"Who the hell is Mrs. Calvin?"

"Lady who lived in 4C before you. She used to bake banana bread every Wednesday and make me a loaf. I don't suppose you bake?"

"Was Mrs. Calvin deaf?" Heather asked, ignoring the baking question. She *did* like to bake, but not for this guy, no matter how great the upper body.

"Definitely," Josh confirmed. "Turned her hearing aid off every night at eight p.m., which is when my band and I started practice."

"Aha!" she said, pointing a finger in his face. "You are in a band."

"Of course."

"Well, I need you guys to knock it off."

"Oh, they're not here tonight," he said simply.

"That was just me practicing along with one of our recordings. Can't get the intro quite right."

"Can you get it right some other time?"

"It's Friday night, babe. You need to loosen up. Want to come in for a beer?"

"No," she said, sounding out the word slowly with what she thought was admirable patience. "What I want is for you to stop the hideous music so that when my alarm goes off in four hours, I won't have to stop by here and kill you before I go to work."

"Work? On a Saturday? Dare I hope this means you're a professional baker and like to get in early to make delicious sweet buns?"

"Do I look like the type that makes delicious sweet buns?"

"You look like the type that *has* delicious sweet buns."

Heather made a face. "You're a pig."

"I'm lashing out," he said with a grin. "My ego's stinging from the fact that you didn't show any appreciation for how hard I work on all of this."

He spread his arms to the side and glanced down at his body.

Heather rolled her eyes. Great body or not, this guy was disgusting. "What normally happens when a woman bangs on your door at two in the morning?" she asked irritably.

He wiggled his eyebrows.

"Never mind," she muttered, embarrassed at having set herself up. "Can you please, *please* just shut up until after I leave at seven tomorrow?"

"To go . . . to the bakery?" he asked hopefully.

Yep. It was official. The new neighbor had to die.

Heather let out an audibly annoyed sigh. "To Park Avenue United Methodist Church to ensure the florist is there with the pew bows and to set up the guest book table, and to the bride room to make sure it doesn't still smell like onions. And then to the Bleecker Hotel to make sure the gift table's under way, that the florist is on time, that the caterers will be able to get into the kitchen, that they set up the good dance floor, not the crappy one that splits right down the middle, because if they do, so help me God—"

"And this is why modern men avoid the altar," Josh interrupted. "You're one scary-ass bride, 4C."

"I'm not the bride," she grumbled, rubbing her increasingly tired eyes. "I'm the assistant wedding planner."

"*Assistant* wedding planner. What does that mean?"

It means I need to get some freaking sleep so I can become the real deal.

"I see," Josh said, even though she hadn't said anything. He leaned toward her. "You want to come in and talk about it?"

"Better idea. How about you go to bed like any normal person over the age of twenty-two," she snapped.

"I thought you'd never ask," he said, stepping aside and sweeping an arm inward as though to usher her inside.

Heather put a hand over her heart and made a dramatic gasping sound. "You mean . . . you mean a big, handsome hunk like you would actually bed little old me?"

"Like I said, gotta verify that the sweet buns are, in fact, sweet," he said, flashing her another one of those easy grins.

Heather's fake smile dropped, and she stepped forward, getting in his face and ignoring—mostly—the heat radiating off him. "I'm going back into my apartment, and I'm going to sleep, and if I hear one more peep from your side of the wall, I'm going to get my hands on a loaf of Mrs. Calvin's glorious banana bread and shove it up your—"

Josh's head dropped to hers, and he stamped a kiss on her mouth. Hard.

Heather lifted her hands to shove him back, and they made it as far as his shoulders before she registered that it was a good kiss. A really good kiss. His mouth was warm and firm and he tasted a bit like chocolate and a *really* good time.

For a second, Heather was tempted. It had been a while since she'd done something fun, just for her. Something that didn't have to do with the Wedding Belles, or moving to Manhattan, or making sure her mom remembered to pay her bills, or . . .

Reality crept back in just as her new neighbor's skilled lips nudged hers open.

She pulled back before he could deepen the kiss and make things *really* interesting. "What the hell was that?" she spat at him, wiping her mouth with the back of her hand.

Josh's shoulders lifted. "The quickest way to shut you up, apparently. Should have tried it five minutes ago before you started rambling about bows and pews."

"Fine," she said through gritted teeth. "Let's make a deal. I'll shut up about bows if you stop the music. Deal?"

"You need to lighten up, Assistant Wedding Planner."

"Yeah, we're not calling me that," she said, already turning toward her apartment.

"Hey, 4C," he called, just as she was about to step back into her place.

In spite of her better judgment, Heather glanced over. "What?"

He winked. "See you around."

His door shut with a firm click, leaving Heather staring like an idiot with her mouth gaping open. She clenched her fists, walked back into her new apartment, locked the door, and got into bed. But while it was finally quiet, her mind was racing a million miles a minute.

What. In the fresh hell. Was *that*?

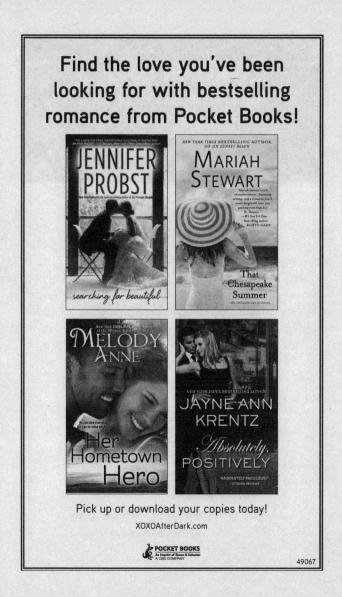